The Celluloid Peach

Derek E Pearson

First published 2019
Published by GB Publishing.org

Copyright © 2019 Derek E Pearson
All rights reserved
ISBN: 978-1-912576-83-8 (hardback)
978-1-912576-84-5 (paperback)
978-1-912576-85-2 (eBook)
978-1-912576-86-9 (Kindle)

Cover Design © 2019 Ruth Hope
Cover Illustration © 2019 Derek E Pearson

GBP

GB Publishing Org
www.gbpublishing.co.uk

To Sue, who inspired some of the fun

Thanks to the folks at GB Publishing who support me with critique and praise

To you, Colin
enjoy

24 - 7 - 19

When the new century roared, she threw a custard pie in its face. When the cameras rolled, she became a star. Some girls made it into the movies because they looked good in a bathing suit, Melia made it because she looked beautiful under the lights. She made the cameraman purr, and she made people laugh. She grabbed me by the heartstrings and played me like a Torres guitar.

Some people have special talents. Some people poke a finger in every pie and make money in their sleep, some fire passion in every loin. That little thief Melia stole your heart the second after she put a smile on your face. She took mine and never gave it back. She took it with her to the grave.

Her parents were itinerant musical folk who chased the buck whenever it fluttered within reach. Melia's Pa was a gifted pianist, a French-speaking Canuck and a handsome enough fellow. Her mother was as Irish as a shamrock on a green hat.

When she was younger, Melia's Ma would sing and dance to accompany her husband's tune in bars and eating houses the whole length of the northeast coast. When she wasn't dancing a jig she was baking babies, six in all. Luckily three of them died young or all of them would have starved. As it was, Melia learned what hunger tasted like when she was still barely old enough to welcome the new century.

By then her folks were living on a steady diet of wishful thinking and scrapings, scratching by in two pokey rooms on Staten Island. The tide washing them down the coast had finally fetched them up at the feet of Lady Liberty but, unlike the Lady with the torch, their feet were still shackled by poverty. The kids had to help bring in the lunch money as soon as they could turn their hands to anything useful, and Melia was no exception.

There would come a time when that little black-haired firebrand would cool her wits with ice cream and Champagne for breakfast, but that was a fair ways off. Fate had to deal a few hands first. She was thirteen when her pretty looks were spotted in the street by an illustrator fellow. He was a commercial guy who put his artistic talents to good use for magazines, fashion houses, and advertising – posters and such.

He introduced the new little darling to his clique and for a while Melia became the favourite of the studio set from Twenty-seventh Street to West Sixty-seventh Street, she even hit Carnegie Hall. She was putting good food on the table by tucking her neat little caboose into anything the clique gave her to pose in, everything from wedding dresses to lingerie to soap bubbles.

And you could always tell where she was posing, you just had to follow your ears. Listen for the sound of laughter. You'd think her big-eyed charm would excite a different reaction in a man's soul. She sure had the fixings, a fine enough figure and legs right up to yay there, but she was too alive to be a tailor's dummy. She had '*IT*' but she never knew it. She put the froth on the beer, the bubbles in the wine, and warmth in your heart.

She was so innocent and wide-eyed and dizzy on life she reached into your chest and sucked that laugh right out of you, dragged it into the open where she could hear it. And she would laugh right back, which somehow made it worse. I've seen her make a hefty brute of a set technician cry with laughter thanks to her malarkey, but he could never explain why.

But excuse me, I'm getting ahead of the story. We need to go back to a time when Melia is still posing for those fellahs keen to put her on the pages of magazines to sell anything from toothpaste to skin cream to umbrellas. I didn't know her then so I guess using her first name all the time is a little familiar.

So, Miss Melia Nord is posing for her 'polite artistic gentlemen', her description. 'They were businessmen with a job to do and they had no time for hanky or panky,' she told me a few years later. 'There was no nudity and none of that funny stuff. No, they were nice, polite artistic gentlemen. And it put a few bucks in the crib without any heavy lifting.

'Then one of the talent guys on the circuit, the modelling circuit, you know? He told me he was getting a few bucks as an "extra" in the moving pictures and offered to take me along...'

It was 1911. Melia was just sixteen. She had been born barely two years after the first purpose-built movie studio, the *Black Maria*, was opened by Thomas Edison in New Jersey. The Maria was so named because it was small, sweaty, cramped, uncomfortable to work in, and, thanks to the tarpaper that covered it, reminded the crew of the black vans the cops used to carry their prisoners around.

Edison had the place demolished in 1903 after he'd built a swanky new studio with a glass roof. He used to call his old studio the Doghouse, but to his people it would always be the Black Maria. I wonder how many of them volunteered to swing a sledge through its walls when it was coming down? How many grabbed themselves a bit of revenge for all the misery it caused. I also wondered if any of them had ever seen the inside of a real Black Maria.

These days people think the movie business sprang from the womb fully grown, but the truth is a lot less surefooted than that. Old man Edison started by filming stage acts, as if it was a fake vaudeville show. He shot trapeze artists and little bits of theatre – like men pretending to be blacksmiths. There was a lot of reliance on scenes of scantily-clad girls, and that came straight from backstreet burlesque.

A pretty girl was like catnip to movie audiences back then. Women were still buttoned into clothes that showed little more than their ears, so to catch a glimpse of something more daring was always worth the price of admission.

Those early films were shown on gadgets called Kinetoscope machines that were more like 'What the butler saw' boxes. They quickly went out of favour. True moving pictures had been projected up on a big screen by the end of the last century, most notably by the Lumière brothers in France; but the first dedicated establishment to show nothing but movies on the big screen was the Nickelodeon in Pittsburgh. That was in 1905.

By the time Melia's model friend had introduced her to the grit under the first rung of the cinematographic ladder we already had Florence Lawrence and Mary Pickford with star billing, and those divas were vying with each other over who was the first true movie star. Before them actors had not been listed on the screen. These were the early days – before close-ups and sound made the people on the screen seem real on the reel.

Melia walked into the studio and introduced herself to a man leaning against the wall. He looked her up and down enquiringly then said, 'You dance?' He was evidently more interested in her legs than her personality.

Melia answered, 'Dance, sing, play the piano. I'll do anything legal and decent for an honest dollar.'

'What you been doing?'

'Modelling.'

'How long?'

'Three years.'

'You don't look old enough.'

'I can get you references if you need 'em.'

'No time.' He raised his voice, 'Boss! We got the showgirl.'

A slender, thickly moustachioed man, with a head of white hair that curled over his narrow head like a wave, put down his megaphone and glanced across. He was packed into a three-piece suit that sported broad, black and white vertical stripes under which was a white shirt and a wide black tie. His wing tips were polished to within an inch of their lives: the shine on those shoes could dazzle eagles out of the mountains on a bright day.

He pulled out a fat Havana, said something to a young fellow at his side, and then ambled towards the new girl on the set. He stuck out his hand, shook hers, then carefully lit his cigar and took a step backwards. At no time did he take his eyes from her face.

Behind him his young assistant was calling, 'Take five, take five, people. Coffee and doughnuts on the table if you're starving. Smoke 'em if you got 'em. Take five and be back in ten.'

The dapper man drew smoke into his mouth, savoured it, and released it in a fragrant stream. 'I'm Lemmon,' he said. 'Carl Lemmon; like the fruit but with two 'M's. I'm the director around here which is why they call me the "Old Man" or "Boss". I'm not old, nor am I a fruit, but, on set, I *am* the Boss. Who are you and why are you here?'

'I'm Melia Nord, a model, and I'm told you need a dancing showgirl. I can do that. What do you pay?'

'Seventy-five cents an hour, cash. More if you're good.'

'Make that a dollar and I'll be better than good.'

'Prove it. Lance, show the little lady to wardrobe and make-up. I'll wind up the boys for scene three, the gunfight in the barroom. Melia, all you got to do is dance on the stage, show a bit of silk, and then run out in a panic when the shooting starts. You can do that without tripping over your bloomers?'

'Yes, Boss.'

'Fine. You start when I holler "ACTION" and you stop when I holler "CUT". You don't need a script. I'll tell you what to do and when to do it as we go along. Go get ready then come back here and earn your dollar. Lance, I want her back here in thirty so no flirting this time. We don't have time to go chasing the cast down the street every time you want to play Romeo and scare them off.'

Lemmon scowled thoughtfully and tasted his cigar. 'Melia, I want to see what the camera thinks of you. If Lance here gets fresh while you're getting ready you tell me and I'll tell the boys to put real bullets in the six guns. You hear what I'm saying?'

'I hear you, boss.'

'Good. I think we'll get by just fine. Now, follow the Corporal to costume and be back here in thirty minutes ready to knock my Stetson to the back of the room. Off you go.'

Lance unpeeled himself from the wall and took Melia's arm. 'He means it about the thirty minutes, hope you can do a quick change and make-up.'

'What did he mean by "show a bit of silk"?'

4

'Stockings, show a bit of leg. Do a few high kicks and point your knee at the camera. The paying folk love to see a bit of what goes under the petticoats.'

'Oh. Okay. Do you really flirt with the cast?'

'Only if they flirt with me first. This is a good crew. The old man has good taste and we rub along together just swell. We all look out for each other. Here we are, costume.'

Lance knocked and a man's voice yelled 'Enter, pray!' The door swung open to display a black man dressed like a jungle savage, complete with a bone through his nose and a spear taller than him. All he was wearing was a grass skirt and woven bands on his arms and ankles.

Lance pointed at Melia, 'Patch, this is Melia. She's new and needs to be a wild west showgirl in twenty minutes. Can do?'

'The old man's wish is my command. Step into my parlour, Melia.'

She turned to Lance, 'Wait, why did he call you "Corporal"? Were you in the army?'

'No. It's because my name's Lance, see? Lance Corporal. His sense of humour is like that. You'll see what I mean if you join the corps. Now, go get ready, clock's ticking.'

'So, what's your real name?'

'Murdoch, Lance Murdoch. And believe me, you can make that "the name's mud" if you're not on set in twenty minutes. Hustle that bustle, lady. Move!'

Yep, you've guessed it. The boy named mud is yours truly, Lance Murdoch. Can't act much, can't dance worth a damn, and couldn't hold a tune without squeezing the life out of it. But I knew carpentry, knew how to carry stuff without breaking it, could paint a realistic looking house on a flat and crank a camera at the right speed. I could also run through a burning building and come out the other end with my cigarette lit by the flames without setting my hair on fire.

Officially they called me the stunt man. I knew how to fall off a horse without busting a leg, and I could die convincingly with my boots on or off. Tell me what you wanted crashed and where you wanted me to crash it and you could leave the rest to me. I lied to Melia that day, Boss called me Corporal because of the punishment I could take without breaking a sweat – or my neck – and I'm mighty pleased to make your acquaintance. Let me tell you a story.

5

You ever seen a herd of rhino stampede out of a railway tunnel when you were expecting a train? No? Me neither. But after seeing what happened in that studio when Melia hit the stage I think I know how it might feel.

Cinematography has inspired thousands of column inches over the years, maybe millions, so forgive me while I add my five-cents worth to the flood. There's not much new to say but I was there and I saw it all. I'll try to make sense of it for you, what little there was of it.

Melia was on time, but, when she walked out onto the set she looked like a little girl playing dress-up in her big sister's party frock. By the look of it, that sister must have been something of a 'Thanksgiving Party Girl', the original good time had by all. Everyone else ignored her. They were getting into their positions, moving about, and practicing the noble art of getting the maximum amount of movie buck for the minimum number of people on set.

Back then the camera didn't move, we did. And there were set rules we had to follow. We had to stay at least twelve feet from the lens but not so far away we were out of focus. We were always in the frame from top to toe.

And there was nothing subtle about Carl Lemmon's productions. Audiences loved his work because it was full of the 'Three Bs': Big, Brash, and Bold. Those of us who had worked with the old man before knew what to expect. We were professionals.

The big shutters in the ceiling were open to provide the maximum amount of natural light. In front of the camera were the tables and chairs of an authentic looking western bar. We had to get that scene looking right on the nose. Out west some potential movie customers were still drinking in places just like that. The so-called 'old west' was still pretty new in a lot of people's minds.

Heck, Butch Cassidy and the Sundance Kid had only met their maker three years previously. Wyatt Earp was still pushing steins of suds at drunks in Tonopah, Nevada; a notorious gunfighter turned barkeep. Yeah, we had to get it right. That set was smoky and gritty and the cast weren't above chewing tobacco to get themselves into the right mood for their roles. The spittoons by the brass-railed bar were real as the rest of the furniture and they were already filling with tarry juice.

Lemmon had once quietly confided to me that most movie roles were filled with 'way too much ham', but not by me. I never pretended to be an actor. I was a brass movie bum and I did what I was told, so he liked me and treated me as his walking confidant. That meant that when the Boss wanted to get something off his chest we'd go for a walk and he would unload whatever was itching under his saddle. Normally it was him grouching about the difference between an honest performance and what finally ended up in the edit.

Lemmon had started in the legitimate theatre and had ideas about what should be up there on the screen. One day he'd be able to afford the talent he needed to make it happen. But not just yet. He had his small group of carefully honed talent – the contracted corps – and when we needed more bodies he hired whatever came in off the street.

A fine example of street pickings was the far from fresh boys recruited for the bar fight. They were growling around each other like a herd of buffalo – and a few of them smelled worse, especially in an enclosed space.

They were hulking brutes aching to cut loose and do their thing, which was tear the place up. Furniture would get smashed, heads might get loosened, and teeth might be lost in the name of art. I thought it was no place for a naive young girl to make her debut. Turns out I was wrong.

The boss turned his megaphone on Melia and bellowed through it, 'There's your stage, lady.' He fetched a hat off one of the background stooges and planted it on his head. 'Here's my Stetson. Let's see what you can do. ACTION!'

The stage for her performance had a few period style limelights pointed at it plus a technician who manhandled a five-hundred-watt Edison lamp to make sure we had enough light to catch the action, if there was any. We waited, but not for long.

That very moment after the boss yelled action Melia moved. She hitched up her skirts and *ran* at the stage. There were wooden steps at either end she could have climbed but instead she kinda skipped and somersaulted up into the limelight. Then she began to dance like a dog that spends time as the holiday home for a flea circus. The lighting technician had to fight to keep her square in his beam.

I couldn't tell you what that dance was called but at one point she did a vertical splits and spun on her toe like a ballerina. That move clearly showed everybody on set that she wasn't wearing bloomers. Don't get me wrong, she wasn't naked under there, but she was wearing little frilly afterthoughts that suggested more than they concealed.

Melia danced for a full five minutes before completing the performance with a standing three-sixty rotation that kicked her legs backwards, up over

7

her head, and ended with her in a full splits flat down on the deck. I tell you, I don't know where Lemmon's Stetson ended up but mine was blown clean to Alaska.

The entire room fell silent. The only sound was that of bristled jaws dropping to the sawdust covered floor. Nobody moved. They were all waiting to see what that little fireball would do next. She stood looking at the Boss, arms akimbo. She was barely breathing heavy. She knew what she'd done.

Eventually Lemmon recovered enough to whimper 'Cut' into his speaking horn, then he tottered over to Bisset the camera wrangler. 'Please tell me you got that,' he said. 'Tell me you got that. Tell me we've got seven hundred and fifty feet of beautifully shot film in the can – or I swear I'll strangle you where you stand. And then I'll kill you.'

Bisset let out a low whistle, 'Boss, I'm keeping a copy of that for my *private* collection. But, yeah, I got it. Say, what happened to the gunfight? Wasn't there meant to be a big punch-up and a gunfight?'

Lemmon grinned, 'Who cares,' he said. 'We got gold.'

We got gold, he said, but what we didn't have was a story to wrap around it. Not yet. He called Melia over to him and, with me by his side, started asking her questions about her home life. No, she had no sisters. She did once, she said, but they both died young from weak chests. So did one of her brothers.

Of the survivors, brother Len was a delivery boy for a Bronx greengrocer, and Bright was in the army. Bright was the only one got regular chow. In his letters he told them about his meals. 'Reading about food,' Melia said, 'don't feed the belly. Sometimes I wish I could eat his words.'

She said her Pa spent most of his time sitting at home looking hungry. And tired, as a man will when he's looking for a good reason to wake up in the morning. Her Ma was made of more robust stock. She did cleaning work for anyone who had a few spare cents to pay for someone else's elbow grease.

She spent so much time cleaning other people's cribs that her own home looked like it had been abandoned and left to rot. Melia dusted and cleaned what she could, but most of the time she was out looking for work too.

Melia told us all this without any trace of emotion. She wasn't looking for pity: she was just answering our questions as honestly as she could. The jolt of feminine electricity she had recently kicked onto the stage still crackled in the air, but here she was again, the young, big-eyed and beautiful girl who was wearing her sister's party frock and looked as if butter wouldn't melt.

Lemmon leaned forward, his elbows on his knees and his chin on his fists. He was scowling like a man who just discovered his favourite kitten had lost its fight with a steamroller when a neighbour slid it under his door. That was a good sign.

When the Boss smiled it meant he'd just thought of a new way to fire a fool; when he scowled he was thinking hard. Melia didn't know that; her lower lip began to quiver and those big eyes glittered with potential rain.

The Boss realised his cigar had gone out and he lit it slowly, carefully directing the smoke away from the girl. He squinted at her, studying her like she was a painting he was thinking might sit just right over his fireplace.

'Melia, what time you got to be home?'

She shrugged, 'When I got something to show for the day.'

'Okay. Good. Do you know what a contract is?'

I sat bolt upright, my eyes flickering from him to her. Melia knew something was up but she didn't understand it. She shrugged, still blinking back tears.

'Melia,' Boss said. 'Do you know how to put your John Hancock on the dotted line?'

She shrugged again. I said, 'Can you sign your name?' She glared at me, I saw a wildcat ready to pounce. Whatever this girl was feeling shone from her face. If there was ever such a thing, Melia was a natural born actress.

'Of course! I've got my letters and I bet I can read better than you! You big lummox!'

I reeled my tongue back into my mouth and held my peace. After all, maybe she could.

Lemmon patted the back of her clenched fist, 'Lance was just being friendly. He didn't mean to insult you. That's what a John Hancock is, your signature. So, are you stuck on this modelling work? Or how does fifty a week sound?'

'Fifty what?'

'Fifty dollars. But you'll have to earn every cent. I'll make you work like a rented mule. You can say goodbye to the easy life posing pretty for the life-stylers. You got a lot of hard graft in front of you. You ready for that?'

Melia had the wind knocked clean out of her. Her mouth was moving but not a peep was coming out. The colour drained from her skin: she could have gone for a white face clown without make-up. I thought she was going to faint but instead she held her right hand up in a fist and her eyes blazed.

'You don't want to be mocking me. I'm not a simple Sally who will sit still for no such a thing. I thought you were a good man.' She aimed her

9

thumb at me, 'He's a lump, I can tell, but I thought you had smarts. Why're you pulling at my tail like this?'

'Fifty dollars a week and meals from the chow wagon. That's the best deal I can offer. Take it or leave it! We got a movie to make and I ain't got time to parley. You're in – or you're back on the posing couch. You choose.'

Melia made a sound like someone blowing a grass whistle. She bounced forward, took the Boss's face in both hands and bussed him full on the lips until he squawked. She released him, squealed, then jiggled up and down like a St Vitus dancer. She said nothing, just made that ear jangling squealing sound.

When the Boss got his breath back he gasped, 'I guess we can take that as a yes.' He almost smiled.

[3]

Sara Bennett couldn't understand Melia's appeal, nor did she want me as her replacement director cum cameraman. She thought her career had earned more than the second banana cranking the film through the box at sixteen frames per second. She wanted the Boss.

She was a professional and believed she deserved the best. According to her professional biography, which she called her Curriculum Vitae, she had been trained in New York City's legitimate theatre. Which was almost true if you accepted Patch's version of it.

He told me once, 'Legitimate? Missy Bennett surely was. In fact she put the longest "leg" into "legitimate" I ever did see. Her performances at Minsky's were legend. She was a tail twisting draw who kept that long, wet bar at Minsky's busy; a fine working girl performing for lucky working stiffs. She set fire to that stage with her act and those boys hollered and stamped and worked up a thirst for over-priced beer.

'When men get excited they got to cool their ardour – and who could do better than kiss goodbye to a few extra cents for a bellyful of Mr Ehret's finest Hell Gate brew while catching an eyeful of Missy Bennett shaking her tail feathers? Still makes me thirsty as a Bedouin just looking at those ice-blue eyes, you know what I mean?'

Sara's ice-cold baby blues were boring into mine that afternoon, and though it was a hot August day I felt the breath of winter in the wings and the promise of a storm just over the horizon. The wind on that set was blowing in from Alaska and chill as December.

Just then I believed I understood what Patch meant, because under that frozen gaze my mouth went dry as a politician's promise. When she was in a good mood, Sara could set a fire in a priest's cassock, but when she was annoyed she could outstare a pawnbroker. She was annoyed.

She barked at me, 'It's bad enough we're paid peanuts. We shouldn't have to dance for the nackle-ass monkey. Get out of here, Corporal. Go sit on a barrel for all I care. I'm doing nothing for you! I'll be waiting right here until the organ-grinder wipes the new girl dust out of his eyes and gets back on the job!'

The Boss had warned me that Missy Bennett might be a 'little agitated' if I took over on scene three of *The Lost Soldier's Letter*, her latest little drama. But, he told me, we had to get it in the can today.

'Fetch a bottle of that good red wine from behind the bathtub in my office and a brace of glasses. Clean ones. Pour her a few glasses and give yourself a sip or two. Do the sorry spaniel face, you're good at that. By the time you pour the dregs in her glass she'll be ready to weep over the funnies in the Tribune.

'It ain't a complicated bit of business. All we need for scene three is the letter, the telegram and the waterworks. Tell her you want a close-up of her weeping. Tell her D. W.'s doing it now so we should follow suit. Tell her it's a poke in my eye and it will make her famous. Tell her she's beautiful and the camera loves her. Tell her anything – but get the scene!'

He laughed, 'Tell her I need that last five minutes or I'll see her later, understood? Tell her she's the maypole around which we dance and a polished diamond professional. That's why I can leave her with a big lug like you while I steer a greenhorn rookie down the right path. Tell her anything you like, but get that shoot finished today! This afternoon. Okay?'

I poured the wine and looked sympathetic while Sara vented her spleen using the kind of language that would make tar boil. It took three glasses to calm her down enough so I could talk and she was ready to listen. When I mentioned the close-up those astonishing eyes of hers lit up like sodium flares. I swear they were bright enough to read by. She was ready.

'The Boss will shit a lake full,' she visibly preened at the image. 'He'll fire you from a cannon. You sure about this, Corporal? You'll do this for me?'

'I've been wanting to put you up there on the silver screen in close-up since I saw what D. W. Griffith was doing. It'll be beautiful, not a dry eye in the house. And you have the face for it, Sara. Please, it'll be worth getting me fired for. Let me make you famous and the Boss can go kick a can or roll a hoop with the rest of the kids. When I'm done you'll be the new Mary Pickford.'

Hey, maybe I *could* act after all.

Sara told me I was talking a man-sized shovelful of the stuff makes the roses grow, but she wasn't quite so polite about it. She had a way with words, did that sweet-faced kid. *Kid*? She was at least in her late thirties, looked as if she was in her late twenties, and could get away with being a late teenager under the right lighting conditions – with very carefully applied make-up.

The Lost Soldier's Letter was written to be a prime heartbreaker in seventeen minutes. It ran across three scenes – and this was scene three where the audience got jerked like a fish on a hook. The plot was so thin you could shave with it, but that was good enough for the paying public – and movie theatres were always clamouring for more fresh content.

They were not very demanding. I saw a masterpiece of understatement called *The Elopement*. The plot went like this: boy climbs ladder up to a window at night. Girl waits for him there, with her suitcase packed, they climb down the ladder together. They kiss.

Girl's father sees them and goes after them with his shotgun. Policeman rushes over to see what all the shooting's about. Policeman joins father in chasing the runaways, but they climb into a goods car behind a passing train and vanish into the sunrise. The end! *Really?* There's more subtlety in a bottle of Mr McIlhenny's hot tabasco sauce.

So, *The Lost Soldier's Letter*, this is how it went. Scene one; boy puts a ring on his sweetheart's finger while they're standing under a tree and surrounded by wheat fields. He's in uniform and has a pack on his back and his rifle over his shoulder. He's riding to war and off to Mexico. Sweetheart promises to wait and stands waving her handkerchief while he marches down the hill to his waiting horse then rides away with his troop.

He looks over his shoulder and blows kisses. She waves until he's out of sight. Scene ends with her looking at the ring on her finger with tears of joy on her flawless cheeks. Sunlight glitters in those big, bright eyes.

Scene two finds the soldier sitting at a table outside his wigwam tent. In the real world he'd be *inside* the tent but we don't do that because the lighting would be lousy. He's writing a letter to his sweetheart; we know what he writes because the words will be put up on the screen during editing. Boy, does he love her. He writes like a college kid, but the beginning has the pair of them in farmland, so he must be a hick. Maybe he's the hick who went to college? See, there's another great movie idea right there.

He seals the envelope, addresses it, puts it in the regimental mail bag – which has 'MAIL' stamped on it just in case you wondered what he was doing – then climbs onto his horse. He joins his troop in a cavalry charge against the foe and the last thing we see is him getting shot out of his saddle. If you ever see the movie, that was me falling off the horse, and not Don Sherwood who was playing the juvenile lead.

Scene three was the shoot Sara performed for me that afternoon. Sweetheart receives a letter: it's from her soldier boy. She reads it, kisses the paper, holds it to her breast, and then admires the sparkler on her ring finger once more. She runs to a cabinet and picks up the framed photograph of her beau who looks like a movie star in his new uniform. Well, of course he would, he was Don Sherwood.

Sweetheart stands at the window looking south, towards where she imagines her soldier boy to be. There's a knock at the door. 'Who is it?' she says. 'Telegram!' She opens the door. We don't see who delivers the telegram, that would cost another five dollars to pay some guy to wear a uniform for a five second performance. Cheaper to pin the telegram to the door and have Sara pull it off.

She tears open the message and reads it. We go close up on her face while she mouths 'The United States Army Regrets To Inform You...' She reads the whole thing, tears well up in her beautiful eyes. Sara could produce the waterworks without resorting to smelling salts or onions – it was a gift. When I asked her how she did it she said she just had to think about some of the men she'd met as a teenager.

She looks up to heaven. We hold the shot, she's lit like an angel. For a heartbeat Sara Bennett is the most luminous lovely in the history of cinematography. Then she collapses in a faint, falling like a gentle feather to the ground, her skirts billowing demurely around her. It is a chaste collapse, as if she knew we were watching.

The last shot is of her hand with the engagement ring on its finger. It is stretching out towards the telegram where we clearly read the words 'Killed In Action'. Fade and go to credits; guaranteed, not a dry seat in the house. Sara kissed me on the cheek and hugged me when we finished, told me she thought she'd done her best work that day and that I was not a monkey after all but a genius.

I agreed about her work but couldn't allow the genius thing. She hugged me, kissed my cheek again, and headed straight for make-up to get out of her costume. She could never wait to get back into her street clothes and go celebrate another reel in the can.

Maybe it's just me but I can't do that. I always feel like I need to come back to ground after shooting a scene. Reality gets tucked behind my ear while I'm working and I don't pull it back out until I feel ready to smoke it again. Sara could breathe a sigh, blink twice, and come crashing back into the here and now like a baseball into a mitt. Maybe it was all that legitimate theatre training she had at Minsky's.

She was right about the work. *The Lost Soldier's Letter* did more for the damp handkerchief industry than anything else we put out that year. The Boss was thinking of giving Sara a raise, but he hesitated a mite too long. A week after it opened in Nickelodeons and movie theatres across the United States of moviedom, Sara was poached by Tri-State Pictures like a breakfast egg. She was served up on toast for a new series of heartbreakers and became the cream in their coffee. Thinking of those amazing eyes, I still get hungry for breakfast.

14

Meanwhile a quiet revolution was taking place in studio two. Boss had his second scene but now he needed scenes one and three. He had the middle, but what was the beginning and the end? The gunfight had been put on hold, that could wait for another movie. Now he needed to work out what a sweet angel like Melia was doing spinning like a sexy little dervish in front of a bunch of beer swilling cowpokes.

He had added a segment at the end of Melia's dance in which the cowpokes showered her with money to show their appreciation. The girl scooped up the dollar bills like a starving squirrel gathering nuts. *That's it*, he realised, *perfect*.

The Dancing Angel was born, and it could be shot on a shoestring.

I was at the premier for both movies. It was easy, they followed each other on the same screen. We were all at the Unique Theatre on Broadway, in the back row and set for a fast getaway if the movies tanked. I had Sara on my left and the Boss on my right. On the other side of him sat Melia. Beyond her was Bisset and next to him was an actor called Pa Greenwich, more of whom later.

We had to suffer through two features and a newsreel before they got around to screening *The Lost Soldier's Letter*. When the title flashed up Sara held my left hand so tight I lost the feeling in my fingers for hours afterwards. I could feel her trembling right through the seats. It gave me an insight I've never lost since, actors are people too. They might fool you into thinking they're always in control but they get a knot in their colons same as everyone else.

She needn't have worried. That last five minutes caught at *my* throat and I'm the man who put it there. The womenfolk wept in sympathy and so did some of the men. I heard one guy say, 'How is it possible for any girl to be that beautiful?' That statement was followed by the ringing sound of a slap; I guess maybe he shouldn't have put that question to the lady he'd walked in with.

I felt the softest kiss on my cheek from Sara, and heard the whispered words, 'Thank you'. The Boss didn't kiss me, but he whispered in my other ear, 'Consider yourself promoted, Lieutenant. Nice work, see me later.' He settled back in his seat and turned his eyes back to the screen. The honky-tonk man up front was playing some popular music hall number I vaguely recognised, but everything I heard sounded like Beethoven's *Ode to Joy*. He'd called me Lieutenant! I'd skipped Sergeant and gone straight for the officer's club. That made it a great day.

And that was when *The Dancing Angel* flashed up onto the screen, and just over fifteen minutes later I was in love. The Boss had taken his own best advice and included close-ups of his new star, Melia Nord, who had been introduced during the opening credits as 'The discovery of the Century'. His style was much like mine but a lot less obvious. I lit Sara like an angel, ethereal and lovely. He lit his angel like the most fresh-faced and exciting girl I'd ever seen.

I heard that odd, grass whistle sound again, like a kettle about to blow. If Melia kept that up throughout the entire film she'd pass out from lack of oxygen. The Boss had the answer. He fetched his silver gilt flask out of his inside pocket and handed her a capful of whatever it held.

She threw the contents into her open mouth and immediately starting choking like a cat with the biggest furball in feline history. Boss quickly poured another and I heard him whisper, 'Sip it or you'll blow your eyes out.' She did, and she finally settled down. I was glued to the story on the screen. That was when I noticed the sound coming from my left-hand side. Sara was grinding her teeth.

Let her, I thought, *she's had her five minutes of glory.* I wanted to watch the movie. I was entranced. Something happened to Melia in front of a camera. She glowed from within and sent a jolt through everyone in the room. She was like God bottled electricity and the cork only got pulled in front of the lens. She looked like the finest cream shaped itself into a girl and everyone wanted a spoonful.

Of course there was the plot, lean as a barber's razor and stropped right down to the ivory grip. In a nutshell; young girl is looking after her father. Father's ailing and there's no money for a doctor. Girl dresses like a tart, dances like a wild thing in a saloon bar – showing a bunch of strangers plenty that she should have saved for her wedding night – and gets a mess of tips from her audience in return.

Final scene shows the girl back in her ordinary clothes and rushing the doctor through a freezing rain to her father's crib. Too late, he's gone to the great banqueting hall in the sky. The doctor shakes his head, pats the girl on the shoulder, and leaves her alone with her father's corpse. What a considerate example of medical thoughtfulness. Doc needs his ass kicking.

Epilogue, cut to a church interior. The girl is seen in close-up stuffing money into the poor-box. It's the money she earned from her dancing spree. She prays for forgiveness and her father's immortal soul. We get a final look at her sweet, tearful face. Fade to black, the end. Wipe salt moisture from the eye and fight the urge to climb up and lick the tears from her twenty-foot cheeks up there on the silver screen.

Of course, I'm sure you understand why the old fellah had to croak. We can't have a good outcome from a girl showing all of her finer points to a bunch of redneck cowpokes. That could be considered downright immoral and might lead our female audience into temptation.

If Melia's sinful display had saved her father's life she might be tempted to do it again just to earn a decent steak dinner. The father *had* to die, it completes his story arc and leads the girl to redemption. Or at least that's what the Boss would say if he was pressed.

The fact that greedy eyes would be ogling every inch of her 'performance' in movie houses up and down this great land of ours – and pouring hard-earned cash into the hungry coffers of Century Pictures Inc. for the privilege – was not a factor. People could keep their morality cake and enjoy a fine view of a young girl's underwear while they were eating it. It all pays the rent.

But, was it really that morally tight? I wonder. There was Pa Greenwich, gurning and smacking his thin old chops like a dying monitor lizard. He played the father. He's easily typecast as a rack of old ribs and plays dead more convincingly than a side of beef in a butcher's window. Next to him, Melia shone like a flaming torch. No, she shone like a star.

The Boss knew what he was doing when he put them on the screen together. Pa's light had been growing dim for a while and Melia's glowed brighter by comparison. Sharp-eyed viewers might even have spotted the old guy throwing money at his half-naked 'daughter' in the saloon. The Boss makes his performers work hard for their five dollars.

They would have had to see through the jungle of false beard Pa was sporting in that scene; and found their way around the flagon of beer he was waving about, wetting more than just his whistle. Boss puts real beer in the barrels. It's cheap and it's weak but it's beer, and it skated over Pa's bottomless thirst faster than a chicken set loose in a dog pound. It lasted about as long too.

Thing is, Pa went back for refills. Lots of refills. When we set the scene where he was languishing on his deathbed in the role of father – sans beard and stein – his bladder was fit to burst and he was hankering for something a little stronger than weak beer. Something that might put hair on his scrawny chest.

Every time Pa gathered up his nightshirt and scampered barefoot to the latrines the Boss shot more close-ups of Melia. Every time Pa came back he was weaving like a grass-snake and his eyes were rolling in their sockets like marbles on a spun plate. It was obvious he had a stash of the hard stuff somewhere, and it sure wasn't tucked away in his costume. The only thing in that long nightshirt was Pa's bony butt.

By the time Boss got to scene three, Pa Greenwich was several sheets to the wind and out colder than Sara's eyes when she took umbrage against the world. Melia told me later that the Boss looked down at the soused bundle of bones and he smiled his happiest smile. He told Bisset to light the deathbed for a final act, told the actor playing the doctor that the father had died, and talked Melia through her act.

After that they left Pa to sleep it off and took the action to the little church up the street a ways. The priest there knew the Boss, he had even appeared in a few single reelers. He was ready to let Melia stuff his poor box and then unlock it to let the Boss take out the false dollar bills – in exchange for a donation of the real stuff.

Edit was completed and the new epic ready for distribution before the end of the month. We watched it debut on a Friday and we saw the standing ovation it received from the folk at the Unique Theatre. We saw it. Sara didn't. She had stalked out halfway through when the cheering started for Melia's dance.

Melia also missed part of the show, whatever was in the Boss's flask had knocked her out cold. She slept through her first ovation with a dreamy smile on her face. She was fully awake for all the others. And there would be plenty.

The Lost Soldier's Letter was the last movie Sara ever made with us, and it was the most successful. America cried a river for that poor sweetheart and her lost soldier boy. Sara's name was up in lights and she would go on to earn a pretty penny for Tri-State, but she never forgave the Boss for putting the rookie first. *The Lost Soldier* was good – for its time it was superb – and it helped haul me up the financial tree as assistant director. But *The Dancing Angel* was better.

Melia never realised how good she was at what she did. She never needed to ask for her motivation. The director told her what he wanted and the little darling did it without hesitating. 'Melia, look brokenhearted!' She would break your heart. 'Melia, look really happy!' She would make you laugh right along with her. 'Melia, look angry! Look thoughtful! Look confused!' Whatever they called for she delivered. Then, as soon as the camera stopped rolling, she'd be larking around like a puppy in a park full of pigeons.

Did I say I was in love with that little bowl of cream? Well, of course I was. But I did nothing about it because she was just sixteen years old and I was tilting my hat closer to thirty. That girl was barely half my age and deserved her chance to meet someone as awkward and fresh as she was. That's what I thought anyway.

Hindsight is a truly wonderful gift. If I'd known then what I know now I might have behaved differently. I might even have copied the soldier boy and put a ring on my sweetheart's finger. But I didn't, and I still didn't, and that's the way the apples fall.

Melia's life was going to change. Into every life a little rain must fall, but in Melia's case the rain fell in galvanised buckets. Two major collisions would impact that sweet lady's happiness and strew broken glass in her path. One was a sandbag on the end of a rope – and the other was the money man behind Century Pictures Inc, one Mr Mason Jarr.

5

For just over five years, Melia's impossible good luck continued. She rode a cresting wave of froth that would have drowned anyone with less energy. The lunatics who made up the corps would create mayhem all around her and she would act like a ringmaster trying to herd cats, big cats. We dressed her as the spunky little girl down on her luck who faced every threat with the same kind of spirit David used the day he gave Goliath a rock in the eye. And the viewing public lapped her up.

Her natural talent for mischief and pretty little face under a mass of black curls won their hearts, but it was her manic antics that had them rocking in their seats. If she got caught and faced the judge in court she'd be sure to find a custard pie in someone's lunch pail and launch it at the old buffoon. She could make it through a window slicker than a hound and hang from a rail thirty feet in the air without a safety net.

Melia could match anything the stunt players could do. They would stand and applaud the little lunatic when she took a lion for a walk as if it was a pet dog, and some would cover their eyes when she climbed up the outside of a three-story building the way you and I would climb the stairs. She never learned to drive but she could perform any stunt we asked while balanced on a speeding vehicle. She lived a charmed life and never stopped smiling.

She had a trick she performed with Ben Usher, who used to be a circus strongman until the Boss saw his potential as a convincing thug. He would put his right arm out like beam of oak. Melia would link her fingers together around his wrist and Ben would lift her off the ground as if she was a balloon filled with fairy dust.

She was light as a feather. In a high wind that girl could fly, and she pulled the rest of us along after her like the ribbons on the tail of a kite. Everyone wanted to be on set with Melia Nord because she made it fun. People were inspired by her, and her movies made money, good money. When some wag put up a sign that said; 'Never work with children, cute animals, or Melia Nord', she had her picture taken under it.

She never reacted badly to stunts off set – twitting each other went with the territory. She got hit with a water balloon she'd pretend to swim underwater; they put mustard in her make-up, they'd find a chilli wiener in their underwear. Someone put down a tripwire, she'd roll over it, do a complex little jig and end up in the splits. Nothing hurt her, nothing upset her.

Her mood was always like the sun coming up on a sweet spring morning. It couldn't last. Nothing that good lasts for ever. It was inevitable that one day something would go wrong and the girl would be hurt. After all, Melia was a mouthful not a full meal.

We all pulled pranks. Some called it high jinks or practical jokes; others called it letting off steam. Boss allowed it, so long as nobody got badly hurt or needed make-up to cover a bruise. Over the years the corps did more damage to itself falling off sets or through stunts that backfired than ever happened through pranks. Most of them were silly and harmless; but the sandbag trick was misjudged – and it was aimed at me.

Sandbags are an aid in lifting things including people, automobiles and props. They swing from ropes through a block and tackle fitted at the end of a hoist or screwed into a beam. An expert will judge the weight of the sandbag to within a few ounces so whatever they're lifting doesn't get launched into space. It's a fine art. Then one day one of those sandbag scientists rigged a door they knew I would walk through.

I got a message that the Boss wanted to discuss a new idea for the next movie, if I had five minutes. He was on stage one. I was on stage two. Between the two was a wide corridor full of boxes and props. Melia followed me out. When she wasn't working she was often with me – she seemed relaxed in my company. I was probably the only guy who hadn't hit on her at some point, well, me and the Boss.

She was at my elbow when we walked out into the corridor, her voice fluttering and chattering like excited birdsong. I never needed to answer her; she was like a pot full of life that kept bubbling through the lid. I couldn't take the grin off my face when she was around me: she made something float in my chest. We got to stage one and I pulled that big door outwards.

I saw something swinging towards me and I automatically got out of its way. It was a sandbag on a slender rope, not a big one, but enough to wind a tall man and bowl him over. It could have been a bucket of water or a pitcher of milk, but it was a sandbag and I got out of its way. I went to my left. Melia was behind me and slightly to my right. She didn't have a stuntman's instincts.

The bag missed her precious face, which was a blessing, but it clouted her hard on the side of her head. I heard it strike like a baseball bat. That glorious mass of midnight hair must have cushioned some of the blow, but enough got through to send her spinning like a ten-pin in a bowling alley. She was thrown completely off her feet, spun in mid-air, slammed bonelessly into the solid wood of the open door and dropped like a stone.

I instantly threw myself down on my knees beside her. My stomach was knotted, my heart pounding. There was a curious buzzing sound in my ears. I pushed the hair away from her face. Her skin was white as paper, and I mean good white paper too. There was no blood. I had a little first aid training that I'd picked up along the way, but none of it included 'things to do when a dot of a girl gets clubbed to the ground by a sandbag'.

A voice rasped out, 'That should never have happened. Leave her, don't move her. She might have a broken neck. Bisset's running for the doctor. What kind of crazy foolishness *is* this? Lance, what happened? Where did Melia come from? Why was she here? Speak up man!'

The Boss's voice was quivering with barely suppressed rage. His face was almost as white as Melia's and his feet were spread and his fists clenched like a boxer looking to throw a punch. He bent over us like a protective wall. I never thought of him as a big man; but looking up at him just then, he was like a grizzly bear. The Boss looked ready to rip a cougar limb from limb.

I tried to answer but my heart was stuck in my throat. He got blurry. He reached down with a handkerchief, 'Have a blow, Lieutenant. Doctor will be here any second. We'll look after her, you bet your boots we will. That little girl is the most precious thing on this set. She could star in a single reel on her own and have them lining up to see it. Damn! That shouldn't have happened. I'm angry!'

I blew my nose and was surprised to find my face wet as if I'd just washed it. Why was my face wet? I looked up to see if the rain was coming in through the skylight windows. No, but the sky was white as Melia's face. I fought to stop shaking but I couldn't help it. It felt like someone had taken the tendons of my spine in a fierce grip and twisted them. I groaned and buckled.

'Lieutenant, why are you crying? Are you alright? Oh, oh dear, you look so sad. Oh, *ouch*! My head. I ache all over, what happened?'

Her big eyes blinked at me. The whites were pink and she was finding it difficult to focus, I could tell because her pupils were roaming around my face like a blind man's fingers.

'Don't move,' I said. 'Doctor's on his way. You'll be fine, there's nothing to worry about, he just wants to take a look at you. Stay still until he arrives.'

'I don't need a doctor.'

She tried to sit up, bad idea. Her eyes rolled back into her head and she went down again in a flat faint. I caught her before she slapped her head against the floor. *Where was that damn-fool doctor?* I wondered. *Was he crawling here on his belly?* I could hear the Boss ripping the hide off everyone on set. He didn't have a specific target, he didn't need one.

Someone had done something dangerous and stupid; someone else must have seen it. Boss would put the screws on the whole pack until one of them cracked.

'Get the hell out my way you baboons! Where's my patient?' I guessed the doctor had got off his belly and arrived at last. His voice cracked like a whip. It was the voice of a man accustomed to being obeyed. I didn't care, just so long as he could find his way around to fixing whatever ailed little Melia.

The great man loomed up like a dark storm cloud, eclipsing all light. My main impression was of a pink egg balanced atop a mass of wire wool, which was perched above a mountain of expensive tweed. He breathed noisily as he squatted down beside us. He reached out with surprisingly long and elegant fingers which were hairy as any ape's, but he didn't touch his supine patient.

He flicked a glance at me, the whites of his eyes were as pink as Melia's. I smelt strong liquor and wondered where Bisset had found this bulky medical paragon. Had he dragged him out of the nearest bar? His poached eyes looked concerned. His voice had become gentle.

'How long has she been unconscious?'

I looked at my watch. With a shock I realised it had been just over fifteen minutes since I had received the call to go see the Boss. It seemed like an eternity. 'Bout a quarter hour, tops.'

'Very good. Has she moved at all? I understand she suffered a blow to the head from a sandbag? Is that true?'

'Yes, she moved. She came around just now and tried to sit up. She spoke to me. She looked dazed, you know? She couldn't focus.' I pointed at the sandbag which still hung like a guilty head from its rope in the middle of the stage. 'That's the bag she was hit with, that one there.'

Doctor looked at the bag, down at Melia's crumpled form, and then at me again. I couldn't see his mouth for all the black wool sprouting from his cheeks, but I could discern the sneer from his narrowed eyes and the barb that sharpened his next words.

'Is this sort of cretinous behaviour a regular occurrence?'

I didn't feel like defending the 'cretin' who had struck down our girl.

'They play the giddy fool and twit each other most days, but this is downright stupid and unusual. I would like to get my hands on whoever did this and give them a sound Ohio thrashing. Is she going to be okay?'

The voice was gentle again, I had obviously not been counted amongst the league of cretinous fools, at least, not entirely. 'Let's take a look, shall we?'

In the background I was aware of Bisset hovering like an agitated crow. A dark suspicion entered my mind but I dismissed it for the time being. The doctor was talking again. I missed his words and apologised. He repeated.

'I need to examine my patient. Can we please clear this scene? This is not one of your little cinematic comedies, get the clowns out of here.'

I looked up, 'Boss, can we get Melia and the Doc a little privacy here?'

Boss bellowed, 'Okay, people. Take five, hit the commissary. Hal, organise the makings. Get coffee and doughnuts on the board.'

A man protested. It was Hal Bisset. He whined, 'I want to see Melia's going to be all right. I'll wait here.'

Boss collared the fool, 'We don't want to cramp the doctor, do we? Get your raggedy ass where I tell you or I'll kick it there! Move it, buster!'

Bisset whimpered something inaudible and the Boss levered an ominous leg at the seat of his trousers. Within seconds the stage was empty of all except the doctor, Melia, and me. I saw the Boss standing for a moment in the commissary doorway. He gave me a thumbs up; and was gone. The door slammed shut.

'Are you her husband?'

I was surprised by the doctor's question and blurted, 'Not yet. I'm her boyfriend.' It was an answer that his enquiry must have shocked all the way up from my boots. It was a secret to me until that moment, but I heard the truth in it as soon as I said it. 'I'm going to pop the question right soon.'

Melia whispered, 'Yes, okay.'

Doctor's eyes crinkled warmly, I felt a sudden gush of affection for him.

'Looks like you have your answer.' I heard the smile in his voice. And then he was all business once more. 'Enough of this. Congratulations and all that, but I need to see what we have here. Hand me my bag, please.'

25

[6]

It was concussion. In fact, the doctor said, Melia had suffered a severe concussion. If the moron who set the trap had taken a lead weighted sap to the back of Melia's head he couldn't have laid her out more soundly.

He told me nothing was broken, which was a mercy, but she would have a headache and uncomfortable bruising for a while. The doctor was loudly scathing about 'idiot pranksters' and 'dangerous lunatics' who would be better kept in restraints and should, he said, learn a lesson by being 'pelted with rotten fruit in the stocks.'

'When you discover who did this, and I'm certain you will, tell him his village called. They want their idiot back. Tell him you are happy to pay for the ticket, one way, cattle class. He is not fit for civilised company.'

He had a quiet chat with Melia, now roused from her stupor, and told her he was prescribing a combination of aspirin and codeine, which should help with any pain.

'They come in tablet form, my dear, easy to swallow. They are not to be taken with a large quantity of alcohol but a glass or two of wine won't hurt. Take one of each whenever you feel uncomfortable. The drugstore on Fifth will have them. Your fiancée will fetch them for you. He seems a good sort. They are quite strong and you might feel a bit dizzy afterwards but that's normal enough. Now, who do I give my invoice to?'

I fetched the Boss from the commissary. He dealt with the doctor then sat with Melia while I ran out and collected her prescription. She seemed in fine spirits when I returned but kept looking at me oddly. She had the air of someone trying to remember where she had left something vitally important. She took two of her tablets and soon settled into a happy daze. She had become her sparkly self again, but as if floating on a fluffy cloud.

'Fiancée?' she mused. 'The doctor said fiancée. Who was he talking about? He said my fiancée would fetch my tablets, but it was you who went to get them, Lieutenant. Are we going to get married?'

The Boss cast a raised eyebrow at both of us. He said, 'I was only out there drinking coffee for a few minutes, and you were out for the count, Melia. What's happened since? You fine folk moved faster than a field full of hares come springtime?' He raised the bottles of tablets. 'You want to be careful with these, boo'ful. Says here "can cause matrimony". The writing's small but it's clear as a bell.'

26

Melia took the bottle and gazed quizzically at the label. 'Izzat so? I think that word says "drowsiness". Are you pulling my leg, Boss?'

He looked affronted. 'And it's such a fine leg. But am I the sort of man to be pulling the leg of a soon to be married person of the female persuasion? I ask you? Am I?'

Melia sat more upright and opened her pink tinged bunny eyes wider. 'Mister Boss, sir. Do you think a lady should be marched to the altar without being asked first? I mean, wouldn't it be best for a girl to have the chance to say yes or no? Don't you think? I would say so, yes sirree! Wouldn't you?'

They both looked at me. Melia was smiling and acting a little drunk, which might have been due to her medicine or the clout to her head. Boss was fighting a grin; made me think I was probably going to be damned or fired or tarred and feathered, no matter what I said next. Like the boss's spring hare I felt the wire snare pulling tight around my ankle.

'Well?' he asked, archly.

'Well?' I replied, astonished at my rapier-like wit.

'Well, the day's a write-off and I've sent the corps home. As you can see, the cameras are not rolling and the writers are right now sitting in some sleazy bar making up a pile of whisky-fuelled claptrap that will never see the light of day. We might as well see some profit at the end of a wasted hour. So, what about it? Everyone knows you two are Romeo and Martha, the farmer's daughter. What about it?'

Melia blinked. 'I thought that was Juliet? I'm sure that was Juliet.'

'You've got the wrong man. Not that Romeo. This is Romeo Mendoza from California, and Martha Ramirez, the farmer's daughter. You know them?'

'Are we going to California?'

Before the conversation went too far down the rabbit hole I jumped onto their mad trolley bus and tried to pull on the brakes with both hands. Boss could steer a conversation into a figure of eight around a fire hydrant when he was of a mind to, and I felt it was time for a saner hand to take a grip on things.

'Well,' I said, rising to the occasion like the man of the hour. That snare had caught my ankle and bit deep, no fighting it now. 'Well,' I repeated. 'Is it such a bad idea?'

'Going to California?' said the Boss. 'Why not? The light would be better, land is cheaper down there, and we'd be away from the Edison patent laws. A lot of studios are making the move. It's a thought.'

'No,' I groaned. 'What about us getting married?'

The Boss squinted at me. 'I like you, Lieutenant, I like you are lot. But this is a little sudden. Can I have a few minutes to think about it?'

I looked at him in horror, 'No, Boss, no! I meant Melia. Melia, will you marry me? I'll get down on one knee.'

Boss scraped his nails across the dark shadow of bristle on his chin. His hair was white as eiderdown but his chin was pure Cajun black before midday.

'Wait a second,' he mused. 'Hang on there, how much can I get by suing you for breach of contract? You asked me first. Don't I get first dibs on the ring?'

Melia said, 'Yes, okay.' She said it in the same dreamy way she had said it when she was still out cold. 'Yes,' she smiled like an angel. 'That would be nice. We *should* get married.'

I couldn't take my eyes off her, I stuttered, 'Yes. I mean, that would be great. Boss, can we have some time off to get married?'

'What? Both of you at the same time? You guys want the whole cake and the cherry on top. What kind of a studio gives key honchoes time off to get spliced? A bankrupt one, that's what. *And* you'll want a honeymoon I bet. Jeeze!'

He clapped his hands, 'Say, can I be the best man? Yeah! If I can't be the bride I can at least be the best man. I still get to wear white, or at least a tuxedo. And spats, I can wear spats. Yeah, wow! I will look so damn good. So will you, Melia. You polish up nice too. We'll make a beautiful couple. My mouth's watering already.'

My bride-to-be spoke up, 'Actually, Boss, if you don't mind, I was wondering if you'd give me away. My pa's ill and I'd be right proud if you'd do the honours. Right proud.'

The Boss was never at a loss for words. His mind was like a ticker tape machine continuously reeling out snappy one-liners. But at that moment he did his finest impersonation of a beached fish and the words stayed caught behind his gaping teeth. The joking stopped right there.

Melia gazed at him with embarrassment painted so large on her face it might have been slapped there with a wallpaper hanger's brush. She took some colour in her cheeks and looked ready to spill the waterworks in earnest.

'I'm sorry, Boss. I shouldn't have asked.' She got to her feet and made as if to run for the hills. She didn't get far before she lurched and staggered to a halt, pressing her hands to her eyes. She groaned, 'What have I done?' Boss was at her side before she said another word.

He hugged her and kissed her cheek. 'Melia, I'd be happy to be a simple usher at your wedding, but you want to give me the star supporting role? Are you sure? I'll try to make sure my feet are big enough to fill your pa's shoes. It would be an honour and a privilege to give you away. Hell, I might even negotiate a few dollars for the transaction. You'd like a decent honeymoon? Let me see what I can do to get a little good time capital behind your wedding plans.'

We got married four months later in Trinity Church near the intersection of Wall Street and Broadway in the lower Manhattan section. Don Sherwood acted as my best man and six of the Century Beauties acted as bridesmaids. The Boss wore white just as he said he would, complete with spats.

Our wedding photographer was some womanish fellow from *Harper's Bazaar*. Boss had been as good as his word in getting us some extra spending money for our honeymoon. He had sold the exclusive rights to our wedding story to the renowned fashion magazine for a pretty penny. They had even supplied Melia's dress and jewellery as part of the package.

My girl looked wonderful without a scrap of make-up, but *Harper's* pushed the boat so far out she stepped off it and into the church looking like God had spent seven days doing nothing but make her look perfect for the occasion. When the Boss walked her to my side and I lifted her veil, my knees turned to water. I had never seen anyone so beautiful.

The rest of the day passed in a daze for me. I know we signed to say we were legal. Don had the rings safely in one of his pockets and we got them on the right fingers at the right time. I kissed the bride and I felt it clean down to my toes. Then everyone else wanted a piece of the lady. Don Sherwood literally lifted Hal Bisset off her to plant his noisy smacker on her lips.

The *Harper's* guy took enough photographs to wallpaper the whole church, including the windows. He seemed in something of a quandary as to whether the new Mrs Murdoch should be posed next to her freshly unwrapped husband or the much prettier Don Sherwood.

He compromised by inviting our best man for a drink after the reception, which Don accepted. Then the photographer remembered our little wedding and got busy with his camera once more.

We rode an open coach and pair to the reception at Keen's Steakhouse, 72 West 36 Street. We ate dinner under the gentle varnished gaze of Mr Abraham Lincoln and some other vintage folks I couldn't identify. The walls were packed with paintings. The rich and the famous through the ages had been hung shoulder to shoulder, something my father would have applauded on any beer-soaked Friday evening. He, however, would have used a gallows. None of them pinned us with a glare to match Hal Bisset's.

Hal could go hang with the rest of them. I would allow nothing to dampen my spirits. I had my best girl to my left and her pleasantly tipsy mother to my right. My Pa was in the opinionated stage of alcohol consumption at her shoulder, directing his barbs at both my new mother-in-law and the maid of honour, one Florence Casey.

Florence was a timorous forest creature Melia had tucked under her wing the minute she cautiously sniffed her way into the wild jungles of Century Pictures. Through the day, she had taken to the wine in an attempt to survive my father's increasingly vitriolic slings and arrows. The watery eyes she pinned on Melia screamed out two things, 'help', and, 'sinking fast, send ships'.

Strong liquor has never been a lure for me. I had seen it take my father's wits too often to wilfully open my door to its temptations. Around the Boss's shoulder my mother was gazing along the table towards Pa with enough fire in her eyes to burn a hole in my father's rented suit – and roast everything it contained. It was clear to me that as soon as Ma finally got the privacy she needed to start laying down her mind, my father would be nothing but a pile of baked meats and charcoal.

I had booked my parents a room in a nearby hotel and already I pitied any neighbours who were hoping for a quiet night's sleep. Pa, in his cups, was an orator to rival Cicero, but Ma, in her righteous fury, was a preacher with a fine line in fire and brimstone.

She could thump louder than any Senator at his tub, and she willingly laid the stones for her husband's certain path to Hell's hottest corner, and always had. And given half a chance she would drag her husband along it and feed him to hellfire damnation without need of any pitchfork. I pitied any demons that might get in her way.

I turned away from the skirmish, took my wife's hand, and pressed my lips to it. She gasped and jumped as if I had drenched her with ice-water. 'Soon,' she whispered to me. 'Soon.'

7

Alone at last we took a cab to The Plaza on Fifth Avenue. The Boss had paid for one night in the bridal suite as our first wedding present. After telling me about it he promised me that our *second* wedding present would be, 'So much hard work for both of you as soon as you get back I might one day be able to afford to pay for it.'

He scowled, 'You think I've ridden you hard before, Lieutenant? That was nothing. You and the good Mrs Murdoch are going to make my fortune. You've the beginnings of talent and she's a born genius. With me cracking the whip and you bleeding in stripes we'll be making so much money we'll soon bleeding dollar bills into the Hudson. Kiss the lady for me, Lance. Anything else you do is up to her husband.' And he shook my hand like he meant it.

We had climbed out of our wedding finery and changed into our going away outfits in a quiet back room at the Steakhouse. Melia got changed behind a Chinese screen. I heard the silken sounds of lingerie on smooth skin while I stood in the middle of the room and buttoned into my lounge suite then wrestled with a fresh collar and tie. My mouth was dry with nerves.

'Hey, Lieutenant,' her voice thrilled from behind the peacock tapestries.

'Hey, wife,' I whispered back.

'Gimme a hand here. I'm all thumbs for some reason.'

I made the long walk to the screen then stepped around it, my heart in my mouth. Melia stood with her bare back to me. She was almost wearing something floral and blue that was just about long enough to cover her behind, if it hadn't been flapping wide open like an invitation. I could see that it clipped together using little buttons and loops, but my eyes explored everything else on show.

'Can you do the buttons up for me, my love? I've never worn anything like this before. Damn, but it's a complicated business.'

I sighed, 'I've never been called "my love" before, and I've never seen a beautiful girl in her unmentionables neither. My Lord but you're lovely.'

Melia turned, her small, pink nippled breasts stood proud of the little outfit. She was as fine and exotic a sight as the peacocks on the screen. She pressed herself against me and chuckled. 'We've got a roomful of guests to say goodbye to, and our wedding night hotel-room to get to. Can you wait just a little longer?'

She rubbed the front of my trousers with her hip. 'We'd better get dressed or we're going to be late for our own honeymoon.' She looked down at my discomfort, which made things worse.

She smiled like a wicked child, 'Oooh! Nice to know the little man can find his way so far north when he has to. I'd be glad to lend him a hand later, but right now I need you to button me up. Then I'll sort out that mess of a collar.'

I fumbled her buttons shut. There were eight of them, I counted each one. The only thing under that thin fabric was Melia, all soft and firm and delicious. My heart was pounding so hard I was surprised it didn't beat it's way out of my chest and pound itself to death on the floor. I could hear my pulse in my breath. I felt delirious, as if I had woken from a dream and found reality to be better.

We got dressed. Melia's trousseau stayed behind with my marriage duds, all of which would be collected by *Harper's Bazaar*. What we walked out to greet our guests in was all our very own. Thing is, my shoes were new and I have big feet. After a few minutes I wanted my feet out of those shoes as much as I wanted my wife out of that little blue number with its eight buttons. Very shortly after that I wanted those shoes off even more than I wanted to see Melia in a state of nature, they were raw agony.

I explained my problem to Don Sherwood. He eyed my spanking new English Loake brogues and then looked down at his stylishly sporty tan and cream wingtips. He always had taste.

'Would a best man be worthy of the name if he didn't make a small sacrifice when required?' He smiled, 'Let's exchange shoes. I'll be fine so long as Clement doesn't want to go dancing. He might, he strikes me as a physical little Ganymede. At least, I do hope so. Yes, I do hope so.'

Clement was our *Harper's* photographer. A million women's hearts would break if they knew the truth about Don Sherwood's taste in lovers. Like so many of the handsomest men listed in the pages of *Variety* he preferred his own sex. However, he had never flirted with me, and one day I asked him why.

'Darling, if I ever develop a taste for beefsteak you'll be the first on my wish list. Until then I'll feed my greed for fluffy little meringues; they melt on the tongue so gratifyingly.'

Don's taste in amours was his own affair, love is too complex a business to have opinions about it, but his footwear fit me like an angel's kiss. I somehow knew he would wear comfortable shoes. I pitied him when I saw him wincing his way across the floor in mine.

'There'll be no dancing tonight, unless it's barefoot,' he said. Across the room the womanish little photographer waved coyly at us and smiled winsomely. Don waved back, 'Or bareback,' he grinned.

My suit was blue and the shoes were brown and cream. That didn't worry me in the least, but my new bride's eyes flared wide when she saw me.

'You borrowed somebody else's feet!' She said, 'Go give them back this instant. You can't wear brown shoes like those with a blue suit! It's practically immoral. They'll spike you for a fake when we reach The Plaza, and they'll be sure to throw you over the falls when we reach The Clifton. Oh, honey, I love you, but when it comes to clothes you really need some urgent education from a strict school marm. It's a fact mister, you married me just in time. Go fetch, get those shoes back, honey.'

I looked around for Don Sherwood to get my torture instruments back, but he and his new beau had already vanished into the Manhattan mist. At that moment a uniformed bellboy under a natty pillbox hat called out from the door to the lobby, 'Mr and Mrs Murdoch? Your cab is here!'

I squared my shoulders and took Melia firmly by the elbow. I looked around the banqueting room at the remaining gang of grinning clowns and spotted Bisset skulking around sucking up any wine left in our guests' glasses and pouring himself the dregs from the bottles.

Scraping the bottom of the barrel as usual, I thought. *I bet* he *wears brown shoes with a blue suit, or blue shoes with a brown suit, or any damn colour shoes with any damn colour suit. Enough of that.*

'Ladies and gentlemen,' I said, loud enough so I could be heard. 'Thank you for making a very special day a real, four-reeler, Century Pictures masterpiece. But now we must be on our way. Your leading lady and her gallant Lieutenant's carriage awaits. Exit stage left. Our honeymoon calls to us like a whippoorwill in the wilderness and we won't leave it lonely another minute. See y'all in a week's time and don't break any more heads until we're back.'

When I made this last statement Bisset gave a guilty little jerk of his shoulders before draining another unfinished glass of fine claret. At that rate he would be spending the night in the drunk tank. It'd be good to see him arrested for something. I wouldn't let him spoil the day, I was already wearing the wrong colour of shoes.

The memory of the iron-like grip of those Loakes on my size twelve feet was enough to make me grimace. I saw Bisset glaring back at me, fine! If Bisset saw my expression and thought it was aimed at him, then so be it. I had no proof he had set the sandbag trap, but as the padre once told me 'a guilty soul finds censure in every glance'.

If he had done it, he'd be his own worse judge and jury and we had places to be. We'd leave his poison behind when we left the Steakhouse. We'd leave him to look for solace in all those half-empty glasses and may the wine turn sour in his belly.

Melia looked askance at me and pursed her fine lips. She wore her heart on her sleeve all right. I must have let my rancour with the Bisset hound bleed onto my face, damn the man!

'Honey,' she said, 'we just got married. I kinda expected you to look happy but you should see your face! You look like you were promised T-bone but got handed the gristle without gravy.'

'Sorry, love. I'm just so over the moon, I was worried it couldn't last. And the thing is,' I lowered my voice, 'we're on honeymoon. And, I want everything to be just right, but I don't have much... The thing is, I'm not... Damn! What I want to say is I've always kept myself to myself, and I haven't run around playing the happy rooster. So if I seem a little awkward in the clinches please be patient, I'll be doing my best.'

She stared up at me with eyes so big I could have fallen into them and drowned in a second. If *I* looked like I got the gristle *she* looked like she had just been goosed with a broom handle. I started to stutter an explanation but she wasn't listening, she just shook her head in amazement. Then she surprised me, which wasn't the first time and it wouldn't be the last. Melia started laughing.

If every angel in heaven and every songbird in Central Park had started making noise at the same time they couldn't have competed with the effect of Melia's laugh on everyone around her. She swamped them with joy. Even the hound Bisset developed a smeary grin.

Melia convulsed with laughter and slapped her thighs. People from the next room came to see what the fuss was all about; and joined in with the jocularity. No-one knew what the joke was, but they laughed until they cried and in the heart of all the fun was the little lady magician casting her magic spell and turning pink as a rose.

Then a gloomy man in a flat cap stepped through the door and said, 'I got a cab out front and the clock's ticking. Any of you ladies and gents a Mr and Mrs Murdoch? Your ride's already cost you a dollar fifty and you ain't gone anywhere yet. I'm happy to spend your money so long as you're happy to waste it. That's all I'm saying. Clock's ticking.'

I grabbed Melia's elbow and steered her through our grinning guests. We followed the gloomy flat cap to the sound of a chorus of farewells and a few whistles. Somewhere at the back someone started singing a song I recognised and hoped Melia didn't. It was a version of 'The boy I love' that had been altered to a lewd effect. Let's just say the boy she loved wasn't up in the gallery, he was much closer than that. And if he was looking down it wasn't to wave his handkerchief.

The flat cap led us out to one of those tall and curvaceous maroon boxes that looked like something from the future, a battery powered Detroit Electric Brougham. He opened the door and let us climb into the back, then he swung himself in behind the tiller, pulled the door closed, and the cab hissed away as silent as a child's prayer. We were on our own at last. The Brougham was as fast as a flats champion racer, and we were warm out of the mist on a comfy leather bench.

Melia snuggled up to me and put her head on my shoulder. 'I love you, mister brown shoes,' she whispered.

'I love you too, Mrs Giggles.'

The flat cap cast a rapid glance at us over his shoulder and beamed a surprisingly broad grin. 'You going to The Plaza on Fifth Avenue? That right?' he asked, his eyes back on the busy road.

'Yes,' I answered.

'Right you are, sir' he replied. 'Lucky you're with such a lovely young lady, if you'd pardon me for saying so, miss.'

'Of course,' replied Melia. 'But why?'

'Well, with a bit of luck the concierge might be so busy looking at you, miss, that he'll ignore the young gentleman's shoes. He's a demon for the correct attire in his hotel is Monsieur Lavell, a proper sergeant major. But, fingers crossed, he won't notice.'

Fingers crossed? I thought. And groaned inwardly.

8

I could have crossed my fingers and also my toes in those traitorous comfortable shoes and it wouldn't have helped. I'd been strongly tempted to cross my eyes, no luck. Melia did her best when we entered the lobby of the Plaza. She positively sparkled trying to create a diversion, and when she engaged her star quality at full blast the general public needed sun glasses or they risked being dazzled. But this time it didn't work.

I worked out that Monsieur Lavell was the tall, reed-thin man standing, no, *lurking* by the reception desk. He had to be. He was as fancy antique French as the hotel's lobby, sporting an immaculate two-tone bouffant and a waxed moustache that could have been used as an offensive weapon. He gleamed.

His eyes crossed the elegant floor and settled on my footwear like a sniper taking aim. His moustache lifted and his nose wrinkled as if an overripe Limburger cheese had unexpectedly roosted under it. He stalked towards me, a glistening vulture swooping down on his helpless prey.

Melia tried to cut him off at the pass by stepping in front of him and raising her hand, but he slid around her, slippery as an eel, and perched before me. The praying mantis about to pounce. I got both nostrils pointed at my forehead, full bore, and behind them his fully loaded eyes were cocked and primed with French disdain. I've noticed the way French folk use disdain like a wild west Texan using a Colt Peacemaker, and both have itchy trigger fingers.

He spoke. Ice tinkled in the air like razor sharp crystal. 'Congratulations, monsieur. You 'ave won your little bet. You 'ave brought your noisy collision of poor taste and sartorial comedy into my 'otel lobby to 'orrify my guests – and you *almost* reached the reception desk. But not quite. Well done. I salute you. But the *petite jeu* is over, you are caught. Please, go away and take those Tin Pan Alley pimp's shoes with you. *Alors*, bye, bye. But, why are you still 'ere?'

A guy in a swallowtail coat and a black cravat bobbed his way around from behind the front desk and cringed into Monsieur Lavell's awesome presence like a minnow approaching a shark. He inserted himself into the great man's shadow, almost melting with fear. I could smell the sweat on him and see the sheen of it on his upper lip.

I wondered what terrible hold the disdainful Frenchman held over his cowed staff. Did he have a torture chamber hidden away below stairs? Even with his little minion rubbing his hands together trying to get his attention Monsieur Lavell kept his vulture's beak of a nose aimed directly at me. I smiled at him, which saw his thin mouth quirk upwards slightly as if caught on a fisherman's hook.

'Mr Lavell,' I said, ignoring the 'monsieur' honorific. After all we were in NYC, not Paris. 'Mr Lavell,' I repeated, 'my wife and I are booked into your bridal suite. I'd be mighty grateful if you could call us a boy to show us to our room, thank you kindly.' His eyes narrowed and glittered dangerously.

I continued, 'I have driven fast cars into burning buildings and walked along telephone wires thirty feet in the air – without a safety net. I have driven motorcycles off cliffs into the sea and clung by my fingertips from the roofs of skyscrapers. I have also married one of the most beautiful women in the world, today, this very afternoon.'

I stepped a little closer, the nostrils flared. I continued, 'Not much scares me, so you can believe that the sight of a Frenchman's nostrils will not set my knees a' knocking. Now, sir, are you going to call that boy?'

Slow as a mill wheel turned by an exhausted donkey, Lavell turned his head and gazed at Melia. She beamed at him. The warmth of her smile froze and died about a foot from his bleak countenance. Swivelling en route back to sneering at me, he found his underling quivering by his side. He turned on the poor man with frigid contempt.

'Monsieur 'Amilton, you are not at your post. You 'ave, perhaps, a very good reason why I shouldn't ask you to 'and in your cravat and seek less enlightened employment elsewhere? Well? Speak up?'

Mr 'Amilton stuttered his reply, 'S, s, sir, I, I, thought it best to warn you sir. I know how much the fine reputation of The Plaza matters to you, sir. I thought it best to warn you, sir.'

'Warn me 'Amilton? Warn me of what? Is this ill-dressed ruffian...' I guessed he meant me. 'Is this ill-attired oaf with his so antic shoes a desperate criminal who will shoot me down in cold blood if I treat him as the comic figure he so plainly is?'

The little man's lips must have got stuck to the seat of his boss's pants for a few seconds because all he managed was a gurgling mumble. Then he rallied. The spirited blood of Lexington and Concord was still pumping around his American veins and he roused himself to face his oppressor.

'No, sir,' he said with a touch of Yankee steel in his eye. 'But this gentleman is Mr Lance Murdoch, a noted director with Century Pictures, and his wife is the famous Melia Nord, now Mrs Murdoch. They have chosen to spend the first night of their famous nuptials with us here in The Plaza, sir. It is a feather in our cap, sir, the newspapers will love it. We wouldn't want to upset the apple cart would we, sir? Not even with a fit of understandable pique, sir. Would we? Sir?'

It was evident that Monsieur Lavell had met his Waterloo, but he didn't go down without a parting shot. He smeared a smile across his face that was as friendly and welcoming as a yellow plague marker; and turned it on poor Melia. She quailed under its chill impact. *The man's a pantomime monster*, I decided, *we must find room for this character in a two-reeler before the year is out.*

'Very well, 'Amilton. I shall escort the good madam to 'er room while you take Mr Murdoch to Johnston and Murphy. There 'e can be provided with more suitable footwear. *Vite*, now, time is wasting and my poor eyes can no longer bear the agony of seeing those... those... things. 'Amilton, make sure you bring them back in a bag. I will not see them again. *Bon, vite. Allez!* Go!'

In a matter of seconds I found myself back outside in the misty chill of a Fifth Avenue late afternoon in early March. The sun had vanished behind the towering bulk of the Avenue's broad-shouldered buildings. Architects must have taken bets on how high they could build and how many windows they could use without the whole house of cards falling on its face. Evening visited in time for tea in those man-made canyons, but the street was still crowded with vehicles and horse buggies.

There were increasingly few horse-drawn transports those days, but such had not always been the case. There had been a time, quite recently, when the streets were lively with a circus of trotting hooves, and horse droppings had become a serious problem on the New York streets. Men were employed to clear them into the gutters, and the stench could be suffocating.

Pedestrians back then walked along narrow gullies formed of horse manure on one side and buildings on the other. Inconsiderate ruffians might push a passer-by into the filth then walk away laughing; and on a hot day women could become overcome by the noxious stink and faint clean away.

The arrival of the automobile was applauded as a stone blessing because it brought with it cleaner air and vastly improved, more sanitary footpaths.

Mr 'Amilton, who I discovered was really named Clarence Hamilton, was a transformed character as soon as he stepped out of the hotel lobby. In fact the further we walked away from Lavell the more human Clarence became. His speech became quite lively.

He accepted a cigarette from me, tapped it on the back of his hand and paused while I lit it for him. He took a grateful pull and sipped on the smoke as if it was mother's milk. I lit one for myself before we continued our amiable stroll in search of suitable shoes.

Clarence chuckled, 'Don't pay no never mind to Monsieur Lavell. His bark is worse than his bite, though I have seen him bring younger housemaids to tears if their apron ain't tied in the exact right kinda bow. And don't let that accent fool you. He's no more French than you or me. He is a particular man though, and will have things just so – to the point where other folks might look at him kinda sideways, if you know what I mean?'

I allowed that I did; and then asked why the hotel owners let Lavell talk to guests like that.

Clarence grinned and shook his head, 'He don't, or at least so rarely it don't make no never mind. Fact is I don't think he's ever seen such a sporty pair of heels on his lobby floor before as those two-tones you're wearing. Yessir, I reckon they turned his weather cock until it was pointing due north, and he couldn't help himself. Man started acting like a crazy bear. Ah, this is it, Johnston and Murphy. Let me introduce you, they know me here.'

I swear I could have purchased my parent's prize bull for the money I paid for that shiny black shoe leather. But the guys in the store knew their stuff and I walked out of there with a fine and comfortable pair of black wingtips that even Lavell's phoney French eyes couldn't fault.

By way of thanks I offered to buy Clarence a drink in the hotel bar once we re-entered The Plaza's French tart of a lobby – I thought that after my latest investment in footwear I'd be welcome anywhere – but he gazed at me with open-mouthed amazement.

'Mr Murdoch, sorry, but you have *Miss Melia Nord* waiting for you in the bridal suite. Miss Melia Nord! And you want to waste time with a *man* in the *bar*? Sir, I've met some cucumbers in my time but you're so cool you put any iceberg to shame.'

He shook his head, 'Sure, I'd be proud to belly up to the brass rail and blow the suds off a cold one with you sometime, and even take a sip of Kentucky's finest at its elbow. But right now you got somewhere you need to be – and that ain't in no bar with me. Come on, sir, follow me to your lovely new wife; and make those smart new shoes of yours step on it like a greyhound to the hare.'

He was right and I didn't argue. When he got me to my door I shook hands and made sure he palmed the five note he had earned from me on pure entertainment value alone. He carried a wise head on narrow shoulders. He grinned and gave me a thumbs up as he walked away and I returned the salute.

I waited until he was out of sight before I rapped on the door. Visions of my beautiful wife danced before my mind's eye, the breath caught in my chest in happy anticipation.

'What the *HELL* is it now?'

Something told me that the harpy's voice battering its way through the door's elegant panelling was not that of a happy woman.

[9]

Lavell gave my feet the full ten-degree inspection before he deigned to raise his eyes to my face. I guessed my footwear must have passed his stringent criteria because he blessed me with a lemon-sucking smile that made me think of a camel's ass puckering tight in a sandstorm.

'Monsieur, I congratulate you on your *tout ensemble*. Voila, you must now feel every inch the *l'homme moderne et à la mode*. But, surely you should be with the very lovely madam? What can I do for you? What is so important that you have left her side for so much as a moment? What ails you?'

I told him what ailed me, and I used short sentences. His narrow eyes snapped wide open and he chewed on my words as if trying to suck the juice out of them, then he led me to a quiet corner. My news had knocked the wind and the Frenchman clean out of him. He spoke low and intense, and he sounded like a civilised American.

'Every fifteen minutes? But this is terrible! Horrible! What? Here in my hotel? And on your honeymoon?' He looked at his pocket watch as if it was a guilty party. 'They'll be at it again! We must do something to put a stop to this mischief, and we must act quickly.'

It had started almost the second Melia had begun to unpack our overnight bag and lay out our knick-knacks on the bed and in the bathroom. There came a knock at the door. She opened it to discover a uniformed hombre carrying a tray containing an ice bucket with a bottle of Champagne and two chilled glasses. He offered to uncork the wine but she said no and sent him away with a dollar tip and a flash of the famous Melia Nord smile.

She had no sooner returned to unpacking when there came another knock at the door. That time it was flowers. Fifteen minutes later it was Belgian chocolates. Five minutes after that it was me. Ten minutes after me, just about the time Melia had finished laying out her suspicions, a maid arrived with bathrobes and slippers.

Somebody was obviously playing the wiseacre with our honeymoon, and I decided to take my grievances to the guy in charge. Lavell proved to be a man of action after all. He called 'Amilton to his side and they butted heads for five minutes behind one of the great lobby pillars. Whatever the plan was, Lavell was taking no chances. The wrongdoers must not be allowed to catch so much as the merest hint of his solution.

Hamilton nodded and grinned, hustled over to the reception desk, and quietly fetched a key from a little box on the wall. Lavell gave him a brisk nod and told me to follow at his heels once he had reached the stairs. I did as I was bid.

We arrived back at the bridal suite just in time to hear Melia using language they don't teach in Sunday School. She was explaining to a black fellah cowering in the doorway that our shoes didn't need polishing. She too spoke in short sentences. The startled shoeshine poke barely escaped with his hide intact.

When she saw me with Lavell, she took a deep breath, obviously planning to let him know what she thought of his gosh-darned hotel, and his gosh-darned staff. But he bowed and held up a hand to still her far from gentle reproof before it melted his eyes from their sockets.

'Madam Murdoch,' he breathed. 'We have no time for explanations, we have just a few minutes. You and your husband must grab whatever is essential and then you must come with me. There's no time to waste. Come on, we must move.'

Hamilton appeared at his elbow and helped us with our stuff. We were just preparing to put a hustle in our bustle and cut out of there when there came a knock at the door. Lavell shooed us all out of sight into the bathroom with flapping hands, ran his fingers through his bouffant, and opened the door. I peeked through a crack in the bathroom door, Melia and Clarence at my elbow.

The uniformed bellboy in the pillbox hat from Keen's Steakhouse stood grinning behind an enormous, beribboned, basket of fruit. The grin slid off his face when he caught the full force of Lavell's French fire. Both nostrils at point blank range, straight into his face. The poor boob didn't stand a chance. He wilted like lettuce on a hot griddle.

He squeaked, 'Delivery for Mr and Mizz Murdoch? I got fruit! See!' He lifted his basket. 'Fresh fruit, in a basket. There are ribbons. Special delivery.'

Lavell quivered, and his Frenchyness fell back onto his shoulders like a cloak. 'Oui, so you 'ave. So what? What is that to me? I run an 'otel, I have plenty of fruit. Go away! And take your fruit with you! *Allez!* Why are you still 'ere? Pouf, be gone! And wherever you go, perhaps you could blow your nose when you get there!'

The boy and his basket vanished without so much as a puff of smoke.

Lavell turned and bowed to us, 'I enjoyed that,' he said. 'Now, if you're ready, let's get the lead out.'

With four of us to carry our slight burden – Melia brought up the rear with the tray of Champagne – we departed our blighted crib for pastures new.

42

Hopefully, I thought, we would be allowed to enjoy an uninterrupted night at last.

Hamilton was in the van and led us down two flights of stairs to a discreet elevator. He unlocked it, we entered it. It had two buttons, one for up and one for down. We went up. When the car came to a smooth stop Hamilton slid the elevator door open. We entered a corridor of beautiful plushness.

The floors gleamed with honey-coloured polished wood and boasted exquisite oriental rugs that politely screamed expensive taste. Lavell took us through into a suite of rooms that could easily have been used as the set for a king's throne room. The leather seats and chaise longues gleamed shinier than my new shoes.

I don't know antiques from Shinola but everything in those rooms looked like it had been auditioned by experts before taking to the stage. I was out of my depth and so was the little lady. I heard Melia's sharp intake of breath while she looked around her in wonder.

'Oh,' she breathed, 'I could get used to this. It's too beautiful. Monsieur Lavell, I've never seen such furnishings.' She ran her hand across the back of deep buttoned calves' leather Chesterfield and purred like a kitten.

Lavell smiled with genuine warmth. I was beginning to like the man. He said, 'Very few people have. This is the Royal Plaza suite. The fittings are genuine Louise XV. Presidents have stayed here, royalty has graced these rooms. Your view is of Fifth Avenue. You even have your own kitchen. You could host a banquet for twelve if you wanted to. For one night you are our guests in what we like to believe are the finest rooms in any hotel in New York; if not the entire United States of America.

He shrugged, 'I'm sorry if it ruins you for any other hotel, but, it is your wedding night, and after the pranks your people have played on you – here in my hotel – I think your memory of your stay with us should be of something special rather than idiotic pranks. Hamilton will give you the tour, and I shall wish you good-night. See you at breakfast, perhaps? Sleep – well?'

He strode from the room, leaving Hamilton to perform his duties as guide while he walked us around the forty-five hundred square feet of luxurious splendour. Melia squeaked with joy when he showed us the beautiful master bedroom with its view over the Pulitzer Fountain and gold-plated fittings in the en-suite bathroom. My wife was still carrying the tray of Champagne as if she needed a shield against being in a place that swanky.

Hamilton reached out and took the tray from her. He touched the bottle. 'This is warm, we can do better than that. May I toast the bride and groom?'

We followed him into the kitchen, where he placed the wine into the door of a man-sized Kelvinator, then took a bottle of chilled Lanson from its nest. He opened the bottle with practised ease and none of that wasteful foaming spurt that throws at least a full glass of expensive fizz into the air – and onto the floor. He tilted three flutes and filled them, handed one to each of us, then raised his own. He smiled and winked at me.

'Mr Murdoch, you offered to buy me a beer. One day I shall take you up on that offer. Mrs Murdoch, you have charmed Monsieur Lavell in a way I have never seen before. You can officially lay claim to have captured the heart of a man I doubted had room in his chest for one. Birds in the trees and the movie-going public of America don't stand a chance.'

He stood tall, we clinked glasses. He said, 'So, to you both. May your new adventure last long and bring prosperity. I wish you more smiles than tears and more joys than fears. To you.'

We drank the good wine and blessed him in return. Melia stood on tip-toe and pecked him on both cheeks. His face glowed, Miss Giggles had that effect on men. And then at last we were on our own. I topped up our glasses.

'Shall we take this through to the bedroom?' I said. 'It's been a long day and we do need to get our stuff ready. For bed, I mean.'

Melia shrugged and said, 'Can we drink it in here? Do you mind? I don't want to risk spilling it on the furniture in there. I'm sorry, but this place makes me nervous.'

I knew what she meant and told her so. We sipped our wine and looked around the room like tourists on a spree, then we placed our glasses on the table and gave ourselves another tour. It was like finding that we were part of a museum exhibit or the most expensive movie set ever. Melia took her shoes off, so I did the same. My stockinged feet slid about on the floorboards.

Melia's voice sounded awed, 'Are we really going to make love in this place? I mean consummate our marriage? I mean, really? I'm scared to sit down here and we're going to... Gosh!'

'Slap me if you don't want to say anything, but have you ever done it before? With a man?'

'Done what? Oh! Yes. I mean no! Gosh. Well, it's a funny thing, I've wanted to, but we weren't married. Ma always made me promise, and anyhow, how do you ask someone about something like that? Well, how do you? I'm asking?'

I looked down at my exquisite doll of a bride. I couldn't give her an answer because I'd never been asked the question either, and I'd never asked anyone. We were both babes in a brand-new wood.

'I've never taken the practical exam beyond a little spooning in high school, spin the bottle and such,' I explained. 'But I'm pretty good on the theory. I do know we best get naked first and then hug or something. Then we see what follows. I guess it must come naturally, or we wouldn't be here. People must have found the way. They don't teach it in class and they never mentioned it in Sunday School. Not even with Adam and Eve – and they were naked.'

We were in the library. 'Naked,' Melia replied, 'in here with all these books? That can't be right. Let's have a little more wine and work this one out.'

Eventually we dropped our clothes on the bed, and then my wife and I went into the bathroom, where we hugged and I kissed her properly for the first time. I was right, we worked it out in the end – quite a few times.

Finally, we saw sunlight spill through the bedroom window while we shared one of the big bathtubs and got ourselves ready to face the morning.

We hadn't touched the bed all night, nor most of the furniture, but we had walked through that Royal Suite in a state of nature. Neither of us wanted to waste our time there by sleeping, and we had each awakened a fire in the other that burned hotter when we fed it. The new day meant our time as royalty had finally come to an end, and then we climbed back into our clothes we dressed ourselves for the real world once more.

We never got a wink of sleep that magical night, but I still remember it as if it was all a tender and passionate dream. We breakfasted on Champagne and ice cream before collecting our stuff and heading towards the elevator. What could a week in Canada do to match our sleepless night in New York? Time to find out.

[10]

The train took an age to deliver us to Niagara Falls but I was too dazed and happy to care. I read about the hotel that was to be our home for the next week while Melia caught up with some completely unnecessary beauty sleep. She was small enough to curl up on the bench next to me and rest her head on my coat, which I had folded on my lap. Her long lashes flickered a few times then roosted gently on the soft curve of her cheeks.

She looked so young and innocent that I could barely believe some of the things we had done to each other the night before. Thinking about it I was glad my coat was there as a cushion between Melia and my errant body. There is, after all, a time and a place for everything. In an attempt to distract myself I returned to reading about the hotel.

Constructed of cut limestone, I discovered, the new Clifton Hotel had been completed in 1906 to replace a previous building that had burned down in 1898. It was a large L-shaped structure with an elegant pillared frontage which butted out towards Clifton Hill and River Road. With 270 rooms, it was larger than the original. It looked to me a little like a White Star luxury liner had somehow become beached on some prime real estate.

We had chosen it for two reasons: one, because it boasted it had 'no superior in the world'. Two, Don Sherwood had been there and described it as the cat's pyjamas for people who have no fancy for nightwear.

'Darlings,' he purred, 'the word discretion is embedded deeply in the Clifton's very stonework. The Canadians share that lovely *laissez-faire* English quality I admire so much. "Do what you like," they say. "We don't mind what you get up to so long as you don't scare the horses or upset the help." They even bring butter to your room if you ask for it. Lovely people.'

Melia blinked in thought, 'What do you use the butter for?'

Don gazed at her with an odd little smile on his ruggedly pretty features, 'Why,' he replied, the picture of wide-eyed innocence, 'to butter up your crumpet. What else?'

Reading up on it we found that its amenities included telephones, an electric elevator, hot and cold running water, and electric light and heating. It also promised elegant parlours and writing rooms, a 'truly magnificent' ballroom, and a dining room capable of seating 600 people. That's a lot of eating irons clashing about on the bone china. Things could get powerful noisy.

46

We only needed a table for two bitty New Yorkers. We wouldn't take up too much space. And I hoped the other 598 diners enjoyed peace and quiet with their meal as much as I did.

We had sent our luggage on ahead and the Canadian authorities would already have checked it for contraband before we arrived. I hoped they'd also put our clothes away in the closets and tidied the place up for us. I learned that British royalty had stayed there, and that suited us just fine. Melia was royalty of a kind. She was a celluloid princess, a true celluloid peach, and I was proud to provide the pillow for her sweet head.

I finally nodded off myself. The next thing I knew a guard was yelling 'Niagara Falls, Union Station, Niagara Falls' and I roused my bleary eyes to the window. There was little to see. The sun had set. I grabbed what little luggage we had under one arm and my confused and sleepy bride under the other, then I followed the signs to the taxi rank on Tenth Street.

Melia dozed off again in the cab and slept all the way to the Canadian border. She barely roused herself to climb out when we reached the Clifton and stumbled on the curved steps as we climbed towards the entrance. I had paid our driver and tipped him as if we were in NYC. His face broke into a wide grin and he happily carried our meagre luggage up the stairs until we were met by a uniformed guy in a tall hat who accepted the burden.

Melia looked up at the pillared entrance and reared back, her head still fuzzy with dreams. 'Oh, my!' she gasped. 'Oh my word! Why are we here? Are we going to meet Mr Woodrow Wilson? We can't, I haven't done my hair. Are these shoes good enough? Ow, where are we?'

In the twilight, and to Melia's sleep fogged eyes, I guessed the place did look a little like the Presidential White House in Washington DC. I reassured my honey that we were in Canada and that the rumbling noise she could hear was the Niagara Falls.

She nodded and said, 'I don't care if the King of England's staying here with all his court. Tonight I'm going to sleep in my bed. That bath tub was hard work last night, and gold taps don't make it any softer, even if they are beautiful.'

The hotel guy looked sideways at us. I got the feeling he'd never heard a crack like that before, but it turned out I was doing him a disservice. In a soft voice that sounded like it was born somewhere in the mid-Atlantic he breathed, 'Madam, I promise you our bathtubs have all been chosen specially for their comfort, but personally, for a good night's sleep, I recommend our beds. They have all been carefully tested by angels who found their clouds a touch too firm for their liking.'

Melia blinked up at him, 'Are you Irish? Or of Irish stock?'

He raised his eyebrows, 'Why, yes. My name's O'Rourke and my people come from Waterford in the province of Munster, like the crystal. Why do you ask?'

'All the snappy story tellers I've ever met have the Blarney in their veins. And the red hair is a clue. Nice to meet you Mr O'Rourke, you should be in the movie business. They pay well for people who know how to shovel the good stuff straight off the back foot.'

'Charmed I'm sure. And are you in the moving picture business, miss...?'

'Murdoch, *Mrs* Melia Murdoch, but until yesterday I was Nord, Melia Nord. I been in a few moving tin types just recently. Then I married this big galoot and we took ourselves a little honeymoon. Good friend told us this was the place to be, and here we are. I'm a Canadian virgin, Mr O'Rourke. Can you tell us the sights to see in this berg?'

There followed a pause while O'Rourke negotiated the entrance to the lobby. I had noticed his shoulders stiffen at the word 'virgin'. Melia takes some people that way. She's like a fastball pitcher who knows all the curves and you just got to hit whichever ball you can reach or duck before it takes your head clean off your shoulders. She'd taken my head off so many times I had it mounted on a spring-loaded hinge. Bounces right back every time.

O'Rourke must have had a similar rig. He grinned, 'Some people say our little splash of a waterfall makes a grand sight when the light hits it just right. And there's a whirlpool sometimes would swallow a politician's promises without gagging on them.

'Personally, I like the post office for a milk-shake with real character; but then, I'm a weak man so Clancy's on Stanley Avenue is a great place for a local beer and it's just a block away. Of course today's Sunday and officially Niagara's dry as Mark Twain's wit on the Sabbath. There should be a little taster in your rooms though.'

He delivered us to the reception desk and I palmed him a tip. We booked a table for two for dinner at eight and a boy grabbed our case and led us up to our room. It wasn't the Royal Suite but it would do. There were chocolates on our pillows, a basket of fruit on a side table and a welcome bottle of fizz in an ice bucket that was still passable cold.

I decided I liked the Clifton Hotel. Melia ate both chocolates, wandered into the bathroom for a while, and then came out and checked the closets.

Someone had packed away our duds in a careful his-n-hers fashion, which she liked. I wondered aloud if it had been the customs men after they searched our tack. Melia thought not. She was of the opinion that no man

48

would fold her silky underthings so carefully. I offered to try, if she'd be so good as to climb out of them first. She called me a few choice names and disappeared back into the bathroom.

By the time she reappeared nearly an hour later, looking like a dream in a towel and smelling fresh as a spring meadow, I was ready to leap over her to get to the water closet. My bladder was fit to burst like a water balloon dropped from a great height. Getting to the porcelain and emptying the tank was sheer bliss. Notch one up for the Plaza, we'd had three bathrooms to choose from there. No waiting.

I bathed, towelled myself down, and then went looking for my shaving gear. I found the soap, brush, and my Ever-Ready safety razor in the middle cabinet. Behind the razor I found an amber bottle half filled with tablets. On the label I read 'Compressed tablets/No. 726/ASPIRIN/PHENACETIN/AND CODEINE by Parke, Davis and Co. Ltd. England'. This was the exact same brand I had bought with the doctor's scrip back when Melia had been clobbered by the sandbag.

I stropped the blade in the razor and shaved carefully as if the little beast was aiming to bite my throat – they do, you know – but all the time my mind was boiling with questions about those tablets. Was Melia still hurting? It had been several months since her concussion: was my brave girl still in pain? If I could only prove it had been Bisset who had rigged it I would give him his blasted sandbag back like a stone hard enema, then strap him to a chair and watch him squirm.

I did okay with the razor, just two little nicks. That was par for the course. Then the bathroom door suddenly burst open and Melia came in with her hair dryer in her fist.

'There are no faucets in the suite,' she declared. 'I need to use the hot water to dry my hair. Are you done yet? I've never known a man take so long at his bathroom business!'

I backed away from the sink and let the puppy see the rabbit. Melia ran the warm water until it was hot enough to melt lead and then she filled the stoneware head of her dryer. She replaced the bung and started combing it through her thick, silken hair. A pleasing fragrance filled the room and I drank deep of my beautiful girl's scent. Her eyes were closed with the pleasure of the heat in her hair.

'Honey,' I said, 'Are you still in pain? You should have told me. What we did last night must have hurt you. You should have said.'

She opened her eyes and gazed owlishly at me. 'What are you talking about? I'm not in any pain. Why do you ask?'

'I found your tablets when I got my razor. Same as the ones I got after that fool stunt with the sandbag. The strong painkillers that doctor wrote the scrip for. You still taking them?'

She hesitated, then smiled her most dazzling smile, 'Of course, silly. Of course they're the same ones. They *are* the tablets you got. I didn't take all of them so I keep some just in case I get a migraine or, well, woman's problems. You know the sort of thing. Forget about them, let's get some dinner. I'm so hungry I could eat a moose or whatever they serve here.'

I smiled back and kissed her on the lips. 'I'll catch one and cook it for you myself. Your dinner awaits, madam.' I held out my arm for her. And all the while I escorted her down to the dining room, I wondered why she was lying.

[11]

A week later I was still asking the question and it was gnawing at my vitals like a rat loose in an abattoir. Don't get me wrong, I'm no saint, but when a man and a woman have shared the kind of things we had shared that week – and one of the pair is keeping secrets and lying... Well, a man has to wonder what else she's keeping from him. Maybe I was overreacting at the time, but I don't think so. Fact is, later events made me certain I was right, and that first lie cast its long shadow into our future.

However I didn't know what to do about my doubts. Melia knew I had something on my mind. If I'd opened up and told her every time she offered me a penny for my thoughts, I would have had enough money to buy us a car and drive all the way home to New York City.

But it was hard to feel resentment for long. Melia looked a million dollars and I discovered new wonderful things about her every hour of every day. Yes, she was a liar, but I didn't love her any less. That secret knowledge added bitter spice to the pot but it didn't spoil the flavour. Not entirely. Not at first.

We had done all the honeymoon things, oohed at the big waterfall, aahed at the whirlpool when it formed, made love in the middle of the day with the windows open and the roar of the falls mingling with a decent ragtime band playing in the hotel gardens. It was an idyllic week and my suspicions didn't curdle the soup.

On the fourth day Melia told me to wait outside a drugstore while she popped in to get some 'girl's intimate things, you know?' I waited for no more than a minute, less time than it took to fire up my Lucky and draw the smoke deep into my lungs before Melia was back with an odd annoyed expression on her face.

I said, 'That was quick.'

She shrugged, 'They don't have the brand I like.'

I had to kick my heels outside another three drugstores before the girl finally realised that she wasn't going to score her lady goods in Niagara. She came out of the last store looking deeply distressed. She glared hopelessly up and down the street as if searching for a solution in the clouds. I followed her gaze. Nope, no sign from the sky that I could see.

Melia plugged her hands into her pockets and her chin into her collar. She looked so downcast I could feel the depth of her misery in my gut. That was part of what made her such a fine actress. The best people in front of a camera are so thin-skinned their emotions beat through into the lens. They don't wear their hearts on their sleeves but on their faces. She looked so heartbreakingly miserable I couldn't stand another second of it.

I made a suggestion. 'Honey, if we can't get your lady things in Canada why don't we climb into a cab and buy them in the U S of A? The home of the brave and the land of the free is only over there. What's to stop us?'

Her face brightened. It was like the sun breaking through a cloud. I swear her eyes shone like happy lamps and she literally skipped on the spot. 'Oh, Lance, you're a genius and a beautiful man. Has anyone ever told you that? Come on, you beautiful genius, let's snag us a taxi.'

Her happiness lit her up like a sodium flare. Melia was so radiant she turned heads from the other side of the street. The miserable little waif had suddenly transformed into an astonishingly beautiful movie star. This was the woman millions of people had paid good money to worship from their grubby seats in a smoke-filled movie house.

With a sick feeling I realised that some folks were now studying her with more than passing curiosity. If she had been recognised, our safest bet was to hightail it out of there, pronto. But there was a long city block between us and the hotel. I wondered if we could make it in one piece if her fans got their hands on us. They wouldn't care about me, of course. They would fling me to one side to get their hands on the tender prize.

I'd heard about one actress, the name doesn't matter, but she had pretended to be dead to stir up some controversy for her next movie. That plan blew up in her face big time when she appeared in public for the publicity reveal. Her fans were so fired up about her being alive, they fell on her and grabbed anything they could as a souvenir.

She lost all her clothes and clumps of her famous auburn hair were torn out. She never tried that stunt again and it cost good money to keep the pictures of her naked hide out of the papers. Newsmen do so love a scandal.

We were in the same boat, and we were surrounded. Well, almost. They didn't run at us like hungry jackals, they simply and quietly approached at a steady pace until we were backed up against the drugstore window. I had my fists balled ready to start throwing punches.

There was about fifteen of them, and they were studying Melia like she was a fine cut of prime rib. Now, I'm the first admit that I'm no fighting man, but I had a female of the species to protect and I vowed to myself I would go down trying my damnedest to do the manly thing and keep her safe. I'd take my bruises if I had to.

Turned out we had nothing to worry about. The only injury I suffered was the scrape I got on my jaw when it hit the sidewalk after what happened next. A middle-aged guy under a brown Derby hat removed it and gave us both a little bow.

He looked around as if asking for permission from the crowd. They nodded, silently egging him on. It was the oddest piece of street theatre I had ever seen. The man held the brim of his hat with the tips of his fingers and turned it like a wheel.

'Excuse me, and us, miss, and you too, sir. Please, forgive the intrusion but my wife here,' he indicated a plump woman beaming at his elbow, 'Helen, here, she said that she believes you to be Miss Melia Nord. I said that if you were, you'd be surrounded by film people. So, I said no, surely not. I told her Miss Nord wouldn't be walking down our street like ordinary folk out for a stroll. But Helen here said she was sure and we should ask. So, miss, are you? Are you Melia Nord?'

The other men in the group had also removed their head gear so I felt it only fair to follow suit. I lifted my hat in a neighbourly fashion and looked at Melia to see what she would say. I was curious. Her eyes went unfocused for the briefest second, and then she pulled herself up to her highest height, which wasn't that far from her lowest.

Her brightest smile suddenly blazed out from under that silky mop of artfully loose curls. 'I'm sorry sir,' she breathed. 'I didn't catch *your* name?'

His knees buckled slightly under the impact of her full star quality, which was all concentrated on him at once. I expected his hair to catch fire. His hat began to crumple in his nervous grip. 'Ma... Ma... Martin, miss. Martin Amesbrook, and this is my wife Helen, Helen Amesbrook. We're married, you see.'

Helen performed a funny little bobbing curtsey when Martin introduced her. Something tight in my chest melted at the sight. *Bless them,* I thought. *These are the folk who paid for our honeymoon.* Melia then got the names of everyone in the group, and after that the names of all the other idlers who had joined the crowd out of curiosity.

A reverent hush fell over the crowd while these introductions took place, but all the time more and more people were pushing their heads forward to see and be seen by the sweet little lady by my side. The press of bodies was beginning to squeeze our original enquirers into a tighter circle.

They were edging ever closer to us. If I didn't do something intelligent for once we would surely be rolled flat by the crowd. However, I had misjudged

Martin and his wife. Before I could utter a word, the lovely Helen bellowed like the football coach of a losing team.

'Back off people! What's Miss Melia Nord and her friend going to think of us Canadians if we act like rubberneckers and trample her into the ground. Come on people, give the lady room to breathe. And I mean it! BACK OFF NOW!'

And Martin joined in, all trace of his stutter vanished. 'That's it folks. Act like civilised citizens, give Miss Nord some air. Get back a ways.'

That did the trick. His words were the lit taper to spark off the fuse. Like a whisper in a cathedral dome I heard the words repeated and spiral around us as they were passed from person to person.

'Melia Nord. Melia Nord. It's the film star Melia Nord? Melia Nord? Where? Where? Let me see. Let me see.' And instead of dispersing the crowd crushed in ever harder. Even the stentorian voice of Helen Amesbrook couldn't hold back the flood any longer. Melia and I were going down together under an avalanche of curious Canadians.

And then the whistles blew and a shudder rippled through the throng. Two smiling giants in dark uniforms with gleaming brass buttons and red stripes down their trousers ambled up to the crowd. The slightly taller of the two touched his right hand to his helmet and smiled with amiable authority that brooked no argument.

'Move along, please,' he said in a firm yet conversational tone. 'The sidewalk must be kept clear. Move along there.'

People obeyed him without demur, and the sidewalk *was* kept clear, although a few people lined up on the curb, anxious to catch at least a glimpse of a famous movie star before moving on. Everybody seemed good humoured toward the big man, whose manner remained impeccably civil throughout.

His colleague corrected the curb line when onlookers wandered out onto the road with, "A little too far out, there. Step back, please, for your own safety. Thank you."

The whole scene was performed with such gentle dignity that I wondered how it might have gone in NYC. I was certain some wiseacre would have cracked a smart line at New York's finest under similar circumstances. But the good people of Niagara patently understood the meaning of the 'civil' part of the word 'civilised'. Under the watchful eye of the uniformed monoliths they began to disperse.

Martin Amesbrook, however, was not about to let his discovery escape. He wanted to take a final sip of Melia Nord's one hundred proof nectar.

'Miss Nord, and you too, my good sir, would you do Helen and me the honour of joining us for a bite and a beer at Clancy's Bar? It is quite the place here in Niagara and is justifiably famous for its hospitality. It would be our treat to stand you to the best steak and the finest brew in town. What do you say?'

Melia graced him with one of her silver service smiles. 'That would be a great pleasure, Martin, thank you. But may we take a rain check until another day? I have some things I need to purchase from a druggist and it looks like we may have to cross the border to fetch them. Could we hold off until tomorrow?'

The man smiled as if he had just been handed Aladdin's lamp and told to take a good rub to make his wish come true. 'What a coincidence! My word, what a coincidence. Come with me, Miss Nord. Fate must have destined our paths to cross. You see, *I* am a pharmacist, how astonishing is that? What a happy circumstance.'

He pointed down the block, 'My store is just a few minutes away from this very spot. I've the key in my pocket. We've just now locked up to step out for a spot of lunch. Please, let me see if I can meet your very particular needs.' He beamed at his wife, 'Helen, please look after the young gentleman for a moment while I serve Miss Nord. We shan't be long.'

I watched the pharmacist disappear down the street with my fresh bride. I'd barely got her housebroken and here she was running away with a new man. Such is fate. Helen sighed heartily and engulfed me with the scent of Parma Violets.

'She is so very beautiful, isn't she? Such natural poise and grace. Good breeding always shows through, don't you think?'

I thought of Melia's folks and swallowed a wry smile before it reached my lips. Her exhausted father and washerwoman mother would never make it onto the society pages, but I could see what my new friend meant.

She continued: 'You must feel blessed to have made Miss Nord's acquaintance. Do you know her well?'

I coughed into my fist and decided to make a clean breast of things. Helen obviously hadn't seen the latest copy of *Harper's Bazaar*. Fact is, I hadn't either. I wondered if our edition was out yet. Down the street a ways I saw Martin stop dead in his tracks and wave his arms at Melia. I think she had just told him what she wanted. He seemed perplexed. The girl pleaded with him, her hands pressed together in entreaty. It was a fine performance.

'So then, sir, do you know Miss Nord well? Are you professional colleagues? It must be *so* exciting to move in such talented circles.'

Martin surrendered with a hearty shrug of his shoulders and the odd little couple continued down the block until he stopped by a store and drew out his key. Melia had got her way.

I turned to look down into Helen's innocently blank eyes. Oh, that Melia's eyes had ever looked so innocent. 'Yes to both,' I explained. I told her that I was Lance Murdoch, a movie director with Century Pictures in New York City, and that Melia and I had been husband and wife since the previous Saturday.

'We're here in Niagara on honeymoon. Say, every day must feel like a honeymoon for folk who live so close to the Falls. It's a fine, romantic place and no mistake. Don't you agree?'

Helen's expression became wistful. 'Martin's a good man and a thoughtful provider. We have a son and a daughter who are both the apples of our eye. Dick is a bit of a mummy's boy I suppose, and Rachel's daddy's favourite. Yes, if I put my hand on my heart life is good. Oh, look, here they are. Did you get what you needed, Mrs Murdoch?'

Melia looked confused for a second then flicked a glance and a smile at me.

She said, 'Lance told you, did he? Well yes, Martin had everything a girl needs to stay comfortable at...' She mouthed the words 'That time' with a slight southwards tilt of her head.

Helen returned a sympathetic nod. 'Don't tell me. I was a martyr to the...' she mouthed 'monthlies'. 'When I was younger, I would have to go lie down in a darkened room. Crippling business. It was a blessing at first when we became pregnant, but then I got morning sickness.'

She pressed her hand against her plump waist, 'And I never really got my figure back even though I starved myself. I lived on nothing but cabbage soup for months afterwards, isn't that right, darling.'

Her husband's face briefly took on a haunted aspect, as if visited by the ghost of a wife eating nothing but cabbage soup. It had evidently left its mark on his memory. But he soon returned to a more bemused, dreamlike state. He seemed subdued since leading Melia back from his store, and there was something odd about the sloppy smile on his face. His wife spotted it too.

'What's that on your mouth? Have you been Rogering again? Bah, he's an addict, can't get enough, can you darling? If I let him, he'd be Rogering day and night. Wipe your face, there's a dear. You look like you're wearing lipstick and that won't do when we get to Clancy's, will it?'

I gazed in confusion from husband to wife, 'I'm sorry, Rogering? What does that mean.'

Martin mopped at his lips with his handkerchief, Helen waited until he finished before she explained, 'Roger's Chocolates. Handmade. We get them from a lovely little shop in Victoria, British Columbia. Martin's a complete glutton for them. He'd rather Roger than have a proper meal sometimes. He's a hopelessly lost cause I'm afraid.'

What Martin was dabbing from his lips wasn't chocolate. Melia's lipstick looked a little smeared and I quickly put two and two together. She was prone to kissing people on the mouth when they had done her a favour, I knew that from personal experience. It was where I had developed a taste for it and decided I wouldn't mind my own personal lifetime supply.

Martin Amesbrook had evidently been treated to a little more Melia nectar than the bee in his bonnet had expected. I'd seen that look before. His feet may be firmly on the ground but his head was lost in that fluffy pink cloud where cherubs go to recover love's arrows.

Melia was back in high spirits and bubbling with energy. She was chattering like a giddy schoolgirl and declared she was in the perfect mood for sinking her teeth into a good thick steak. She put her arm around Helen's broad shoulders.

'I'm in the mind for meat and lots of it, with perhaps a glass or two of fizz to wash it down. But we can't let you buy lunch, darling. It's so sweet of you to offer, but no. You've been so kind, but really! We can't let you waste your money like that, not on little old us. Please, let lunch be on us. Don't you agree, Lance?'

I did and I said so, but Helen wasn't having any of it. 'Lance, my dear man, Melia, dear girl, you accepted our invitation and it was made in good faith. Lunch is on us and that's flat.' She raised her face to her husband who was gazing at Melia like a dog at a roast chicken. She coughed to get his attention. 'Ahem! Don't you agree, darling?'

The man turned his smile away from Melia and beamed at his wife. Something had robbed him of the power of speech and I had a good idea what, or who, it was. I fought the urge to laugh out loud at the poor besotted fellow.

In the end we came to a compromise. Whatever ended up on the plate would be provided by the good Mr and Mrs Amesbrook, if it came in a glass, it would be supplied by those frivolous and crazy movie people, the Murdochs.

I was still getting used to being part of a plural entity. I had – for better or for worse – hitched my wagon to one of the most gorgeous fillies in God's kingdom. When the wind filled her sails Melia was a ninety-eight-pound force of nature with an impact like an April tornado in Kansas. As Clancy's and the Amesbrooks were about to discover.

Melia considered herself to be an adventurer in the world of alcohol, but she had no head for booze. Her barometer would set to 'stormy and tipsy' after a few drinks, but her thirst would remain unabated until she arrived at 'absolute riot'. The thing is, she would do it with such charm and grace that her audience would urge her on until the curtain came down with a crash.

We started with Champagne, by which I mean *we* started with Champagne. Martin and Helen plumped for a stein of light beer for him and a schooner of sweet sherry for her. The steaks were everything we had been promised, thick and juicy with a side of fried potatoes and fried eggs, sunny side up. We mopped up the yolks and juices with soft hunks of fresh baked bread with a crust baked in bread heaven.

I remembered the guy in the tall hat at the Clifton had recommended Clancy's as the best place for a good local brew – what he had omitted to mention was that it had a lot more on the drinks menu that an explorer could sample – if she was of a mind to. Melia was in the mood for celebrating, and she was ready to toast the Amesbrooks with whatever sounded most exotic on the list. After the fizz she moved on to more adventurous choices.

Have you ever heard of a toxic combination called the *Widow's Kiss*? I asked the barkeep what was in it while he was stirring the potion up for Melia. Then I asked him to repeat the recipe in disbelief.

What kind of maniac mixes together apple brandy with yellow Chartreuse then spikes it with Benedictine and angostura bitters? A fine haze floated above the glass when he'd finished, and he delivered it to his victim with an air of amused expectation.

After he'd mixed it for the fifth time and strained it through some ice, he cautiously approached Melia with the glass on a tray as if expecting her to explode or burst into flame. She came close. Instead she threw back her drink, got to her feet, and addressed the simple drinkers who made up Clancy's clientele. I prepared to pick up the pieces when the gauge hit the red line.

'Ladies and gentlemen of Clancy's bar in the fine city of Niagara. My name is Melia Nord and I'm right proud to make your acquaintance. My

58

good friends Martin and Helen here have treated my husband and me to a steak dinner that I would set against any other steak dinner in the world...'

She didn't slur her words or stagger. The alcohol lit her like a lamp and she just burned brighter, along with whatever usually guided her feet along the more sensible path. The born entertainer, who filled that big heart of hers with the love of a smiling audience, would step out and take centre stage. Until the curtain came down with a crash.

She flipped into one of her incredibly athletic dances that had her somersaulting across the sawdust like a circus act, only to fetch up coquettishly perched on a complete stranger's knee. The man made a grab for her but she was already on the move and he ended up sprawled, face down on the floor. And then she began to sing. What she lacked in vocal power she made up for with passion and feeling.

When she sang 'My Mother's Smile' the tears sparkled in the eyes of the hardest men. 'The Sloop John B' got them on their feet, and 'When Irish Eyes Are Smiling' saw then joining in with gusto. Meanwhile I quietly paid our share of the bill and waited for the curtain call. 'Over The Hills And Far Away' meant the end was near, and the denouement followed with 'The Boy I Love Is Up In The Gallery'.

The whole barroom fluttered with men of all ages waving their 'andkerchiefs to show their love of my little prize performer. At the end she curtsied and bowed, kissed Martin and Helen on both cheeks, and then held her hand out to me.

'I think I need a little nap in our room,' she whispered. 'And I want you there with me while I take it.'

She walked out of Clancy's to a standing ovation, spinning like a dervish and waving to everyone. As soon as she hit the cool evening air she collapsed in a heap. I caught her before she hit the sidewalk. The curtain had fallen once more.

[13]

The sound of vomiting has never been the ideal prelude to love play. Call me old-fashioned but I'd rather listen to a barber shop quartet singing 'Sweet Adeline' than hear my wife noisily surrendering her steak and potatoes to the Clifton Hotel's plumbing, while I held her hair out of her face. And I dearly hate that song.

Melia's slight frame heaved mightily for maximum effect, her retching sounds echoed from the toilet bowl, and her partly digested meal slapped hard and wet against the porcelain. My own stomach began to churn in protest. The urge to vomit can be as infectious as a yawn on a hot day under the right circumstances.

By the time I had her shucked out of her day clothes and dressed in her cotton pyjamas, face freshly washed and teeth brushed, and then tucked her into bed, I had begun to feel oddly disconnected from the day. It was as if I was watching everything as an outsider. I was watching the rushes of a movie over which I had no control but had been given the job of editing. Melia rolled over and mumbled something, then fell silent.

I felt trapped – a bit player in a silent movie performance – and I hadn't been handed the script. The late afternoon light took on a cool monochrome air. I could even hear the clack, clack, clack of the editing suite's spooling mechanism. The illusion was complete. I walked to the room's French windows and leaned out for a breath of fresh, cold air. Below me I saw the man mowing the lawns. There it was, clack, clack, clack.

Over the days I had become inured to the ceaseless roar of the great waterfalls. My mind had filtered it out. I heard instead the silence that hangs like a shroud behind all sound. I sensed the utter stillness that waits for us after a lifetime of frantic activity.

A cloak of melancholy settled across my shoulders and gently pressed me down into the plump chair I had positioned to get the best view of the landscape. I breathed slowly. My eyes drooped; and closed. I slept.

When I awoke it was night and the French windows had been shut. An icy mist coated the glass and made it look opaque in the darkness. My mind wandered. I vaguely supposed that, while I slept, I had somehow become entombed in a lightless, soundless box.

But no, I realised, the box was not entirely silent, I could hear a dripping sound. Fat wet drops splashing onto fabric. I reached out my hand and switched on a lamp.

The girl was sitting on a narrow dining chair she had pulled out into the middle of the room until it faced me. The dripping sound was caused by fat tears rolling down her cheeks onto the sleeves of her pyjamas. Her hands were clenched in her lap and her pretty face bowed earthwards as if dragged down under the weight of her silken hair.

She was an abject picture of misery, a figure shrunken by anguish, and I was helpless to do anything about it. The melancholy air I had breathed before I settled into my dreamless sleep still lay firmly across my mind. It sealed my lips shut. A mournful exhaustion bound my limbs with great chains. My eyes were open and I could see she needed me, but I had neither the energy nor any desire to leap up and comfort her distress.

I had become a dispassionate eye, an unfeeling lens. Although I was able to capture every single glorious hair on her head and follow the sweet curve of her cheek I was incapable of any emotion.

I could record the cupid's bow of her lovely mouth, illuminate her exquisite grace, but I felt nothing for the woman in front of me. I watched her suffering as if through a wall, all the while feeling distant and alien to her needs. Something vital in me had broken.

'Why didn't you come to bed?' She choked the words out, bowed low as if speaking to her hands. They twisted and turned in her lap. She was knotting the hem of her pyjama jacket. It was coffee-coloured and suited her complexion perfectly. I recorded the fact but still felt nothing.

'Why didn't you come to bed? I woke up and you weren't there. The bed was cold and I was alone. I was afraid you'd gone. I thought that you'd left me and I was alone. Why didn't you come to bed? Why didn't you come to bed with me?'

It was a timeless moment, a pause in the relentless pace that had energised the rhythm of our lives all through the previous week. Something had faltered and stuttered to a stop in the screaming engine driving us from one madcap escapade to another. It had come to a head in Clancy's when she had turned our honeymoon into a show. That night, that moment, it finally came to a stop.

Then the girl lifted her head and it was Melia who turned her great dark eyes onto my face. Her eyes were lamps lit with a bitter light. Bottomless wells of pain. And I crumbled. A storm of weeping surged up and shuddered through me, my mouth stretched open soundlessly; and the tears came.

61

I didn't know why and I could do nothing to stop them. The dam had burst and I was drowning in an agony of tears. I was caught up in a whirlpool of emotion and sucked down into despair.

Melia sobbed, sprang to her feet, ran to me, and climbed onto my lap. She circled my neck with her thin arms and buried her face against my stubbled cheek.

Her voice sounded small and desperate in my ear. 'Oh, oh, no, no, you mustn't. You mustn't. You're my strong man, you're my anchor. You're the rock I cling to. I'll die without you, I'll die. I'm sorry, I love you. I love you. Please, please don't cry. I love you, I need you. Please.'

And, as if her voice was the key that unlocked those heavy chains that bound me to that chair, I felt myself released. My life coursed back into my veins and my heart beat once more. I took my wife in my arms and we let salt tears mingle on our lips while we kissed. I never said a word, but I stood up and carried her back to our bed. It was a while before we slept once more.

Sunshine streamed through the windows when I woke to a new morning feeling hungry. My mouth was dry. The colours in the room were those of spring, fresh and green. The French windows were open again and the air was redolent with the scent of cut grass.

I was alone in the bed but I could hear Melia singing in the bathroom. I stretched hugely and rubbed my belly before I climbed out from under the blankets and pushed myself up on my feet.

Melia emerged from the bathroom in a cloud of perfumed steam, her hair piled up on her head in a damp mound that looked heavy enough to snap her slender neck. She smiled at me and raised herself on tiptoe to deliver a kiss in passing.

The robe she was wearing was one of my favourites. It was striped red, gold, and white and styled in the oriental fashion, with a round collar and long sleeves she had rolled up to her elbows. It tied with little bows at the front and its hem barely reached the top of her thighs.

She looked fabulously indecent, like an under-the-counter postcard come to life, and her smile promised more mischief than a tree full of monkeys. However, my bladder had other ideas and promised to hurt me if I didn't do something about it. So, I kissed her like I meant it, patted her bare behind under her short robe, and scampered into the bathroom.

Within half an hour I was bathed, and my teeth had been brushed to sparkling whiteness. I fetched out my razor and shaving soap and then spotted Melia's amber bottle of tablets. When I last saw it the bottle had been less than a quarter full. Now it was packed to the brim. Amesbrook had earned his smear of lipstick, and he had probably broken the local pharmacy laws to get it.

I couldn't know for sure but I had a strong suspicion that there are things you can buy over the counter in the US of A that you need a doctor's scrip for in Canada. And one of them would likely be Compressed tablets/No. 726/ASPIRIN/PHENACETIN/AND CODEINE by Parke, Davis and Co. Ltd. England.

Back in our room Melia was dressed. She looked as young and innocent as a convent girl. She had dressed in her light blue morning frock with a white bow tied on the upper slope of her pert little behind. She wore white lace stockings and white buckled shoes, and had gone for a careful, fresh-faced look to her make-up that made her a true threat to any man's blood pressure.

'After breakfast,' she said, 'can we do a little shopping in town?'

'Why?' I asked curtly, stripping off my towel and reaching for my clothes. 'You planning on making friends with a few more druggists before we leave tomorrow?'

She cast me a curiously guarded look, 'No,' she said as if doling out molasses, slow and sweet. 'No, not at all. I want to find a bookshop. I bet our friend in the tall hat knows if there's a good one around here we can get to on foot. We can ask him after we've eaten. Come on get ready. I'm starved.'

I bit back my response that she'd feel better if she kept her food in her belly instead of sharing it with the plumbing. That would have been a cheap shot and not worthy of either of us. Like a coward I also decided that asking about that bottle of pills could wait until the time was right. I dressed quickly while she chattered about whether she would choose pancakes or ham and eggs.

We entered the great dining hall at the tail end of breakfast and the place was nearly empty. The waitress led us to a table and fetched us orange juice and coffee while we debated our choices. I went for ham, eggs, and sausage patties with toast and preserves on the side. Melia chose a stack of pancakes and bacon with a jug of maple syrup. How that girl stayed so trim remained a mystery to me.

We were the last customers to be served and we were still eating when the polite staff began to prepare tables for lunch. All the while they flicked covert glances at us to see how much longer we were going to be. Melia was completely unaware of everything. She ate her pancakes slowly and chattered away with no sense of urgency. She even asked for more coffee.

I realised then that she created a bubble of Melia-shaped magic around herself. That the world had to fit itself to her requirements wherever she happened to be. According to Melia magic, whatever she did was the right thing to do, and whatever she wanted would always be supplied. Melia's whim was the world's command, even though the sweet little despot hadn't the first clue that that was what she was doing. I wondered what would happen when the magic ran out.

As we were leaving, she smiled and waved at the two crisply aproned women who instantly pounced and began clearing our table. They smiled like constipated ducks and waved back with an evident lack of enthusiasm. I noticed their displeasure with us, but Melia was oblivious. Her mind was already on the next important event in her day's packed schedule. The bookshop.

[14]

Quite a few passers-by on East Street performed a classic double-take when they spotted us during our post-breakfast constitutional. We were two people innocently out walking while on the hunt for fine literature, but we were also becoming the focus for a lot of attention. Some people even waved and smiled with genuine warmth – more warmth than the table girls in the hotel dining room.

Melia waved and smiled back with a bashful air, while I acknowledged the strangers with a civil nod of the head. I wasn't in the right frame of mind to be sociable and wished the day had been cold enough for balaclavas, or at least hoods. Any kind of disguise would have suited me.

At first, I thought all that interest was the result of Melia's malarkey in Clancy's Bar the day before, but then I began to wonder. Would there really have been so many people taking lunch there on a Thursday? Nah! So, then, if not that, what else? What had made us so instantly recognisable?

When we entered Niagara News and Books a few blocks from the hotel, just as Ryan, the hotel guy in the tall hat, had promised, we found our answer. *Harper's Bazaar* was out and we were plastered all over the cover in our wedding-day glory. Melia looked devastating in her white, figure hugging dress. Even I managed to look dapper, despite standing next to Don Sherwood, who had somehow made it into nearly every frame.

I bought a copy of the magazine from the grinning lady proprietor, who then coyly asked if we would both sign her personal issue. We borrowed her pen and both scribbled our John Hancock, I added 'To Beth with love' above our signatures. I guess we were famous – at least while it lasted.

I sat in a quiet corner and waded stickily through the honeyed prose of the *Harper's* article, while Beth helped Melia navigate around the bookstore's shelves. I never knew there were so many variations on the word 'pretty' but the author must have used them all when describing the 'winsomely exquisite' and 'gracefully alluring' bride.

She didn't spend quite so many column inches on me, but when she did I couldn't honestly agree with her when she described me as 'ruggedly handsome'. I was proud to be described as 'pleasantly unaffected and modest'. I decided I'd take that for a dollar.

Some of the text I agreed with. Don *is* suave and debonair, and he's so 'modish' that his shoes nearly got me thrown out of The Plaza. But does he truly have the 'regal manner of one of the great crown princes of moviedom'? I'd have to check him out next time I saw him. In fact, I thought, I should ask the Boss! After all, he's paid the big bucks to know everything.

I had to bite back a shock of laughter when I read that Don was also a 'notorious ladies' man' who was often seen in the latest hot nightspots with one of 'cinema's leading lovelies on his arm'. If that was an indication of editorial accuracy, I guessed I should take that crack about me being ruggedly handsome with a pinch of salt the size of my fist.

I wondered what the *Harper's* photographer made of the article. I supposed he might actually consider himself one of the 'leading lovelies'. He was certainly prettier than some of the women I've kissed in front of the camera, and probably more feminine.

I finished reading the piece just as Melia came back to the front of house with Beth. They were already nattering like old friends. *The Melia Magic strikes again*, I thought.

Beth piled up four portentous looking tomes by the cash register. I suffered from a serious sense of foreboding when I saw the thickness and size of the blessed things, and I didn't need to read the spines to know that I wasn't looking at *Anne of Green Gables*, or *Jane Eyre*. Those old romances were weighty enough for me, but Melia was buying books you could use to poleaxe a mule!

The books were wrapped in brown paper and tied with string before I could get a better look at them, but I recognised one of the authors, *Sigmund Freud*. What was my girl up to now? Melia had jumped on more bandwagons in her brief career than most itinerant piccolo players, but, I wondered, what was gnawing at her bump of curiosity now? It must be a new passion.

I'm not saying Melia was flighty. She took all of her passions seriously – while they lasted. I remembered the time she took to knitting between takes. By the time she got bored with it every member of the Century corps had a new scarf; and they were well knitted too. I still had mine.

Then there was the season for poetry, everyone from Chaucer to Keats. It wasn't enough that she enjoyed reading the stuff, she believed it had to be read out loud to anyone who couldn't get out of the way fast enough. When she started in on *Childe Harold's Pilgrimage* by Byron, the carpenters began building her a soundproof box, and they found plenty of volunteers to hold the nails. Luckily, poetry went the way of the knitting needles before things got too heated.

She didn't need a rhyme or a reason for her passions, she would just take the lid off whichever pot had taken her fancy and climb inside, then hunker down until she was deep in the *soup du jour*. She would chow down until she was full, and then she'd climb out and never sample the dish ever again.

I'll give you an example, the knitting thing. About six months after the last colourful scarf came off the production line, one of our writers asked Melia if she would knit one for his girlfriend.

He was willing to pay for the wool and her time, whatever the cost, he said – he was happy to foot the bill. He simply thought a bespoke Melia Nord neck decoration would be the most 'delicious Christmas gift for the (most recent) woman of his dreams'. I added the 'most recent' bit, he was a famous serial dreamer when it came to the ladies.

Now, when Melia was turning balls of wool into winter warmers, she just gave them away to whoever took her fancy. And here she had a huge fan willing to part with a bundle of hard-earned cabbage to commission one of the things. She could have asked whatever she liked. Think of a number and put a dollar sign in front of it – he wanted one of those scarves.

You're ahead of me, aren't you? You know she said no. She told him she didn't know how to knit, couldn't even remember how to hold the needles. She told him the sheep hadn't been born that made wool worth using, it just tore her hands to shreds. So, sorry, but you see, she just couldn't do it. That man pleaded with her, he got down on his knees and crawled, but no dice.

You'd find it easier to turn the Empire State building with a windlass than change Melia's mind once it was set. Stone runs like water by comparison. In frustration, the dreamer then went around the cast and crew until he found someone willing to part with their Melia original for cold cash – and that started a trend. Melia's handicraft suddenly had financial value.

Last Christmas a Century Pictures philanthropist auctioned her scarf for charity, and it fetched enough cash to keep the orphanage in caviar for a year. The things hit the headlines and people offered silly money if the girl would just take up those magic needles once more. Remember what I said about the Empire State? It would be easier to tear down Mount Rushmore with a glass teaspoon.

Melia was beautiful, sweet, and fun to be with if you weren't too set on how you wanted to do things. She would approach everything as if her very life depended on it and she would always do it *her* way. I loved her with every bone in my skull; she took the sinews of my heart and played them like a concert violinist. We made wonderful music together; but looking back she always called the tune – even when it was me who paid the piper.

And now it looked as if she wanted to lift the lid on the human mind. I'd heard of Herr Freud; just a few years before he'd come to the US and visited with the folk at Clark University in Worcester, Massachusetts. He was in all the papers for a while, and he was attacked by some of the establishment for his crazy ideas about crazy people.

He said everything in the mind was to do with sex, and that got up the noses of some of the more conservative thinkers like ground black pepper on a handkerchief. They wanted him tarred, feathered, and run out of Dodge on a rail… and I can see their point.

When I see prairie grass filled with spring flowers I am not thinking about sex. When I see a sunrise turning fair weather clouds pink in the dawn sky, I'm not thinking about sex. When I watch a kitten playing, I'm not thinking about sex, but I guess that if Mr Freud *is*, then he's not the man I want to get stuck in an elevator with.

And those four books weighed enough to be a mighty pain before anyone read a single word from them. They might be Melia's new passion for the next few months but they were going to turn my spine into a pretzel if I had to carry them for those two long blocks back to our hotel room. I had looked forward to enjoying a lot of things during our honeymoon, but a triple hernia was none of them.

I flagged down a cab which delivered us the short distance to the Clifton faster than the terrier took the hare. His tip was bigger than the fare and he happily offered to carry my brown paper parcel up the stairs into the hotel lobby.

He changed his mind after the first few steps. The prospect of putting his spine into traction cast a longer shadow than getting another tip from the Yankee bank of damn fool tourist.

Ryan saw me hefting that parcel like Sisyphus with his boulder and rushed to my aid with a wheeled luggage cart. 'What do you have in there?' he whispered when he took it from my hands and almost dumped it on my foot in shock. The weight threatened to drag his arms from their sockets.

'Melia fancied a little light reading on the train tomorrow. She's got a taste for Mr Edgar Allan Poe.'

'Yes, but did she have to purchase the entire House of Usher? Including the basements? This weighs a ton!'

I shrugged, grinned and followed my mentalist wife towards our room. I congratulated myself on my taste for women. *At least,* I thought, *I'm never going to get bored.* How right I was.

[15]

The trip back to the Big Apple was to prove very different from our trip out. *Harper's* had reached the newsdesks of the local press, as had word of Melia's performance at Clancy's. There was rumour of a cast iron, star-spangled, celebrity in town – and she was about to make her escape.

Ryan warned us when we came down to breakfast for the last time. He said to expect newshounds on the scent of the 'Hottest Queen of the Silver Screen'.

'Those are their words,' he explained, 'not mine. The reporters can't get anywhere with the senior staff so they bribe the maids. Maids don't make much as a rule. You can't blame them if some hack passes them a few dollars in exchange for some juicy morsels of gossip. So, the cameras will be waiting for you when you leave the hotel – and again at the train station.'

He studied Melia for a thoughtful moment, then he punched the air with a balled fist. 'That's it,' he said. 'Mrs Murdoch, I've had an idea. You're a very fine actress and I'm sure we can pull the wool over the reporters' eyes – but only if that's what you want. So, first, do you want to be the fox for a pack of newshounds? Or would you prefer to slip past unnoticed. Your choice.'

Melia looked at me. I mouthed, 'It's up to you.'

She sighed, 'When I'm in the right frame of mind, I'd love to be the fox. And believe me, I'd knock their hats clean off their heads.'

She performed a sweet little bump and a grind to demonstrate. She took a few steps and her hips flipped – a one and a two and a one and a two! I flicked my head so my hat flew into the air, and I grabbed it with both hands, pressing it to my heart. You got to follow through with a gag like that or it hangs around forever and stinks up the place. Like a dead mouse under the floor.

Ryan waited, then said, 'Is that a yes or a no?'

Melia gave him her most beguiling smile, 'I like pulling wool, it's therapeutic. How do we slip past them unnoticed?'

Ryan told her; and was rewarded with an appreciative peal of laughter. We had just under two hours to get ready.

Ryan was right. Photographers clustered around the hotel steps like mountain men around an illegal still; all thirsty for a sip of that sweet Melia nectar. They didn't care about any of the other guests or the hotel staff.

Several carried copies of *Harper's* in their clawed fists and compared the photos with any woman who ventured out into the open.

We had enjoyed good weather throughout our week, but the gods had decided to conjure up a slick, greasy, cold mist for our last day. It wasn't quite rain but it wasn't just fog. It was icy and wet and seeped into everything. The reporters and cameramen were having a miserable morning, but they hoped to catch a candid photo of a movie star to make their misery worthwhile. And perhaps a few words. The front pages were all on hold awaiting news of Melia Nord.

An anonymous man in a trenchcoat with his hat tilted down over his eyes and his hands thrust deep in his pockets, obviously seeking protection from the damp chill, barely got a second glance. Neither did the bellboy in his tight uniform and pillbox hat, scampering behind the man with a leather valise clasped in both fists.

No-one questioned it when the bellboy climbed into the cab with the anonymous man. Why should they? They knew the hotel provided a full luggage service from room to train carriage. The cab pulled away and headed towards the station.

Meanwhile, a petite girl and a tall, well-built man in a flat cap had tried to sneak away from the Clifton without being noticed. The girl was slender and tastefully elegant in her tight-waisted maroon jacket and flared grey skirts.

She wore big, dark glasses perched on her button nose and a bright, feathered concoction balanced on her tousled mop of jet coloured curls. The cry rang out as soon as they appeared and hurried up East Street. The view halloo was up and so were the newshounds' tails. They urged their cameramen into a sprint.

Cameras were heavy back then, but the photographers' could taste the heat of the story on the chill, damp air. They ran after the couple, howling like jackals after their prey. They caught them and surrounded them outside Clancy's. The couple didn't hesitate, they fell backwards through the entrance door, wove a path across the sawdust covered dining room floor, and darted through into the kitchens at the back.

The pack were baying for blood and in hot pursuit. They followed at the heels of the couple. Some of them didn't know the right-hand door rule when entering or leaving a kitchen and pushed open the left door. It slammed into the face of a waiter bringing out a large tray filled with bowls of hot soup. They, the waiter, and everyone in the immediate vicinity, was spattered with chicken and vegetable broth, that day's special.

A number of cooks had worked hard to make that soup, and they didn't take too kindly to it being thrown around the kitchen. The waiter was understandably annoyed at becoming an unwilling ingredient. Even some of the baying newshounds had become distracted by receiving a bowl of soup in the kisser. Tempers flared and fists began to fly.

However, one dedicated scribe saw his prey exiting the kitchen through a back door that opened onto an alleyway at the rear. He grabbed his cameraman and sidestepped the melee to follow the couple. He flew out of that back door with reckless haste; and was instantly upended over a waste bin filled to the brim with a mess of stinking, rotting vegetables that even pigs would reject.

Meanwhile, at the station the man and his bellboy paid the cabbie, tipped him well, and quietly made their way onto the train and into their compartment. The few reporters on the platform were drinking second-rate coffee while warily keeping their eyes peeled for any sighting of the luminous goddess depicted in the pages of *Harper's Bazaar*.

They knew from their sources that Melia Nord would be leaving for New York on the twelve-thirty train. They kept glancing up at the station clock. She was going to be late.

On the stroke of twelve-thirty the whistle blew, then, in a cloud of steam and to the protesting screech of steel rimmed wheels, the great train jerkily hauled its carriages into motion. It took it a few seconds to gain traction then it got its shoulders to the job and pulled away.

It was at that precise moment that the bellboy appeared in the open doorway at the end of one of the carriages. He waved and shouted to attract attention, then pulled off his pillbox hat to release a cascade of midnight curls surrounding the dazzling smile of a mischievous and beautiful face they all recognised. It was Melia Nord.

As the train gathered pace and the reporters scrabbled to point their cameras Melia yelled, 'So long boys! See you in the funny papers!' Then she turned her back and waggled her neat, uniformed behind at them. The train hooted its goodbye to Canadian soil, and within moments Melia was gone from view. And so was the story.

Back in town Clancy's was in chaos. Customers coming in for lunch were greeted by a crowd of soup-soaked, shouting men grappling with kitchen staff in the kitchen doorway. The language was fruitier than the blueberry slump and custard chalked up on the dessert menu. Most of the diners recognised free theatre when they saw it and settled down at their tables to watch.

One of the customers, however, was more interested in her meal than the floor show. She scuttled out into the street and hunted down a constable. He listened to her complaint, nodded, and blew his whistle. Within minutes a scrum of Niagara's finest and largest police officers arrived at Clancy's then waded into the brawl with cries of 'What's all this?' and 'Do you want us to fetch you to the station house, gentlemen?'

One of the officers received a wild and painful blow to the side of his head which knocked his helmet off. He responded with a decisive and well-aimed strike to the guilty party's jaw. The man went down as if he'd been pole-axed. As he collapsed his bulk dragged down several of his journalistic peers and they all collapsed in a heap on the floor.

The white-coated kitchen staff had slunk away to their stations at the first sight of the approaching police uniforms, carefully disguising bruised knuckles under handy cloths while stirring whichever pot was closest to hand, even some of the empty ones.

The newsmen eventually realised they were fighting amongst themselves and the heat of battle soon subsided in the face of the calm, monolithic bulk of the police constables in their midst. Those still standing helped their fellows to their feet. Grinning kitchen porters provided towels so they could mop the worst of the soup from their clothes.

Clancy's owner, one Rachel Morrison, a hard-headed spinster of Scottish stock, estimated the damages. She added fifty per cent for luck and presented the bill to the chastened crowd of bruised newsmen in her kitchen doorway. Money exchanged hands.

No charges were brought, the newshounds slunk away, and the policemen lumbered over to a discreet corner of the dining room, where they were treated to a good lunch on the house.

The newsmen silently limped out onto the sidewalk to a round of applause, wolf whistles, and fruity Bronx cheers. The men tried to put a brave face on it, but inside they were seething. A little Yank flutterbug had put a spoke in their wheels; and that had turned their world inside out. It couldn't be allowed. They would find some way to reap their revenge.

On the other side of the road a small, slender and pretty blonde girl called Hattie Pacer made her way back to her job in the accounts offices of the Clifton Hotel. In her canvas bag she carried a brunette wig and a feathered cap along with a pair of dark glasses and a smart maroon jacket.

Her boyfriend, Ryan, had removed his flat cap and stuffed it in the pocket of his coat. He walked through the sullen crowd of reporters with a hearty, 'Good afternoon, chaps' and was greeted with a sullen, 'What's good about it?' Once he was clear of the crowd, he began to whistle a passable rendition of 'Men of Harlech', one of his favourite songs.

Ryan quickened his stride and crossed the road to Hattie. They covered the rest of the distance to the hotel arm-in-arm. Behind them a newsman who smelt strongly of rotting vegetables squinted suspiciously at their retreating backs, then muttered, 'No, it couldn't be. I'm being an idiot.' But he couldn't entirely lay his suspicions to rest.

The thwarted newspaper crew from the train station gathered with the victims from the front of the hotel at the notorious journalists' watering hole *The Quill and Parchment* on West Street. Those who smelt most strongly of soup or rotted vegetation were politely asked to take their drinks out into the fresh air – just as a steady, drenching rain began to fall. Which then progressed into a heavy downpour.

They clustered in the bar's doorway so they could hear their colleagues describe how Melia Nord had made her escape in disguise and taunted her pursuers from the train.

'That little minx waved goodbye then shook her butt at us as if we were the clowns in one of her movies. What can we do about it?'

One of the soup men in the porch took a stream of water down the back of his neck and cursed, fluently. 'Listen up, guys,' he snarled. 'I've had an idea, and I think you're going to like it.'

16

When Melia returned to me she took a moment to recover her composure. She was flushed with excitement and her eyes were bright. She drew the curtains that closed off our compartment from the train's corridor and threw herself down onto the cushioned bench facing me.

She lay on her back and chuckled to herself, and then she closed her eyes and ran her hands through her hair while arching her back. The pose was artless yet potent; and the bellboy outfit flattered her curves. How anyone had not seen through that disguise to the woman beneath was a mystery to me.

I suddenly realised that her eyes were open and she was gazing at me as if trying to read my thoughts. Her lips were pressed together in a thoughtful pout, while she allowed her eyes to rove over my head. She seemed to be performing an intense, almost forensic examination.

I couldn't fathom her expression, and for a moment she looked as if a stranger had climbed into her mind and was looking out through her suddenly unfamiliar eyes. It was difficult to believe that that stern-mouthed, stony face could ever break into a smile. It seemed frozen.

She spoke and her voice was slow and dreamy. 'People used to think you could tell what someone was like by the shape of their heads, you know, their character. Phrenology they called it. It was nonsense of course. If it worked you would have been able to feel the bumps on a baby's head and hang it before it committed murder. Or lock up a thief before he stole anything.'

She sat up and unbuttoned her tight jacket. It was a careless gesture, as if she was alone. She wore a silky, cream coloured camisole underneath it. The act would have been powerfully erotic if her facial expression hadn't been so completely blank. I became confused while trying to read the signals she was sending me. She lifted her hair and piled it on top of her head, exposing the slim column of her neck.

'Should I get my hair cut into a bob like Hattie Pacer? You liked her, didn't you? Should I go blonde to look more like her? Do you want me to cut my hair? I will if you like.'

I was caught unawares and didn't know what to say. She seemed to be throwing random thoughts at me and they fluttered around in my head like butterflies escaping from a jar.

'I like your hair like that,' I said. 'It suits you the way it is. It looks beautiful. You look beautiful. Don't change a thing.'

She shrugged and let her hair tumble around her shoulders once more. 'You thought Hattie looked beautiful too. I could tell. I could see how much you liked her when we met her with Ryan. You kept smiling at her.'

She paused and worked her mouth, then said, 'Are you going to cry again?'

'She was nice, yes, Hattie was okay, but not as beautiful as you. And no, I mean, I don't know. How can you know? What is this?'

Then it was as if a window had been thrown open and allowed the sunshine back into her soul. She grinned at me and held the wings of her jacket open to reveal more of what was underneath. Her eyes sparkled with her old familiar mischief and she wriggled like an impatient child eager for a promised treat.

God, she was lovely; how could she compare herself to Hattie Pacer? She was comparing gold with gilt, cheese with chalk, good salt beef with baloney. I realised I was hungry.

'Hey,' she said. 'You ever done it on a train? Well? Have you?'

'No, never. And I don't plan to start now. The ticket guy might come in and catch us. We can't do that.'

There was a little lever lock on the sliding door from the passageway. Melia pressed it closed. She looked at me. There was nothing frozen about her expression now. 'Not any more he can't,' she said. For the next hour I forgot I was hungry. Melia was a very athletic girl, have I told you that? Very athletic.

And very uninhibited. And impossible not to love. The liquid silver sun of a northern March afternoon framed her while we made love and I wanted the vision of her in front of me always, just like that. Melia in her primal glory. Her concentration would have better suited a chess game, but I was real grateful she paid so much attention to what she was doing – twice.

She was back in her more feminine attire and I was neat as a bank clerk on a Sunday spree when we finally slid that sliding door open and let some of the heat from our passion out into the passageway. Funny thing, I opened that door and it slid open free as a child's conscience. I could swear it had never been locked. I glanced down at Melia and she gave me a look that made me blush to the roots of my hair. *She was hoping someone would come in!*

Hunger growled in my belly like a cat's complaint so I put my suspicions to one side and we made our way to the first-class dining car. We were met at the door by a guy in black tails wearing a bow tie and an old-fashioned high collar. He looked like he'd boarded the train when the English Queen Victoria was still on the throne and had never known when to get off.

He checked and punched our tickets then called out for someone named Horace to show us to the table reserved for our compartment. Our waiter and guide was a beaming black man in a bleached, tightly buttoned white jacket, and I could hear the chuckle in his voice when he spoke.

He sounded like molasses and spring water tickling its way across pebbles. And yes, I said tickling. That voice didn't *trickle* it teased its way out of his mouth, flirting and tickling at the joys of the day.

He welcomed us to the flyer and handed us stiff-boarded menus just like the ones in the Clifton dining room, then he went to service his other tables while we made our choices. Melia pulled a face at the idea of steak; and finally plumped for a quail's egg in mayonnaise starter followed by charcoal broiled chicken with all the trimmings. I chose a hot ham hock *vol au vent* in a white sauce and then prime rib *au jus* with vegetables and potatoes. The jus was great, it tasted like gravy. I like good gravy, it makes meat a meal.

I drank a healthy portion from a bottle of good Claret, my lady ordered a decent glass of white Burgundy, followed by a second. Horace pointed out that two glasses of wine cost the same as a bottle. So, why not go the whole banana?

'Lady,' he grinned. 'You're travelling on the finest ship ever sailed on rails, and we don't hit no nasty swells or high seas. Your sea legs are safe and this wine don't take you poorly like some. What you don't drink at the table, you can take back to the private comfort of your cabin and enjoy it in your own sweet time.'

He whispered as if sharing a secret, 'Every mile to old New York's a miracle, don't waste a second of the trip fretting whether you've done the right thing. Enjoy your wine in good health and with old Horace's blessing. You paid for it.'

How could she say no to that? I'd like to share a little observation about 'old' Horace, who was actually a younger man. Horace gathered his chestnuts where he may.

When he bent to offer something to me, he did so quietly, with a white smile big as a slice of watermelon. When he bowed to Melia, he did so with his mouth closed and his nostrils flared as if he wanted to experience her with all his senses; sight, sound, and smell. I wondered when he would get around to touch. And what I would do about it.

He handed her a rose, a rose without a thorn. He snipped the thorns from the stem before handing it over. I ask you, how cute was that! And he held her hand for the briefest touch when he did so, after first asking my permission and calling *me* 'sir'!

76

'A rose for the finest flower on the ship,' he sighed. 'Living proof that the Lord sits on His throne in Heaven and loves we poor sinners. Despite everything we do to turn his face against us.'

Melia arched a perfectly manicured brow. 'Horace,' she said, 'Have you done some theatre work? I get a faint whiff of the thespian rolling off your shoulders, and I sense a touch of the greasepaint in your delivery. You still walk the limelight path.'

'Could one pull the wool over Miss Melia's celebrated eyes? You are right, madam, I have indeed trod the boards when the opportunity affords itself. I would starve for my art but the flesh is weak and one can't live on the free buffet at Brady's on Seventh Avenue. And so I fill my rest times with a little waiting on tables. The pay's okay and the tips pay the way. I can't complain.'

'You ever been in front of the camera? Lemmon's always looking for talent but he gets more chaff than grain. He's a man who knows quality, as does his Lieutenant. And that Lieutenant would be my husband. Him, sitting right there, drinking everything in like a thirsty man at the well. He never misses a mark, do you, darling?'

Horace's eyes grew round as saucers and he puffed out his cheeks. 'Mr Murdoch, sir! I'm right proud to make your acquaintance. Are you looking for bodies right now, sir? I can read and recite my lines and I can sing notes that would grow hair on the bald fellah in the back row of the gods. I contract on this ship by the day, so I can be standing on your fo'c'sle at dawn tomorrow.'

'Horace,' I grinned, 'there's a lady over there with an empty glass just aching to get your attention. You're still contracted on this charter and you've got the sour eye of that fellow in the bow tie; best shimmy and shine my friend – before the bow tie bites. When you've got a moment, I'd be grateful for another bottle of that Claret, please. This one's gone the way of all good things. We'll talk later, I promise.'

You don't escape a thespian as easily as a pack of newshounds. After we paid our bill (and left a good tip, I heard what Horace was saying) we got to our feet and made a grab for our wine and the glasses. Our new best buddy was at our side in a flash – he collected everything together on a black laminated tray then led us out into the passageway under the lizard gaze of Mr Bow Tie.

Bow Tie didn't move his head much, I supposed he was afraid that tight, high collar would saw his head clean off his shoulders if he swivelled it too fast, but those berry eyes of his swept around the room like black flies looking for somewhere tasty to settle.

Horace got my card off me, and a promise that I'd see him at Century Pictures on Monday. So at least I still had one more day of freedom before the clapperboard bit once more. He opened our cabin door one-handed and preceded us into the cramped space. He raised the little folding table under the window and propped it up. He arranged our bottles and glasses to his satisfaction and then stood tall, surveying his handiwork.

It was then that I noticed his nostrils flare like a blowing mule and that white, watermelon grin split his round face. He beamed at us like a proud parent.

'Let me show you something,' he said. He slid the door shut and moved the little lever Melia had used to lock it earlier. 'You do this and you think you've locked the door,' he explained, 'but you ain't done no such thing. The lever just falls down again if you don't prop it, just like that table there.'

He slid the lever up then propped it with a little clip lying almost flush with the mechanism. There came a firm snap. 'Did you see what I did there? Mr Murdoch, please, you do it while I watch.'

I unlocked the door then locked it again to Horace's satisfaction. He nodded and then unclipped it so he could make his exit. He turned that radiant smile on us as he stepped out. 'Lock it when I leave,' he growled, 'that way you're certain of your privacy all the way to the Apple.'

He winked. 'You young people enjoy the rest of your *ride* with old Horace's blessing.' And he was gone.

I burst out laughing. Melia hadn't left the door unlocked on purpose – and Horace's connoisseur nose had evidently detected evidence of what we were doing before dinner. What a day! But it wasn't over yet.

17

Melia looked shocked while I carefully clipped our door firmly closed and then poured her some of her wine. Her eyes were wide as she gazed at the sliding door's locking mechanism and sipped at her glass. I could see what she was thinking and she confirmed it with a strangled gasp.

'*Anyone* could have come in on us! Anyone! What if one of those news guys with a photographer had walked in and caught us? They would have thought all their birthdays and Christmases had arrived at once. Melia Nord and Lance Murdoch naked, and... and...' She shuddered.

I reassured her, 'Nobody did, that's the main thing. Nobody did and we're fine. We're just dandy. Anyway, you posed for those artists back in the day. They must have seen some of what made Staten Island famous. Your lovely little figure's out there right now on posters for shampoo and bathroom soap. Where's the harm?'

'Harm?' she hissed. 'Harm? Can't you see it? Back then I was little Melia the sometimes model. It was art, and they were gentlemen. Some wanted French style work, straight nudity, but it was too naughty for me even though the money was twice what I got from the commercial guys. That was *my* choice. Some of the studios peddled pure filth and my artists told me who they were, they warned me to stay away and I steered clear.

'Even when their dirty little pimps followed me in the street and offered me handfuls of cash, I turned a deaf ear. I never did anything would make my momma blush and my artist gentlemen looked after me like family. I put food on the table and I never did anything I didn't want to. So you roll that and you smoke it, Mr High & Mighty Murdoch. I was, and I still am a good girl!'

I kept stomping around on those egg shells looking for the right way to apologise, but I knew I'd kicked Melia's favourite kitten in the tail when she rose with exaggerated dignity and unclipped the lock on the door.

She left the curtains drawn but made it plain we were open to visitors if the world came calling. Sorry to disappoint you, Horace, but the only ride I'd be taking that evening was the trip home to the Apple.

I poured my Claret and gazed out at darkening skies. The sun was setting on yet another day I'd managed to ruin with my stupid mouth. It was a chastening thought that I'd had to marry Melia Nord before I could make her angry. I needed to think it through. Then she hit me with another hammer blow.

'When will I see you again after we get home?'

'I'm sorry?'

'I said, when will I see you again after we get home? Shall we have lunch somewhere on Sunday? That would be nice.'

'What? Wait. I don't get it, sorry. What are you saying? Of course we'll be together, we're *married*. Husband and wife, you know? You were there in the church. We'll wake up together and spend the day together. I'll be with you. Husbands and wives don't make dates to be together, they live together. We'll be having breakfast, lunch and dinner together! Won't we?'

'I don't think so. You've got your apartment and I've got my loft. We don't have to live under each other's feet like that. Really, that would drive us both crazy. Surely you can hear what I'm saying? Can I have some of your Claret?'

I was numb. I said nothing while I poured her wine. The bottle was almost to the dregs. At this rate I'd have to ask Horace to bring more. I wondered what he would say about this situation?

I felt my mind spinning around Melia's question, looking for the simple, hard-nosed statement that would collapse her grand theory. I sure couldn't say what I was really thinking, that the noodles had slipped off Melia's knife and she was talking loon crazy. Then I had it.

'Your Ma and Pa, see, they live together. They're happy, why shouldn't we?'

She sniffed, 'They got no choice, they have to. They couldn't afford to live apart. They hate the way they have to climb around each other if they so much as want to go from one end of the room to the other. I know Mom would move out to her own place like a shot if she had the money.'

She sniffed again, sounding exasperated. 'Anyway, keeping us in the same cage wouldn't work, our egos would clash. We'd be suffocated. And why should we? We've got the money and we can afford to make room for each other. Surely you can see it makes sense?'

'But, honey! Look, see, no! Wait, we can't do that! I love you, I want to be with you. We *can* make it work. I'll do anything you like to make it work, I promise. We'll be happy as fish in the sea.'

'Absence makes the heart grow fonder. If we spend too much time together, we'll fight, I'm sure of it. And if we live in the same house, we won't be able to get away from each other, and, I'm sorry, but that would be horrible. I love you too and I always want to look forward to being with you, but, I don't want to feel like I don't have any choice about it.'

She sighed as if she was talking the most obvious sense in the world. 'I don't want to be like Mom with Pop, stuck together like dumb animals caught in a trap. That can't be the way we live our lives, it would be too terrible! Surely you must see that?'

I must have gazed at her like a baffled ape for about a minute. I know I'm a goofball with words, but I can normally string a few pearls into a line when I have to. But all I could think right then was that I was married to a March hare and here it was – the month of March. I'd have to keep a careful look out that I didn't skate across the cabin on all the marbles she was shaking loose.

My mouth was dry and the bottle was empty. How many bottles had we drunk? Not near enough if the whirring noise in my head was anything to go by. I hadn't felt that sober since watching the great British Shakespearian actress Dame Agatha Covington make her stab at conquering the silver screen by bellowing her way through some horrible *Cleopatra* thing she'd written.

I believe that was the first time the piece had been performed in front of a movie camera – especially a *silent* movie camera. I tell you that mad woman's roaring storm of sound shook dust from the rafters and blasted me straight through despair and out the other side – it truly was that awful. She had reached a ripe age without gaining the first inkling about how to put a script together.

When she tore open her tweedy bodice to expose her venerable breast to the sting of an imagined asp, and the world at large, the Boss ran up to her, pulled her clothes together, and thanked her.

He advised the poor woman, 'Please, dear. Button up, there's a sweetie, and hurry back to the stage where you will always remain a shining beacon of English reserve and culture.

'The camera,' he said, 'is not yet ready for you. The lens has not yet been fashioned that can contain such a stellar performance.'

Once Dame Agatha, who was not fooled for a second, had finally ceased quivering with outrage, she gathered her dignity around her substantial person like a cloak, snorted at the Boss, and vacated the studio in the manner of a dreadnought under full steam.

We heard her bellowing like a moose in season at anyone who crossed her path. I think GETTAHTAHMOOWHAY roughly translated as 'get out of my way', but if the pale faces of her victims were any gauge, she could have been howling, 'I'll kill you where you stand!'

Lemmon ambled over to me and said, 'You heard me. I told her to get back to the stage. If she hurries, she should be in plenty of time to get herself on the next flyer to the Hudson where she can catch a steamer to England. The London stage inspired that drivel she was howling, *they* should be the ones who have to listen to it.'

That old British dame was so rabid-dog crazy she made me feel sane and sober as a temperance preacher by comparison. Melia's oddness in that railway carriage was having the same effect. I told her I'd be back, grabbed the empty Claret bottle and slid open that unlocked door.

Horace spotted me as soon as I entered the dining car and hurried to fetch me a replacement bottle of the finest overpriced vintage, which I paid for while he pulled the cork.

He leaned in and whispered conspiratorially, 'Didn't think we'd see you again this side of the Apple, sir. What with you and Mrs Murdoch having so much to *talk* about and all. Thought you'd be engaged in *deep* conversation for the rest of the trip, if you see what I mean? Real *deep* conversation.'

My soul shrivelled in my chest. We had become the subject for a waiter's bawdy imaginings, and he was doing everything but offer me broad vaudevillian winks and an elbow in the ribs. For the remainder of our miserable train journey, Melia might as well be dressed as a French tart and me as a randy ploughboy. I heard a drum roll every time Horace spoke, Brrrrrrrp-pah!

When I got back to our compartment, I found Melia leafing through a book entitled *The Interpretation of Dreams* by Sigmund Freud. I might have guessed old Sigmund had hitched a ride with us on our journey home. I poured our drinks and took my place on the opposite bench.

Melia lowered her book and gazed first at our newly filled glasses and then at me. I'd seen that look before, just before the schoolmarm back in my home town of Powell, Ohio, took a hazel switch to the seat of my pants. I think she used me for practice before beating her carpets. She liked clean carpets.

'It won't work, you know,' Melia said, coolly.

Now I was really getting flummoxed, 'What won't?'

'Getting me skylarked on wine. If I drink too much, I just fall asleep. So, you won't be able to have your way with me unless you do it while I'm sleeping; and I think you're too much of a gentleman to do something like that. At least, I hope so. Anyway, I'm reading.'

I decided to side-step her inferred slur on my character.

'So, what are you reading?'

She held up the book. I reread the gold lettering on the blue cloth covers.

'Why're you reading that? You having problem dreams?'

'I never dream. In here Freud says, "The virtuous man contents himself with dreaming that which the wicked man does in actual life." I never dream, I guess that's why I do the things I do. Maybe I'm a little crazy. What do you think?'

'Crazy because you don't dream? That's nuts! You're no crazier than I am, and I'm as sane as the next person.'

'Yes, but Lance, the next person in this compartment is me. And I'm not talking about what I do or don't dream about. I'm talking about the things I do. Am I normal? Or do I need the talking cure? Lots of people are batty as a church belfry, why not me? I'm not immune. And anyway, I hear voices.'

'Okay, that's worrying. What do they say?'

'Pretty much the same thing every time. That I'm fooling myself and everyone else if I think I'm any good as an actress. They say that I'm no good in front of the camera, and that in general I'm a talentless nobody and everybody will work it out one day.'

Her beautiful mouth twisted. She was close to tears. 'Then they'll stop laughing because they think I'm funny and start laughing because they know I'm stupid. And when that happens the only thing to do is kill myself. That's what the voices say. And see, now you're not laughing either.'

18

I liked my apartment. I'd lived there quite happily for a few years and it felt comfortable. I'd never felt alone there before – in fact it was my bolthole away from studio madness and New York's frantic pace – but that evening I felt abandoned.

It was too quiet. I'd got used to being around that explosive, boiling personality kettle called Melia Nord, and no, even I couldn't think of her as Melia Murdoch. She could marry a dozen men and she would still always be Miss Melia Nord.

And all alone she was heading home to her loft where she would be at the mercy of those quiet, seductive voices. Voices telling her she should kill herself before the truth about her lack of talent got dragged out into the light. I hadn't been able to get her to understand how wrong she was, and when she had got fed up listening to me, she had dipped her head down for a touch more Sigmund.

She had used that book like a shield, immersing herself in its words so she wouldn't have to listen to mine. And I had wondered whether her voices were weaving themselves into Freud's text, whispering to her all the while.

I've never read Sigmund, I choose not to understand how my mind works. I would no more dip into psychiatry than tinker with the workings of the human body – or try to build a house. Or an airplane.

The way I see it, there are people out there who dedicate their lives to doing the thing right. If I tried to join them I'd just be yet another dilettante hovering around the edges and getting in their light.

I'll give you an example of the kind of people I mean. When I was a young boy back in Powell, Ohio, there was this guy who called himself Walking Bear. Said he was a Pawnee and hailed from Nebraska.

He had a talent, a gift, he could talk any animal quiet. I saw him calm a rabid coon once. The animal was crazy, trying to bite its own ears off, and Walking Bear got it calm long enough so the town constable could shoot the poor beast and release it from its misery.

I thought Walking Bear brought big medicine to a turbulent world, he was a star performer. He could gentle a horse by whispering a few words in its ear, whistle a yapping dog into tail-wagging silence, and bring a peaceful smile to a howling child.

He carried an air around with him that was tranquil like a woodland glade, but I was so in awe of the man that I never knew how to approach him. Until one day I was having a beer in the post office – Powell was that sort of town – and he came in and stood at the bar next to me. He took his beer and swallowed a long draught, then he turned to study me.

'Lance Murdoch,' he said. 'I've seen you. I've seen you watching me whenever we cast our shadows on the same patch of ground. You watch what I do, you got your eyes on me tighter than a snake bite, but you never say anything. What you looking for, young man?'

And I offered to buy him another beer and we took our jugs to a table in the corner where we could talk privately, away from prying ears. I told him how I was impressed by his mastery over animals, and over most people. I told him how what he did looked like magic to me, and how I would love to learn at the master's elbow, if he'd teach me.

Then I told Walking Bear I'd pay anything he asked, at least, as much as I could afford, if he would show me how it was done. That was when he laughed out loud and patted me on the shoulder as if I'd just made a great joke. Folk in the post office looked across at us and grinned. Walking Bear had that kind of laugh. Big and unapologetic.

'How old are you?' he asked when his amusement quietened a little. I still remember the way his eyes danced with light and the maze of fine lines traced across his leathery features. It takes a long while for a man's life to write lines on his skin like that. 'Tell me,' he repeated, 'how old are you?'

I told him I would be nineteen in two weeks and three days. He nodded. 'You should have asked me when you was two. That's how old I was when my grandfather started teaching me. And for all I know he had started telling me things when I was curled up in the womb.

'It's too late to be really good at something when you're two weeks and three days away from nineteen. You got to start real young. Say what, tell me, what do you like doing most? Most in all the world. And are you any good at it?'

I reached into my heart and I told Walking Bear the truth. 'More than anything else I love telling stories, you know? Making things up. I write them down. The schoolmarm used to beat me because I'd rather dream up a new story than listen to the old tales she read out to the class. Well, sir, I took the beatings but I never stopped telling my stories. That's what I like doing and that's what I'm best at.'

He held his hand out to me and I shook it, right proud. Then he said to me, 'Lance Murdoch, seems to me you're already on your path, and you set your feet on it some long years ago. And your path has been hard, you took beatings, but you never faltered. That takes something special.

'So, now, when you've gone so far, why would you want to go back to the beginning? Why should you follow an old man and try to learn something that even he's still not sure about? Truth be to tell, I'm kinda too busy finding stuff out myself to be a good teacher. Go, you go be the best storyteller you can be, and one day I'll tell people how I once had a beer with the famous Lance Murdoch.'

I wonder if he ever did? I learned two important lessons from Walking Bear that day. The first was that it takes a lifetime to be the best – and even then, you don't know all the answers. The second? The best of the best are too busy learning more about their art to find time to teach. A teacher has to provide all the answers for the class, but the man who thinks he knows all the answers hasn't yet heard all the questions.

I guess what I'm saying is that all Melia was doing with her books was picking at the loose threads of psychiatry. It was too late for her to really understand how her mind works, how my mind works, how anybody's mind works. After spending a week with her as her husband I knew I'd never really understand her. I was an open window and she was a locked door.

I poured some good whisky into a heavy glass and sat looking out at the night through my window. The drapes were pulled open but I couldn't see anything out there in the darkness. All I could see was my reflection in the glass: my face had become a landscape of shadows and secrets. I was an open window? Who was I trying to fool? No man is an island they say, but the waters between one soul and another run fearful deep.

I realised I was in no mood for whisky. I was too maudlin to muddle my senses any more than they already had been by the recent rash of events. I poured the spirit back into its bottle and got myself ready for bed.

I looked at the clock. Had it really only been that morning that Melia and I had escaped from the Clifton Hotel in disguise? It seemed impossible. I had woken up in Canada with my wife and now I was going to bed in New York all alone with too many questions fighting for my attention.

For a while my thoughts rattled around inside my skull like a wild bird in a cramped cage, but eventually the long day took its toll and I sank into slumber. I didn't dream at first, not that I can remember. Why should I? I was asleep where Sigmund couldn't find me to shine a light on my mind. But then I found myself listening to the shrieks of a shrill, parrot-faced woman who was trying to give me an urgent message.

86

The sound was a complete nonsense but the message must have been important – she was working so hard to give it to me. The woman's parrot face was purple with effort and her neck was corded like a bundle of thick cables. Her lethal-looking hooked beak was hinged wide open. It got wider and wider until it was open wide enough to swallow my head. I could see her little blue tongue standing out like a small stiff finger.

Then the beak closed over my head and she gulped me down like a pumpkin seed. I opened my eyes in a rush of sweaty panic. My phone was ringing. I cursed and went out into the hallway, still barely awake. I unhooked the earpiece from the mount and pressed it against my ear.

I was not feeling too generous towards my midnight caller. In reality I had no idea what the time was, but my head ached, my tongue was furry, and my bladder bursting. I was in no mood for a long conversation.

'Hold your darned water,' I spat at the mouthpiece. 'I'll be with you in a coupla shakes. Wait for me right there.'

I left the earpiece dangling from its cord and stumbled to the bathroom to ease the pressure that had taken such a firm grip on my concentration. By the time I returned, much relieved, I carried a tumbler of cold water to sooth my head and smooth my tongue. I screwed the earpiece back into place at the side of my head. In a calmer tone of voice I said, 'Okay, waddissit? Waddayawant?' I was not feeling particularly poetical.

The forlorn voice in my ear sounded as if it was calling up from the bottom of a deep and dark well. It sent shivers through my bones and I felt the hairs stand to attention on the back of my neck.

'I woke up and you weren't here. Why aren't you here? I woke up and called out for you but you didn't answer. I looked everywhere. I looked under the bed and in the closets; but you're not here, you're there! Oh, Lieutenant, what have I done? Have I done something stupid? Have you left me?'

I took a sip of water and marshalled my scattered wits. My crazy wife was on the phone asking me where I was as if the conversation on the train had never happened. She was still talking but I wasn't listening too well, my head was pounding trying to get up to speed and I was thinking fast.

Her loft was on the Heights and I was in Manhattan. I could get dressed and be with her in half an hour. She was crying down the line at me.

I told her, 'Listen, honey, I'm on my way, okay? Don't worry, I'll be with you in about half an hour. Pour yourself a drink and relax. I'll see you soon. Don't worry, I'll be with you soon.'

I caught a late-night cab and kept my promise. I knocked at her door looking like a hobo, hair wild, chin coarse with stubble, eyes red with exhaustion. I wouldn't have to spend any time in make-up to look like a back-street bum. The door flew open and Melia threw herself into my arms. She said nothing, she was too busy searching my lips with hers.

I shut the door behind me and locked it with my girl still dangling around my neck like a warm scarf. You can never be too careful. Then I took her into my arms and carried her to the bedroom. We were late for breakfast the next morning.

19

That Sunday swallowed the clock whole, the same way the parrot-faced woman had swallowed my head. One minute we were greeting the dull Sunday morning like two young animals in love and the next it was Monday and we were facing our first day back at the studio since our wedding.

Melia was reluctant for us to arrive together. She was worried that people might get the wrong idea, which, I pointed out, was, in fact, the right idea and perfectly normal for a married couple.

I was still wearing the same clothes I'd been wearing when I arrived at her door that strange night. Melia was dressed like a fashion plate in the latest Parisian style. Nobody on the set noticed me, why should they? But they welcomed the leading lady as if she'd been to the moon and back.

She had to endure the embrace of so many pairs of open arms – and it took so long – that the Boss called a halt to proceedings by threatening to pay a half day rate if we didn't get back to work. I was grateful that at least he still had his head on straight. He thrust a script into Melia's hands, told her to be ready on stage one in twenty minutes, and then grabbed my arm and tugged me into his office.

'Good to see you both back in one piece, Lieutenant. You're on stage two. Bisset's already there and he'll bring you up to speed. But tell me, what were you two thinking of up there in Canada? What if you'd been arrested? You must be crazy pulling a stunt like that! Were you drunk?'

'What stunt?' My mind reeled. 'You mean Melia singing in Clancy's Bar? I tell you, Boss, she brought the house down. If they ever do crack the sound thing for the movies, she'd be a natural. Or are you talking about us breaking out of the hotel in disguise? Melia looked cute as a button dressed as a bellboy. You should use that in a two reeler. Cute as a button.'

I grinned like a besotted ape at the memory; but the Boss wiped the smile off my face by thrusting a broadsheet into my face. The headline read 'Naked Beauty Causes Mayhem!' Another paper blared 'Melia Nord Goes Lady Godiva!' One of the sheets had a blurred photograph of a pale shape on the roof terrace of the Clifton Hotel. It might have been a naked woman with dark hair.

I read the story at high speed, then blurted, 'That wasn't her. Melia never left my side. Why would she do that? Anyhow, we were on the train by then. This is baloney with a capital C! The newspapers set it up.'

According to the newsmen a woman, believed to be movie actress Melia Nord, had appeared on the roof terrace of the Clifton Hotel on the Canadian side of Niagara. She had been naked as a new-born and performed several astonishing acts of athleticism while in a state of nature, which brought traffic to a standstill and caused a large crowd to form in front of the hotel. There were a few incidents, some vehicle collisions and startled horses, but no fatalities.

By the time local constables and the hotel management reached the roof the woman had disappeared. It was a mystery, said the slavering newshounds, she must have vanished into mid-air. Or had she, I wondered. What if she just got dressed and blended in?

Failing to catch the naked athlete in the act another paper printed a shot of the hotel people posing with the police on the terrace. The pert grin on the face of the diminutive and athletic looking Hattie Pacer caught my eye and a suspicion bloomed in my breast. What if the little accounts lady had reprised her role – but with added sauce?

'I'll get our people on it,' said the Boss, 'We'll talk over lunch. Now let's get at it, the days a' wasting and time is moolah. Move it Lieutenant.'

I moved. Bisset and I were scheduled to shoot a caper involving Emily Cooper and Bert Savage in an airplane. Boss and I had talked about it before the wedding and the money people had given it the thumbs up while we were away.

Flying machines had been falling out of the sky for ten years but ours was perched firmly on its tower in the centre of stage two. The sky was a painted canvas drop on rollers. One of our guys cranked the handle and clouds rolled past the stationary airplane to add the illusion of speed.

Bert was the kind of guy who could play any role and he was gentle and generous to a fault, but thanks to his incredible dark eyes and a carefully applied waxed moustache and straggly black beard, he was perfect as a rogue and a villain. He was invariably scripted to be up to no good with foul designs on the virtue of any feisty heroine. Pure pantomime.

He gave great moustache twirl did Bert, and he made a hissable bad guy. His eyes bugged out of his head, he clenched his teeth, twirled the 'tache, and he would clutch at the fair maiden *de jour* like a hungry gorilla at a bunch of bananas.

Emily made a great foil for Bert's bad boy schtick. Clean looking, she was boyish and vulnerable in equal measure, with a thick shag of light-coloured hair that flopped into her remarkable lilac eyes.

Emily made a convincing aviatrix. Her lean look recalled the late, lamented Harriet Quimby, and she was wearing a figure-hugging white flight suit that did wonders for her spare, long-legged figure.

The jodhpur-style pants enhanced a fine pair of hips and her nicely shaped jacket made it clear that what was underneath might have been slender but it was all woman. She wasn't a patch on Melia but she lit up the screen in her own way. I liked her and she was easy to work with.

'Lights,' I yelled through my megaphone. 'Roll camera, action!' The storyline was all my idea and took advantage of a special effect I'd seen in a competitor movie. In short, Bert was a passenger in a two-seater airplane. He was seated behind pretty Miss Emily, the pilot. But Bert wanted to enjoy a bit more with his pilot than just the view.

He had tied his top hat to his head with a scarf, otherwise he was in his trademark black frock coat and pants, striped waistcoat, high collar dress shirt and string tie. Beyond that his only nod towards the correct costume for a man taking to the skies was a huge pair of goggles. Bert had originally fought against the goggles. He was worried people wouldn't be able to see him 'emoting his vile intentions towards sweet Emily'. I told him to go for added twirl.

The plane was based on a Wright Brothers flyer, a big open kite with an engine behind the passenger. Bert's job was to unclip his seatbelt and lean forward to make a grab at Emily. She had to fight him off, and then they would clamber all over the airplane. Emily's suit had specially designed sections that Bert could tear away to give the audience an added touch of frisson. That was the theory.

When I yelled 'action' the sky whirled past on its rollers and two carpenters pushed and pulled at long poles that rocked the mocked-up plane on a big gimbal. The illusion was completed when the technician cranked up our wind machine and fired up the plane's rotor.

Bert and Emily's sham aircraft bucketed around at the top of a tower which put them fifteen or so feet in the air. Bisset and I were the same height on a scaffold twelve feet away. The camera was on rails so that Bisset could follow the action in a smooth tracking shot.

It was looking good. Bert lurched out of his seat and leaned into the wind to embrace the plucky girl. She fought him off bravely, unbuckled her lap belt and eased herself away from his advances. She climbed out into the open triangular nose of the craft and up onto the – for want of a better word – fuselage.

Perhaps Patch in wardrobe had been a little too enthusiastic with his tear-away sections, perhaps the wind machine was a little too fierce. Whatever the reason, one moment Emily was modestly attired in her white flight suit and the next she was gaping open mouthed as her outfit was torn from her body by the wind and flung into the airplane's prop where it was sliced into confetti.

Thankfully she was a sensible girl when it came to underwear, and the team were only gifted with the sight of her lean figure in high boots, stockings, long drawers and a camisole top, finished off with the incongruous touch of her goggles and the sort of stylish flight cowl made famous by Miss Quimby.

Bert was a darling and a gentleman. As soon as he realised Emily's quandary he struggled out of his frock coat and handed it up to her. She was buttoning it up carefully even as I was yelling 'Cut, cut for mercy's sake, CUT!'

Patch couldn't have been more apologetic. He was mortified. He'd never had a wardrobe failure of such magnitude before and offered his resignation on the spot. The Boss wouldn't think of it, Patch was family, and anyway he could prepare a new outfit for Emily and have it ready straight after lunch – couldn't he? He could. Boss had a persuasive glint in his eye and a threatening grin.

The afternoon shoot went without a hitch. We got enough yards in the can for me to edit into shape, but Emily couldn't understand the storyline.

'I don't get it. I can see the stunt on the airplane okay, but what happens next? You got Bert looking terrified like he's just seen a mad bull coming straight at him, and you got me grinning like I just won the pot – and I'm back at the controls. What happened next? Where's the punchline?'

I gave her a hug, 'Emily,' I said, 'you're a brick. I love the way you handled things this morning and I promise you it's all going to be worthwhile. Sorry we all got to see your scanties, but you climbed back into the rig and acted your pants off...' I felt a sudden heat in my face, I shrugged. 'Maybe that was the wrong thing to say in the circumstances.'

Emily grinned like a sunrise, 'Okay, Lance. I hear what you're saying. Say, wait though. What happened to that footage?'

'What footage? Oh, this morning! Good question.'

'See, I'd rather that sequence didn't go stag. You know what I mean?'

'Yes, I'll go find Bisset. And don't worry about the punchline, you'll love it I promise you. Be a surprise for you.'

I found our cameraman by following the sound of raised voices to the reinforced film storage room. Film is explosively inflammable and must be stored in a flame proof facility, and there was plenty of heat on show when I entered.

I discovered Bisset glaring white-faced at Bert Savage. Savage's face held an expression of pure contempt, Bisset looked on the point of murder. Both jumped when I asked, 'Okay guys, what's this about?'

Bisset uttered an oath under his breath, offered me a withering scowl, and stormed out of the room. Bert laughed at the man's vanishing back. 'Good riddance to poor rubbish,' he said, and turned a sour smile on me.

The moustache and beard of his screen persona had been removed, and what remained was unrecognisable as the same character who had been pawing Emily just hours earlier. He had a pleasant, open face, one I instantly trusted.

I asked again, 'What was that all about? Bisset was fit to bust a gut, why?'

Bert turned and indicated a pile of exposed film on the room's cement floor. 'I thought to make sure our favourite camera jockey didn't keep the footage of Emily's little mishap for his private collection. He does have one you know. He caught me exposing the reel to the light and blew up like a firecracker.'

He grinned, 'I quietly and politely explained how I was protecting a lady's privacy. Well, I can't tell you what the nasty little hound called me – but you tootled up just as I was about to dust his behind with my boot.'

I thanked him warmly and shook his hand. I worked with good people, I knew that. But, I wondered, what was I going to do about Bisset?

'By the way,' asked Bert, 'what's happening with that footage we got this afternoon. I don't understand, where's the punchline?'

I grinned and told him what I'd told Emily, I promised that he too would be the first to know as soon as I had something to show them. Then I asked him if he could meet me on stage two early the next morning to shoot some vital extra footage. 'We'll be going on location,' I said. 'Just the two of us.'

20

I cranked my own handle for the few minutes of location footage I shot the next morning. Bert was in full costume but there would be precious little twirling during this shoot. There was no time. When I told him what I wanted to get in the can that day he took off his top hat and ran his fingers through his thick mop of hair. He gazed at me for several seconds as if trying to gauge my sanity, then he looked over his shoulder at the railway tunnel behind him.

He sighed, then spoke slowly as if talking to a simpleton, 'Let me get this straight,' he said. 'You want me to wait in that tunnel until a train comes along, then you want me to run out just in front of it and throw myself to one side at the last minute. Is that right?'

'That's right. But, if you'd rather not I'll understand. I can dress in your rig and I'll do it instead. With the goggles and all no-one will know it's me. And you know how to crank the camera as well as I do. What do you say?'

Bert addressed me in his most solemn tone, his sombre eyes spoke volumes. He shuddered. 'One should never ask an artist to allow another to mime his work. Never! The art is about more than just costume, it is about modelling the truth of the character. Bert Savage is more than a mere waxed moustache, he lives here,' he tapped his head, 'and here,' he placed his hand over his heart.

He turned his gaze on the tunnel, 'By the way, how can we be sure which direction the train will be coming from? I want to read my reviews, not my obituary. I'll never outrun an engine for the entire length of that tunnel.'

'I checked the timetables. Next one is due in fifteen minutes and it's heading thataway. I checked them twice so I'm sure as certain can be.'

'Very well. I shall prepare for my grand entrance and trust that it shall not also prove to be my great finale. If it is, make sure the vile Bisset doesn't get the footage for his private collection. Give it to Emily. If I must haunt someone, I should prefer they at least be clean and attractive. However, I am very curious to discover how I ended up in that railway tunnel when yesterday I was up in an aeroplane!'

He pulled his goggles into place and tied his scarf around his top hat. Then, costume continuity taken care of, he descended towards the mouth of the tunnel and edged his head in to take stock of the situation. He held up his thumb and stepped out onto the rail. Then he vanished into the gloom.

I whispered 'action' to myself and started cranking at sixteen frames a second. I needed a few seconds of just the tunnel mouth anyway so it wasn't wasted film. It would all lend itself to the famous 'punchline' that only the Boss, me, and one other person knew about. Then, after a minute or two, I felt the rumble through my shoes. The train was coming.

The sound crescendoed until it filled the air with a terrifying racket, I heard the engine's whistle howl with piercing urgency and had to fight an urge to speed up the crank of the camera's handle. 'Come on, Bert!' The ground was shaking and little rivulets of soil trickled down over the tunnel mouth like a fine curtain of dust. My mouth grew dry but I kept cranking that damn handle. 'Come *on* Bert!'

Then it happened. It happened at breakneck speed and I caught it all. Bert was right, I could never have mimed his insane spurt of speed and his pinwheeling flight out of the tunnel's mouth just yards ahead of the rolling tonnes of roaring steel monster.

I could never have matched his oddly elegant leap to one side, his spreadeagled roll in the dirt, or the way he came to rest sitting down with his legs splayed wide and his hat tilted to one side.

And there followed a magnificent final shake of his head that flung dust around him in billows, and concluded when he got to his feet, battered the choking dust from his clothes, straightened his hat, and gave his moustaches a final defiant twirl. It was perfect, but I couldn't resist what I did next.

After whispering 'cut, print' to myself, I walked to Bert's side and put my arm around his shoulders. He gave me a triumphant grin.

'That was great,' I said. 'Perfect rehearsal. Can we do it again when I've got some film in the camera? Just like that. Picture perfect.'

Bert literally deflated in front of me and his legs buckled. His jaw swung open and his eyes flared wide in shock. He made an odd huffing noise and he tilted his head to one side and examined me as if I was a strange insect he'd just found in his sandwich. 'Buh, buh, buh, buh...'

I realised I'd overegged the pudding and quickly put him out of his misery, 'Bert, I'm joking. I got it. I got it all. You were magnificent. You were amazing! They're going to give you an award for this, *I'm* going to give you an award for this! It was incredible.'

And that was when I saw tears making tracks down the filth on his face and I realised that some things will never be as funny in real life as they seemed in my head. I hugged my friend and told him I was sorry. We wept onto each other's shoulders until we started laughing.

Bert pulled away and punched me on the arm, hard. 'Don't ever do that to me again,' he said, 'If you ever do, I'll clout you such a fierce one that Melia will have to kiss the back of your head to find your lips. You hear me, you scoundrel?' He mussed my hair, 'You daft scoundrel!'

That day I made him a promise that I kept for all the remaining time I knew him. Never again would I pull a stunt like that, not on him or anyone else. I'd leave practical jokes to the folk who thought they were funny. I think I grew up a little that day.

It was almost a month later that I kept my other promise to him and Emily. I called them both into the screening room. It had taken a while to complete *Airborne Antics* and the pair of them had been asking me about the hold-up – it was time for them to discover why.

I gave them each a carton of salty, hot buttered popcorn, which had become something of a tradition during screenings at Century Pictures. I never could fathom why, I couldn't stand the stuff. Then I invited them to take their seats and gave the projectionist a wave. The lights went down and the screen lit up. The credits rolled.

Bert chuckled when he read the title, 'I'd almost forgotten I was in this one,' he said. 'Remind me, did Emily keep her clothes on right to the end this time?'

'Oi,' laughed Emily, 'I was wearing more than you and Horace put together in that thing *The Passion of Salome*. And as for Melia! Brazen I call it.'

I felt myself grow hot with embarrassment at the thought of the recent biblical epic that had seen my wife parading around in what one newspaper had described as 'feathers and fancy little else' and another as 'her birthday suited gift to her audience'. 'Shhh,' I whispered, 'you're missing your film.' Emily snickered, an unprepossessing sound that belied her clean, good-sort image.

On my desk I had pencilled an insane script which had been difficult to cast because its core business involved a girl fighting off a giant octopus in her bathtub. In the interests of 'reality' her decency is protected by nothing more than a few well applied bubbles. Who would do such a thing? I decided I had found my principal cast member.

Up on the screen Bert was pursuing his prey – a few pieces of Emily's costume came away in his hand whenever he came close enough to take a grab at her. The action was fast and looked dangerous as they swung and tumbled their way around an apparently airborne flyer. The wind whipped furiously around them and the clouds sped past too fast for anyone to realise that they were seeing them for the umpteenth time.

They moved close to the airplane's whirling propeller and for the umpteenth time I wondered what might have happened if either of them had fallen into the blades. With a sick feeling I remembered how Emily's flight suit had been sliced to ribbons, and my imagination presented me with nightmare images of what those blades might do to tender flesh and bone.

Around a mouthful of popcorn Emily said, 'This is good, Lieutenant, but how do you finish it? You need a grand finale to make it sing.'

'You watch,' muttered Bert. 'You watch this.'

No, I thought, *this will be as much a surprise for you, Bert, as it'll be for the lady.* I whispered, 'Both of you, watch this!'

And that was when the pair performed the stunts they hadn't understood. Emily climbed down into the pilot's seat and grabbed the joystick. She pushed it forward. Above her on the plane's frame Bert reared up as if he was going to dive down through the open fuselage and take a big armful of warm and vulnerable woman. There followed a close-up of Emily's determined face.

Then the scene cut away and we saw the airplane winging down in an arc towards the infamous railway tunnel. Close-up of Bert's horrified expression. The plane entered the tunnel. There followed a beat, beat, beat where nothing happened except the camera held that tunnel long and steady in centre frame.

I couldn't hear my audience breathing. A quick glance showed me both of them lit up like silver ghosts and gazing open-mouthed at the action on the screen. Neither was interested in popcorn or banter at that moment.

Like a bullet from a gun the Wright's flyer burst back out from the tunnel and soared up towards the clouds. There came a close-up of Emily's triumphant expression as she punched the air like a home-running baseball star. Then the camera cut back to the tunnel.

Bert's wonderful business in front of the roaring train concluded the presentation exactly as he had performed it on the day. The only addition was that his last triumphant moustache twirl was directed towards the departing aircraft we could clearly see above the horizon – instead of the great steam engine that had so nearly mown him down.

I had expected any number of reactions when the movie finished and the lights came up, what I hadn't allowed for was stunned silence. Bert and Emily were both still squinting at the empty white screen as if looking for answers up there. Emily raised her empty right hand to her mouth and pressed the fingers between her lips, then looked around to see where her popcorn had gone.

Bert asked the question both wanted answered, 'How, in the name of all that's holy, and yes I do mean D W Griffiths, did you do that?'

I basked in their astonishment, 'It was good, yes?'

Emily crowed, 'It was good, hell yes! Better than good! How did you do that? We're going to be famous! Bert, the Lieutenant here's going to make us famous. It's amazing. I loved your business with the train, Bert, but, Lance, darling, how did you get the airplane to do that? It was incredible.'

I told them about a fantastic artist named Art Cobal, who used to work with Melia. He had contacted me through her because he had discovered a way of painting directly onto processed film, frame by frame. He had some crazy idea of creating an entire movie that way with moving pictures, wacky animals, dancing ducks, anything he could imagine.

'This movie will be his calling card. This is his proof of the pudding. Boss calls it "added mechanical effects" or 'frame painting'. This is just the beginning. Impressive yes?'

They agreed, impressive yes and then some. My happiness at that moment nearly helped me forget that Melia and I were living apart once more; and that she didn't even want to talk to me unless other people were present. Our marriage was only just over a couple of months old, and it had already gone colder than an Alaskan winter. All over that movie, *The Passion of Salome*.

[21]

The problem had started not long after we got back from honeymoon; and was a direct result of that business on the roof terrace of the Clifton. The idea of Melia dancing naked had apparently become box office gold. The Boss didn't go for it straightaway, he thought it disrespectful. He had often told me that we weren't in the business of making stag burlesque and if men wanted to see girls in the raw there were plenty of places they could go.

But Boss wasn't the producer. He was top of the pile to us players, but, to the money, he was just another member of the talent. Mr Mason Jarr was the voice behind the money – and he could smell a ripe profit coming off the idea of putting Melia's sweet hide on display.

I was in Boss's office when Jarr first made his pitch. He was one of those square-built, flabby, soft guys who have too much fluid under their skin and too many teeth in their mouths. The fluid dripped from his flesh as sweat and his teeth came out in a smile that wouldn't convince an alligator.

He could afford good clothes but wore them tight as a two-bit collar. They were stretched taut around him and shaped his body into circular bulges of fat. I'd met the man before and had never wanted to shake his hand.

When it came to Mason Jarr, any room was too small to contain the both of us. I would be happy to leave it to him, but it was the Boss who had sent the invitation so I had to stay put. Jarr's voice suited his looks. It was heavy and unappealing with an oily, wet quality that licked around the inside of my ears like a fat worm.

'You're a lucky man Mr Murdoch. You're married to the woman every other man would love to take on a cakewalk. She's the prize of the Century, every penny paper says so. The prize of the Century! I mean Century Pictures, get it? Yes? You're a lucky man. Don't you agree Carl? Isn't he a lucky, lucky man?'

'They make a nice couple. Lance is very talented and works hard, he's my right-hand man. And Melia? Yes, Melia has a natural charisma that the camera fell in love with at first sight. She's easy on the eye, sure, but any hat-check girl can be easy on the eye. Melia has that magic quality you can't teach and can't buy with easy dollars.'

He smiled, 'By the way, waddaya mean by calling her a "cakewalk", Mase? Melia's no pushover. And don't forget, she's a married woman now.'

I wanted to know the answer to that 'cakewalk' question too. I didn't like Jarr, and to hear him talk about my girl was making my knuckles itch. I knew he was the studio cash monkey, and, if I cranked his arm hard enough, he would probably spit hot pennies. But I didn't need to cuddle up to him. It wasn't as if I was looking to him for someone to share a cold beer with.

He grinned at the Boss like he was scraping the flesh from an artichoke leaf with his teeth, 'She's the *prize*, Carl. *The* prize. That's all I mean. Darkies on the plantation used to take their best girls to the swept floor on a Saturday evening and they would step out to the sounds of a banjo or a washboard played with metal thimbles. The best dancers won a fine cake. A delicious cake. That's the cakewalk. Melia's the prize now, just like that cake.'

He wiped sweat from his upper lip, 'Her dance on the roof of that hotel in Niagara set a fire that won't go out. The lion's share of that delicious cake has been taken by the newspapers; I say it's time we got a good slice for ourselves.'

I blurted, 'That wasn't even her. Melia wouldn't do something stupid like that. That was some imposter sent up there as a stunt by the papers. Melia had spoofed them, she'd thumbed her nose at them, and that stupid dancer was their way of getting their own back. Hacks are like hyenas, they need to get the last laugh! You hear what *I'm* saying, Mr Jarr?'

That earned me a look that made me feel sad for myself for being so unforgivably solid in the skull. It was the kind of look some people reserved for simple folk who had never learned to use a soup spoon in polite company. There was no pity in it. My knuckles itched even more and I ached to sink them hard into the man's flabby jowls. I'd had warmer feelings towards a skunk.

He hissed, 'My dear, Lance. I mean no disrespect towards your lovely wife, and I intend nothing but the most tasteful display. A creative man like you must surely understand the artistic pedigree behind putting the female form on display? A woman's body is nature's greatest gift to the human eye. We intend nothing lewd, you know? I'm talking fine art for the masses. Tastefully done, fine art.'

I couldn't keep the distaste out of my voice. 'I know some men are happy to show off their women to other men. I think the word I'm looking for here is "pimps". You want me to *pimp* Melia? Yeah? Is that it? You're talking to the wrong man, *Mr* Jarr. My wife, she's an actress, a fine one. She's not a backstreet, burlesque whore. Isn't that right, Boss?'

Carl Lemmon didn't answer, Jarr did. 'We're not suggesting we sell your wife's virtue, Murdoch. And we think you need to think carefully about how you talk to the people who put meat on your plate. We're businessmen, not flesh peddlers. Perhaps this discussion would be better served if you were elsewhere. Please, could you go ask *Miss* Melia Nord to join us. Thank you for your time. We'll let you go now.'

I glanced at the Boss, he nodded without looking me in the eye. I was sure he was feeling the same acid burn as me. I got out of that room without another word. I was angry, and worried that I was too close to answering Jarr with both fists rather than civilised words.

I found Melia on stage one. She was involved in some complicated business involving Horace, who had kept his promise and arrived bright on the first Monday afternoon after we got back. Melia was dressed as a society lady out walking her dog and Horace was playing a postman. Dogs don't like postmen in the movie world.

The dog, a terrier called Brutus, kept sinking his teeth into Horace's pants belt. Brutus was trained not to actually bite actors, but he could hold on like the devil, and, with his front legs braced against his quarry, he would stick out at right angles which was visually hilarious.

Horace tried to swat Brutus off and Melia was beating Horace with her parasol every time he made a move at the pooch. All the while everyone was getting more and more tangled in the lead.

The timing was perfect and Horace had a way of rolling his eyes that was pure comedy gold – if you were in the right frame of mind for a laugh. I wasn't, and I broke every on-set rule by walking straight out in front of the camera during an ongoing shoot.

Bert was cranking that one to get some footage while waiting for the Boss to come out of his meeting. He greeted my appearance in front of his lens with some choice comments you won't find on the back of a cereal carton. The friendliest of them indicated that my parents had never been legally married.

I put a lot of energy into my apology, levered Brutus off Horace, untangled everyone from the dog's lead, and led my wife to a quiet corner. She was livid, and I couldn't blame her. To cut filming like that felt like a mental slap in the face to an actress who put as much into her work as Melia did.

She let me have her opinions regarding my thoughtless, stupid, block-headed and downright idiotic actions with both barrels, but then something in my mute, hang-dog demeanour brought her up short. She became silent and reached out to touch my cheek.

'What is it Lieutenant? You look like someone ate your apple and left you with the pip. What's happened?'

I told her about Jarr's idea, that he wanted to put her out there in front of the camera, naked as a jaybird, to titillate the crowds who'd missed the show in Niagara and would be lining up at the movie houses with their five cents burning a hole in their palms.

I told her exactly what I thought of it and said that if she wanted to walk away from Century to a studio with more respect for its stars, I'd take the walk with her. We'd manage, I said, and they could keep their damn contract!

Melia listened to me without comment but her face grew pale and her lips thin. The storm warning flags were flying. Somebody had better batten down the hatches and man the pumps because Storm Melia was going to touch down hard. I thought Mason Jarr was going to get his pipes cleaned – and my girl knew how to handle a pipe cleaner that was just his size.

I was wrong. It was me she was riled with, and if I thought Brutus got his teeth into a target – well that terrier wasn't a patch on the woman I'd married. In no uncertain terms she told me that when we stood at the altar we had promised to love and honour each other. She said she would stick with me in sickness and in health; and was happy to go along with the 'richer' part of the list (she'd already had a bellyful of the 'poorer' bit, thank you very much).

'But where?' her voice was low and flat, 'Where did it say you could negotiate my career? Where did it say you decide my movie roles for me? What am I? Some soft-headed spoilt kid who needs a big brother to fight for me? Well think again, *Mr* Murdoch! I've been making my own decisions for a few years now. You weren't there to hold my hand when I was twelve. Why should I need you now?'

She stepped up to me and stuck her finger into my ribs, 'This isn't finished, mister! We've got more we need to talk about. I'll see you after I've finished with Mason Jarr and the Boss. Now, I'll thank you to keep your over-inflated ego out of my affairs and to shift your dumb, pretty-boy face out of my way.'

She pushed me to one side and strode like a fury towards the stairs up to the Boss's office. Bert, Horace and Brutus watched her leave. The dog crouched down, whimpered, and covered its eyes with its front paws. I knew how it felt.

By the close of play that day Melia had, agreed to play the part of *Salome* on a closed set. The press would get carefully posed photographs that offered a salacious hint about what was to come. I saw them. I wanted to break

Mason Jarr's legs with the photographer's head. I also went home to my own apartment which seemed a cold, lifeless place after my weeks with Melia in her loft.

I was to have nothing to do with the new movie. To keep me occupied the Boss had put me in charge of the *Airborne Antics* project and the follow-up movies. I liaised between the studio and Art Cobal, and soon got caught up with the fantastic opportunities his new technique would provide.

But, no matter how wonderful and successful our work might have been, even Cobal's imagination couldn't match the blockbusting attraction that was my wife dancing in her birthday suit. And I grew sick of the whole thing.

22

Salome broke box office records. I helped by joining the queue of sad saps who wanted to ogle the only girl I had ever loved. I ask you, is it right that a man should stand in line and hand over his nickel to see his wife on the big screen? Well, is it? I still caught glimpses of her at Century if I walked through studio one; but all too often it was a closed set and my imagination ran riot trying to guess what was happening behind those locked doors.

Bert and Horace joined me for a beer sometimes after the day's shoot, and Bert told me that Melia wasn't really naked under those veils. She was wearing a kind of body stocking affair that he swore disguised her tenderest parts and effectively screened her from prying eyes. Technicians on set had to wear blindfolds.

Only the director, it was the Boss, of course, and the cameraman, Bisset, kept their eyes on the prize. Members of the cast couldn't stumble about blindfolded, but their numbers were kept to a minimum. Don Sherwood played John the Baptist, Bert and Horace played guards with little more than loincloths and exotic hats to preserve their dignity, and Mason Jarr sat in as Herod the Great.

Herod the Great Sweaty Pudding. God, I hated to see him there. He squatted like a toad on his throne and sweated under the lights until streaks of pale flesh began to appear on his carefully bronzed belly. It didn't matter, when Melia took the stage nobody was looking at him anyway. She stormed the screen and burned a smoky, woman shaped after-image into her audience's retinas. She was magnificent.

Boss had put all his storytelling genius up there on the screen and Bisset filmed everything with a lover's touch. It was tasteful; the lighting was seductive rather than revealing, but Melia performed a sinuous ballet that would put a kink in the spine of a saint. The real Herod wouldn't have stood a chance.

The dance was introduced by specially written music played on a phonograph recorded for the purpose. It began when Melia's hand appeared to one side of the screen and dropped the first veil, the signal to the lug cranking the music box to get going. A high haunting flute began a wild composition that perfectly accented Melia's movements. It was a masterpiece.

She dropped that last veil and pirouetted slowly in front of her king then threw a high kick at the camera. You could hear strangled groans from men all over the theatre. When she bowed and her pert little behind was revealed under those lights it didn't look to me like she was wearing any body stocking.

The hoots and cheers from all around me told me I wasn't alone in thinking that. She looked the way Jarr wanted her to be, naked, and the folk lapped her up like candy. I was the only man watching her performance with a broken heart and a sick feeling in my stomach.

When I left the theatre I heard a man telling his friend, 'I'm going to buy me that music and get my wife to take dancing lessons. Hell, it won't cost much to buy the costume.'

His companion laughed, 'Damn, Frank, after watching that Salome it ain't dancing I'm thinking about. I'm telling Bessie dinner can wait until I've had some Turkish delight.'

On my way back home I bought a bottle of good whisky. I felt I'd earned it, but I was too wretched to drink more than a few glasses without becoming maudlin.

The next evening I was there in the back row and I watched the thing all over again. And the evening after that, and the one after that. Melia played to packed houses, night after night. There seemed no way to sate the public's appetite for her flesh. They ate her up with the biggest spoons they could find and then came back for second helpings. *Salome* was a phenomenon and stayed that way for months. Salome's dance sold a million phonograph recordings.

That is, until *Bathsheba* hit the screens and the world joined King David in watching a beautiful woman taking her bath. Jarr had begun mining the gospels for nudity and the Testaments had provided a lucrative seam of usable scripts.

The newspapers loved it. They invented the scandal of Melia Nord. She was the 'Scripture Siren' or the 'Biblical Babe'. She created a frothing frenzy of alliterative descriptions and a screaming demand for more, more, MORE!

Some of the more respectable papers had left the Melia question to their arts reviewers, there were more important things going on in the world. But for others she was a big enough draw to push the fact that the US had joined France and Britain's never-ending war against Germany off the front pages.

There followed the inevitable backlash. In some parts of the Bible Belt, naked Melia effigies were left hanging from telegraph poles or carried burning through the streets. Her name was thundered from the pulpits, and fire and brimstone was cast down upon her lovely head. She was adored and reviled in equal measure. Something had to give.

Melia was working like a slave, getting into the studio early and going home late, but somebody was watching for her. Waiting until she was vulnerable and out in the open. She had spent another long day on a closed set, working on *Jezebel*, her third movie in a year. It was November and the streets were dirty with rotting ice and horse droppings. It was bitterly cold.

Horace was walking her home. He had taken a brotherly shine to Melia and enjoyed spending downtime with her. She shared her worries with him and he, in turn, secretly shared them with me. Melia's greatest concern that evening was where Jarr would turn once he ran out of scandalous women from the gospels.

'What do you think? Will I get to be Lady Godiva? Cleopatra bathing in ass's milk? How many women are notorious and naked enough to get Mason Jarr's juices flowing? How long will it be before I just get asked to vamp it up as a showgirl or a stripper?'

She paused, 'You know something, Horace? I wonder if the Lieutenant wasn't right when he tried to warn me back then. Maybe these movies were a bad idea. I feel like I'm on some kind of a nightmare treadmill and the only bits of me people want to see on screen these days are below the neck. I'm an actress not a...'

Something hit her in the face and exploded like an overripe fruit, spattering her and Horace with a sticky liquid that looked black in the orange lamplight. They heard footsteps pounding down the street and a voice called out 'Next time it will be a bullet, you stinking bitch!' Horace started after their attacker but stopped when he heard Melia scream.

He ran back to her side; her eyes were wide in horror. 'It's blood, Horace. They're throwing blood at me! Why? What have I done to them? Why?'

Horace told me later that all trace of the sophisticated actress was washed away by the assault. He quickly put his arms around the shoulders of a young woman quivering and helpless with fear, trying to comfort her.

'Let's get you home, darling,' he said. 'Whatever it is he threw at us will wash clean away, don't you worry. See, old Horace is here. I'll make sure you're safe right enough. That dirty coward ran away. He won't hurt you. Okay? Come on, let's go. One foot in front of the other, that's the way. Let's get you home.'

While Melia was in her bath scrubbing at her skin and hair with a hard brush, Horace rang me and told me what had happened. I was at her door within twenty minutes. Horace opened it to me and I was shocked to see the blood still in his hair and spattered across his face and shoulders. It was beginning to crust.

He shook his head at my expression of horror, 'It looks worse than it is. I think it was a toy balloon filled with animal blood. Neither of us was hurt, but it made a mess and scared the sap out of Melia.'

He looked back into the loft, 'She's been in her bathroom for over half an hour now. Is it okay if I leave things to you and go home? I'd like to get into my own bathtub and wash up, but I don't think she should be left alone just now. That okay with you? I can stay awhile longer if you want.'

I thanked him and took his hand in mine. I would have given him a hug if it wasn't for the mess of clotting gore crusting across his upper body. I shut the door behind him with a heartfelt goodnight, hung my coat on the hook by the door, and then walked towards Melia's bathroom. Would I be welcome or would she scream abuse at me? Time to find out.

The loft smelled sweetly of perfume and soap and that was all. There was no trace of any cooking smells. My apartment always held aromatic reminders of my last meals, and, since Melia, no woman had been there to scent it with her fragrance. I realised how much I missed it. I knocked on the bathroom door, called out 'It's me,' and pushed it open.

Almost without thinking I caught the scrubbing brush Melia had thrown at my head. The red raw girl slid down into the tub full of suds, covered herself the best she could, and gasped, 'Horace, what...' Then she did a double take. She gazed at me and sat back up. I got a free show of the body everyone was queuing to leer at. It looked mottled and sore from hard scrubbing.

'Oh,' she said, 'it's you.'

'Yes,' I replied. 'Horace rang me and told me you guys had been attacked, I came straight over. Horace went home, he's a mess but he's okay.'

Melia made a hoarse moaning sound and pushed herself to her feet. The next second, I held an armful of sopping wet, naked woman and our lips were welded firmly together.

I had not spoken to her for the months we had been apart. We didn't say much for that next hour either, at least, not in words. But our actions spoke volumes. Eventually we slept.

Everything of mine I had left at the loft, clothes, toiletries, underwear, shoes, was still there. All neat and cared for. The next morning Melia remained asleep in bed while I performed my ablutions, shaved, and put a pot of mocha coffee on the stove before getting dressed. There were no fixings for breakfast. Either Melia didn't eat anymore or she always ate out.

While the coffee brewed, I studied the bookshelves that filled half the long wall facing the windows. I noticed that Sigmund had invited some mentalist friends along to the party, but there was also a collection of leather-bound editions of literary classics.

I still hadn't dipped so much as a toe into the subject of psychiatry, but I was pleased to recognise names such as Homer, Kipling, Twain, and Joséph Conrad. I grinned to myself, thinking the girl would learn more about the human condition from authors like that than she ever would from the talking cure brigade.

Then I heard her call out from the bedroom and my heart missed a beat. I ran to her side and took her in my arms. She was panting in panic, 'You weren't here. You weren't here when I woke up and I thought I must have dreamt you. Where did you go? Why weren't you here? I thought I'd dreamt you, it was horrible.'

I tried to make light of it, 'I see, so I'm a horrible dream, am I?'

Yep, that earned me a flood of tears. You'd think I'd learn when to keep my flapping mouth shut and hold an upset girl until she calmed down. I already knew I was an idiot; did I have to try so hard and so often to prove it?

I sat on the bed and held her, making meaningless shushing noises until her weeping stopped. I buried my face in her thick mop of tousled hair. 'Honey,' I mumbled, 'I'm making coffee. Want some?'

She brought her face up to mine and smiled, 'Please, that would be lovely.'

I released her, kissed her lightly, and ambled back into the kitchen. I heard her light step behind me and turned to see her tying a bow into the belt of a long white robe. She looked so small and vulnerable I wanted to lift her up and tuck her into my pocket where she would always be safe.

I poured our coffee and joined her at the solid, waxed oak table I had liked from the first day I saw it. Mom and Pop had one just like it at home. Melia blew on her coffee to cool it a little. We were drinking it black. I had found no cream in her chill box. In fact there was nothing in there.

'We have to move.'

At first, I missed what she said, I was thinking about breakfast and wondering if I could leave Melia alone for long enough to run to the corner delicatessen and get some fixings. Ham and eggs seemed like a great idea and my empty stomach was threatening to go into business for itself if I didn't address the situation right soon.

I said, 'Are you okay if I go get us some breakfast? I can just finish this coffee and get some stuff from the NYD on the corner. Abramovich always opens early, I seem to remember. Or would you rather eat out? Either's good for me. What do you say?'

'We have to move. We can't stay here. We have to move. They're going to kill me if I stay here. We have to move, Lance, promise me.'

Without thinking what it would mean, I promised. I took her hands in mine, and I promised. She was shivering like a fever victim and kept turning her eyes towards the big windows on the gabled south side of her loft. I looked out there too. If you stood on a chair and gazed down, you could see New York laid out below you like a rich counterpane, but from where we sat you could only see the sky.

The clouds broke and a shaft of light lanced down like a spear. It was heartbreakingly beautiful. I wished I had a camera to film it. Melia gasped and covered her eyes. I asked her what was wrong. She pointed at the window with a shaking finger.

'See, they're trying to find me. They've got lights in the sky and cameras everywhere, they want to film me in bed and in the bath. They'll sell the pictures. Everyone wants to see me naked, they'll pay anything, anything. Oh, Lance, and they'll pay more if I'm dead. Can't you see I'm right? They want me dead. We have to move – or they'll kill me.'

23

The studio must have been listening. We were a little late for the start of the day's filming but that was fine with the crew. We arrived to find everyone in the commissary drinking coffee and eating breakfast. The place was alive with the hubbub of lively conversation. I saw Horace sitting at a long table beside Bert and Don Sherwood. They looked a little nonplussed as if trying to digest unexpected news.

When Horace saw us walk in together his face brightened into a grin. He strode over and took Melia in his arms, lifting her off the floor. At the same time he thrust out his paw to me. 'Good to see you together again. Made my heart ache to see you two so far apart. You sleep okay?'

Melia giggled like a naughty schoolgirl. Her moods were swinging around like a flag in a storm. My head spun trying to keep up. She was like one of those tiny birds that levitate around a tree without lighting in any one particular spot for more than a second. The tree must get dizzy after a while, I knew I was.

'We did eventually,' she replied with a throaty chuckle. 'The Lieutenant had to help me out of the bath and I slipped on the soap and we got kind of mixed up. Took us an hour to get untangled and we slept where we lay. You know how it is?'

'I wish I did, darling. The only body I get to help out of the tub is this, mine very own. I don't get to tangle with anyone.'

Melia pouted, 'That's very sad. Lance, don't you thank that's very sad? We should buy Horace a cat. Would that help?' She lowered her voice, 'We're going to move so those people can't find us. We'll tell *you* where we go but you've got to keep it a secret. Cross your heart? Secret.'

Horace leaned forward and whispered back, 'We're all moving, darling. You and the Lieutenant here made the studio so much money we can all join the gold rush and head south.'

I raised my hand, 'Woah there, puh-dner, what gold rush we talkin' 'bout?' I pretended to spit tobacco juice into a spittoon and wiped my hand across my mouth. Come the talkies, I could make a living as a prize idiot. I was born for the role and could step into the part without any auditions. Horace rolled his eyes and grinned.

'Golden sunlight is what I'm saying. The smart money says go south young man and get the best light for making movies without paying the utility companies a single penny. We're just a little late in taking the plunge. The pottery pot says this is the best time so we move.'

'Who's the pottery pot?'

'Your favourite movie producer and mine,' he paused, 'Mr Mason Jarr.'

'Oh,' said Melia with a cold expression on her face, 'him.'

'Are we all excited about the move?' The sly voice insinuated itself into the conversation without warning or greeting. I wondered if Jarr was like the devil himself, mention his name and he pops up through the floor. He sidled over to our little group with his arms held out as if ready to embrace us all, but the plump palms landed on Melia's shoulders and gave her a proprietary squeeze.

'This little lady's hard work has paved our way clear to California, and the Century train's wheels are rolling towards a new, brighter horizon.'

He cupped his hand and dropped it as if he was ready to take a firm hold of Melia's behind. I set to slap it away but Horace was faster than me. He took the offending paw in his fist before it could make contact with her sit upon and shook it like the handle of a water pump. Melia accepted that as an invitation to dance nimbly out of the man's reach and tucked herself behind me.

Jarr's face took on the expressive look of a mangy cur just had his dinner bone lifted from between his jaws at the same second he got his tongue to the marrow. He gritted his teeth and almost snarled at Horace who was still pumping that limp, damp handle for all it was worth – which was precious little in my opinion.

Melia whispered in my ear, 'You know you told me about that script with Emily and the octopus in the bathtub?' I nodded, she chuckled, 'I know who could play the octopus. Problem is, he'd really enjoy it.'

I shook my head, 'I wouldn't put that grasper in a tub with Brutus, let alone a bona fide girl of the feminine persuasion. What's he been like around you on set? I see he got himself an invitation to the party as King Herod and again as one of King David's advisors. Did he get close?'

'He would have liked to, but the Boss keeps him in line the best he can and Horace gets in his way. That man still makes my flesh crawl. He uses his little piggy eyes like fingers. They touch everywhere, and then they linger...' She shuddered.

We turned at the mention of my name to see the Boss walking our way with Art Cobal at his shoulder. Art and I had become great friends during our work together and we had swapped crazy ideas and much laughter over the previous few months. He was an easy man to like, and I knew he loved Melia like a daughter.

It was mutual. She squealed and ran at him, flying the last few feet to throw her arms around his neck. He held his arms out like a tightrope walker and took a few steps with her just hanging there. He wasn't a big man but Melia was a small girl and didn't weigh much. She was a 'little scrap of beauty' he told me once. 'She's like a treasure you want to keep somewhere you can always see it.'

'Hey, Lance, can I borrow your necktie? I hear everyone's wearing them these days.' Then he gave Melia a hug and placed her carefully by my side, his hands on her waist where they could cause no offence.

Boss wore a rare grin around the big Cuban cigar jutting out under the thin moustache he had started to favour recently. Tattle had it that his latest lady friend had shaved his thicker 'tache down to a pencil line for fun and he'd taken a shine to the rakish look. It gave him a piratical air he quite liked.

'Lance,' he beamed, 'I've offered Art here his own little studio at the new place and he said yes. We're calling it "The Art Studio".' He paused for the inevitable groans and choking sounds. 'Okay people, enough. Thing is, Lieutenant, we've had so much financial success with the projects you two guys have come up with that I've had a little idea. Art says yes, so, what about you?'

I shrugged, 'What about me what?'

'Dumb,' he said. 'Dumb! Sometimes an idea is so plain and so damn obvious you think everybody either already knows about it or can see it coming, but no. I'm so dumb. Lieutenant, I thought a smart guy like you could see this coming a mile away. Fact is, you and Art here are making great movies that make money, and more important you're making pure movie magic.'

He pulled the cigar from his mouth, examined it as if he couldn't remember where it had come from, then pressed it back between his teeth. 'We're talking about giving you your own brand name, and, okay, we may be crazier than a bull in a drugstore but we want you to work on your own scripts in your own studio space and pay you a percentage of the take. What do you say?'

He scowled, 'And don't think we're giving away the whole farm through the warmth of our philanthropic hearts. We want to nail your hides to the barn door before someone else poaches you away. Well, what do you say?'

'Will this make me a Captain?'

'Damn, son, this will make you a Major! As in major player and major asset, at least until you run out of ideas. You think you're going to run out of ideas any time soon? Well, waddaya say?'

What could I say? I said yes!

Cobal rocked back and forth on his heels with his hands in his pants pockets and whistled between his teeth. 'I got a thirst for something that ain't coffee,' he said to the ceiling. 'Time to celebrate. Come on folks!'

'Later,' said Jarr harshly, 'there's work to do and these clowns have been swinging the lead all morning.'

A few hardier souls pointed out that they had been ordered off set and into the commissary to await an announcement, they weren't swinging anything. Jarr was evidently not in the mood for making friends.

'Quit your bellyaching! Get your noses back to the grindstone or I'll have your asses on toast.'

One or two of the larger carpenters looked Jarr over with amused contempt. It was a poor stab at tough guy talk. He had rarely showed his face in the studio until Melia began starring in the biblical dramas, but since the first, *Salome*, began shooting, he had been there every day. It didn't take a genius to put those twos and twos together to make a peeping Tom.

Melia followed the Boss to spend yet another day under the camera's greedy eye. No wonder she was having nightmares about cameras and lights in the sky. Acting in nothing but her skin was getting to her – that much was obvious, as was Jarr drooling all over her on set. It burned me up – and it was unprofessional. I wondered how long it could last before she went crazy.

Jarr gave me a hooded stare and a pig-faced sloppy grin that made me want to pound him with a chair, then he followed after Melia like a hound on the scent. My mouth went dry. A quiet voice in my head wondered if the creep was worth my attention. Didn't I have better things to spend my time on? Better people? But I couldn't help it. I despised him with a passion.

The commissary emptied except for Art Cobal and me. He put an arm around my shoulders and soundlessly steered me towards the exit. I paused and gazed back towards the door that led to studio one. It was closed and I could see the sign that said, 'Locked Session'. Melia was probably already dressing down for her part, and Jarr would soon be running those fat, fingering eyes all over her.

Cobal sighed, 'You're an honest man, Lance. I can see what you feel writ plain as day on your face. So can that pig, Jarr. Don't let him rile you. He's doing it on purpose. Forget him. Let's go celebrate your promotion to Major and mine to artistic genius first class. Then we can take Melia to dinner after

113

she finishes. She'll probably need something to remind her of who she is and what she's worth.'

I made him detour to studio two where Bert and Emily were rehearsing for our next antic four reeler. I wanted them to meet Cobal and get some idea of the things we were planning for the movie. Emily was in her bubble costume and splashing about in a big wooden tub filled with bubbles and lukewarm water. Bert was working a couple of thick rubber tentacles using wires.

To make things look more animated Emily was pretending to fight the tentacles off while actually grabbing them and wrapping them more tightly around herself. Cobal would add the octopus and another six tentacles in his studio. He watched the performance in the tub for a few minutes. His face creased in a thoughtful frown. Then he buried his chin in his hand.

He wandered over to the tub and had a quiet word with Emily. I couldn't hear what he said but she grinned and nodded. He said something to Bert who shrugged and pointed at Emily. Then he came back to me.

'I've had an idea,' he said. 'Let me buy you that beer and I'll tell you what we can do. I know you'll like this. Come on, partner.

24

I don't normally drink that early in the day and I knew from experience that Cobal was no lush, but we had things to celebrate and I wanted some fresh air after my encounter with Mason Jarr. Maybe a tall one would help wash some of the bitterness out of my throat. I had a bad taste in my mouth from having to swallow the man's gall.

I steered Cobal to The Albany, a fine bar I knew on East Fourteenth Street that served fresh, Lion Brewery light beer. It also promised good steak and eggs. And it was clean, comfortable and quiet. It was a good place for Art and me to hole up for an hour and talk about the new script.

There was a time when some bars attracted their patrons with a free buffet of bread, ham and cheese so long as they invested what little cash they had over the bar. Such establishments were everything you might expect, and the smell in most of them was like used kitty litter stored in a warm, men's locker room. I'd eaten in them when I had to, but I never liked it. The Albany was more my style.

We found ourselves a wooden booth away from the few drinkers at the bar, men who were working hard to put a little alcoholic tenderness into the day's harsh reality. We sipped our beers and talked while we waited for our steak, eggs and fried potatoes. I jotted notes while Cobal outlined his vision.

Everywhere I go I carry my ideas book around with me because if you have a great idea and don't write it down it will fade from your mind like ink on water. I'd had some wonderful ideas make their escape before I could nail them down on paper, so, I carried my book with me and I wrote things down.

He liked the octopus in the tub, he admitted, but we could do more with the idea if we added some madness, as we had with the airplane flying into the train tunnel and impossibly turning around to come back out just in front of Bert and the train.

He said, 'Emily's told me she'll do whatever it takes to make a great picture, and Bert said she calls the shots on what we do with her. So, if she's happy he's happy. She's happy. You know those two are an item, don't you?'

I didn't and said so, then I asked what Emily had agreed to. I explained that I thought the story was already a done deal. Emily in the tub, octopus attacks, she fights it off and then it lifts her into the air and drags her under the water. Emily wakes up on a park bench to find Bert had been trying to get fresh while she was asleep.

The octopus had been a bad dream brought on by his moustache-twirling villain trying to get our plucky heroine into his vile clutches. Heroine clouts the villain with her handbag and knocks him cross-eyed, stars circle his head courtesy of Mr Cobal. She leaps to her feet and makes her escape while he's dazed.

Emily smiles to camera, opens her bag, pulls out a horseshoe, kisses it and puts it back. Then we see her walking lightly away and behind her the villain's moustaches droop forlornly and his eyes are still crossed. Close-up of crossed eyes, fade to black and credits. Twenty minutes of magic.

Our food arrived and we took a break while we made a start on our steaks. Art made noises of appreciation, The Albany had just entered his short list of Cobal-approved eating establishments. He admitted it was a shame I had introduced the place to him just before we moved to California. All too soon he would have to start a brand-new list.

Then he told me what he had planned for Emily and Bert. 'We still start in the tub,' he explained, 'and Emily gets lifted up and then dragged down into the water. So far so everything planned for the original. Okay, then the camera follows the octopus and its victim under the water, but now we find ourselves under the sea.'

He squinted at me, 'See, this is where we needed Emily to be happy. The seawater would wash the bubbles off her and she would be naked in the tentacles. Nothing tawdry, and the tentacles will save her blushes, but we already know how much the viewing public enjoys a little feminine exposure with their popcorn. Melia's movies proved that and so have the numbers.'

He cut some fat off his steak and dipped it into his egg yolk, popped it into his mouth then chewed with a blissful expression on his face. 'So good,' he said. 'And so, back to the story, Emily is under the sea in the grip of the octopus. She's struggling like crazy but begins to weaken. She's drowning. The octopus starts to pull her towards its terrible beak. It's going to eat the girl! Oh no, what's going to happen next?'

I was caught up by the energy of his storytelling, he'd got me. 'Yeah?'

'Yes, what?'

'So, what happens next?'

'King Neptune comes to the rescue with his trident, what else? That would be Bert with a different kind of beard. Emily doesn't mind if Bert rescues her while she's naked. In fact she won't allow anyone else near her. Anyway, Neptune fights and kills the ravening octopus, which releases Emily who floats to the seabed. Nothing too revealing, the octopus has fired a cloud of ink so we can't see her.'

He chuckled, 'At least not all of her, not all at once. Anyway, Neptune looks around and sees her draped across some seaweed and he dives down to her side. She looks dead but he kisses her and blows bubbles of air into her lungs while he brings her back to the surface. But, now, she's no longer in her tub – she's out on the ocean.'

He waved his steak knife, 'She and Neptune kiss while they bob about on the waves, and that's when Emily wakes up on the park bench to find our moustachioed villain trying to get fresh once more. But this time he's too strong for her and moves in to have his wicked way. On the screen we see his face change to be replaced by the dreadful beak of that octopus, Emily's nightmare is coming true. She screams!"

Cobal left me on tenterhooks while he forked more meat into his mouth and chewed. I took the opportunity to sip my beer. I ask, 'What happens?'

Cobal swallowed and took a pull on his Lion brew before answering. 'And then the picture switches between the octopus beak and the villain's slobbering lips, getting closer and closer. His face fills the camera, there's no escape. Then suddenly the man is yanked backwards. We see a hand has grabbed his shoulder and pulled him away. A man who looks just like King Neptune has arrived to save the day.'

Cobal waved his fork in the air for emphasis, 'Our hero boxes the villain's ears for him then kicks the man's cowardly butt down the path. The villain runs like the cur he is, jumping in the air after every kick. The hero strides back to the girl and helps her to her feet, they embrace. They kiss. We hold a close up of his left hand holding hers. We see the identical wedding rings on their fingers. They are husband and wife! Close and credits.'

He mopped egg yolk and meat juices with his potatoes while I applauded his performance. I asked, 'How much of that's going to be you and how much in the camera?'

'Dear partner, we just have to work out what can be done. As much as possible in the camera, it is so much quicker. I can add bubbles easily enough and use them to make sure Emily doesn't show anything her mother wouldn't approve of. Best laid plans and all that, things will pop out sometimes no matter how careful we are.'

He shrugged, 'I'll do the octopus, of course, but we'll need to build its beak. And it has to look frightening. Can do?'

We could and would. If we were going to turn Bert into a hero, I'd need someone else to play the moustache twirler. Jarr would be perfect, it would be wonderful to see that creep kicked down the path, and he was born to play a bad hat. But, no. He wasn't an actor, he was just a natural born slime-ball.

Horace was no good. He was an actor, true, a fine one, but if we had a black man molesting a white girl that would give a completely different slant to the story. We'd be talking to the Klan. They were already burning Melia in effigy down south, we didn't want them using Horace for kindling.

Don Sherwood was already tied up in the biblical epics, and anyway, he was wrong for the character. We needed someone threatening – or someone who could dress the part. Someone like, yes, like *Ben Usher*. Big Ben would be perfect for the role, and he had the comedy chops to make the butt kicking look painful *and* funny.

Art and I returned to the studio and found an intimate atmosphere had descended on the room. Our two stars were sitting by the tub talking close and quiet like sweethearts. Emily was wrapped in a dressing gown. Bert's hand was resting lightly on her knee.

Now that Cobal had pointed out that Emily and Bert were 'an item' it was so patently obvious I wondered how I'd never seen it before. And Bert was a very good-looking guy, why hadn't I noticed *that* before? I thought I must walk around all day with my eyes shut.

I asked Bert if he knew where Ben Usher might be found and if he was free for work. Actors knew each other, the good ones looked out for each other whenever they could.

It turned out Bert knew exactly where Ben was 'resting'. He'd taken a job as a plongeur – an up-market dishwasher – at the Waldorf Astoria. And sure, Bert would take a cab to find out if he wanted to join us as part of a brand-new movie team.

'I'll tell him we're a "family",' grinned Bert, 'I'll tell him he's my brother from another mother. I'll bring him back in chains if I have to. He got me my first job with Century, did know that? I owe him. He'll be cock-a-hoop!'

He almost ran from the studio in his eagerness to deliver Ben the good news. I realised how very lucky I was with the big-hearted people I had somehow pulled around me, they were great folk. We *were* family, in all but name.

I left Art Cobal to explain the new script to Emily and went to find some carpenters. They were having a coffee break in the little hut they'd built in the workshops. I loved the carpentry guys, they knew their craft and worked hard to get things done, but I'd never yet caught any of them doing anything but drink coffee. The sets seem to get built by magic.

I sat with Maurice, the foreman and offered him a Lucky Strike. He suggested we step outside where we were less likely to burn the place down. 'Come into my office,' he said and steered me towards the 'can'. This was a metal drum about four feet tall where we could flick our ash without catching the store on fire.

'We're always just one careless cigarette away from the great fire of New York,' said the foreman. 'And I guess now we're moving we can start worrying about the great fire of Los Angeles.'

'Is that where we're going?'

'Yeah, they always tell the guys like us first. We got to manhandle stuff to make things happen. So, what can I do for you today, Mr Murdoch? You got something interesting for me? The boys still talk about that totem pole we built for yah, and that ship's stern, that was sweet.'

I told him I needed Neptune's trident and a giant octopus' beak. I showed him the drawings Cobal had made in my book.

He whistled, 'The boys are going to love this. It will get their juices flowing. All the Boss wants these days is thrones and benches from old Egypt, which is okay, I guess but a bit flat, you know? Furniture is furniture, whether it's from Macy's or King Tut's palace. You give us the crazy creative projects. When do you need it?'

When I told him I needed it as soon as possible, if not sooner, he grinned like I'd just told him it was his birthday.

'One day, Mr Murdoch, you'll say, Maurice, you take your time. Just make sure you do it right. But, hey, you know we'll do it fast for you – and we'll *still* do it right. Give me forty eight hours then come back and see me.'

He spat on his palm and shook my hand. We enjoyed another cigarette together, this time from his pack of Chesterfields. We smoked slowly in amiable silence, comfortable in each other's company.

You know something? If I hadn't been promoted, I think I might have ended up in those workshops full time. I always felt at home with those men, and in that place of pride and workmanship. Maybe I should ask them to build me a box I could nail Mason Jarr into? Looked like they had enough wood – and enough nails.

Life felt good that day. How soon everything would change, and not for the better.

25

Undersea Terror would finally be finished in the brand-new Century studios on Allesandro Street in Edendale, a little place on the outer fringes of Los Angeles. We had already begun shooting the script for *Babe in the Woods*, another starring vehicle for Emily Cooper and Bert Savage – with added mayhem from Ben Usher.

Bert had taken to his new heroic persona with dignity and dash, and I was confident that once *Undersea Terror* was out, we'd have another sure-fire winner on our hands. And every day Art was adding more magic to the mix, I had seen the rushes. Wow!

Ben Usher was a revelation and a great addition to the 'family'. He was tall, powerful, and came with his own moustache. Add the beard and he looked like the Devil on skates with extra mustard. He was hot stuff. He looked like he ate Kodiak bears for lunch and was convincing as the black hat. In life he was as sweet and civilised as pink Moscato and just as welcome to the table.

So, the Major had his core troupe of players, but there was a problem. I was trying to do too much and there weren't enough hours in the day. I was liaising with the Boss and the pottery pot, writing scripts with Art Cobal, directing the scenes and guiding the players, while also dealing with the carpenters, and shooting the footage.

Something had to give before my mind snapped under the strain and I ended up as a character study in one of Melia's psychiatric reference books. I shared my concerns with the troupe over mid-morning coffee and biscuits in the long marquee we used as a commissary while Century Edendale took shape around us. The troupe had no easy answers for me. But they promised to think about it.

Ben thought about my logistical problem just long enough to make a phone call before he joined us back in our studio for the rest of the morning's shoot. He wandered about with a pleased expression on his face that quickly evaporated when he realised that I had stopped filming and was grinning at him.

'Hey, Ben,' I said. 'Get that goofy smile out from under the beard, I can't take you seriously looking like that. You got a feather up your kilt or something? Remember, in this epic you're the Laird, the bad guy. Look fierce!'

He jolted upright and grinned back at me, 'Cain't help it. I feel so lucky to have fallen on my feet with you guys. I guess I must've wished on a lucky star and the wish came true. That's all it is, Major, I'm so happy I'm busting clean out of my skin.'

'Well if you do, we'll film it and use it in the movie. Save Art a piece of studio time.' Meanwhile, I was filing away 'wishing on a lucky star' and 'so happy he busts out of his skin' in my ideas book.

Ben *was* wearing a kilt and all the traditional trappings of a Scottish Laird, including a knife in his sock and a mad floppy hat with a long feather that Patch swore was authentic. The black beard and his wig of long black hair nailed his character. He was perfect as a wild, passionate, and cruel man from the Highlands. Emily, meanwhile, was playing the lovely and innocent daughter of a highland sheep crofter.

Babe in the Woods was a typical example of our particular and unusual genius. It was insane – but in a good way. We start with Emily out in the fields looking after her father's lambs. No crofter's daughter in history had ever treated lambs the way she did. She was hugging them and dancing around with the woolly little beasts in her arms as if they were children.

The sun picked out her radiant loveliness and she was spotted by the passing Ben Usher, who gazed at her as if all his birthdays had come at once and he knew which present he wanted to unwrap first. I swear if they ever include moustache twirling alongside caber tossing in the Highland games my money's on Mr Usher.

All unawares Emily bent to pick up one of her lambs and the sight of her tight skirt hit the man like a taper to the blue touch paper. He leapt the fence and screamed as he ran for her. She saw him coming and fled. It wasn't long before she was pursued into the dark woods by the lust-crazed Laird. He was after taking her virtue, and he didn't care how she felt about it.

The intertitles were already drawn up for the piece and consisted of passages such as, 'I shall have you', 'You can't escape me, wench', and even 'I shall drive your father out of his cottage if you don't surrender to me that which is mine by tradition and law.' Emily was also stuck with her own pedestrian lines including, 'I would rather die,' and, 'Not while I have a single breath in my body, you scoundrel'.

It was riveting stuff, if you're amused by rivets. We weren't. It was a work in progress. So far, so ordinary. Exciting enough for any other studio but not enough meat on those bones for a production by the newly named *Tremendous Tales* team, which consisted of, me, the troupe, and Art Cobal's magic artistic touch.

Here's how we told the story – the Laird chases the shepherdess into the depths of the forest until she's lost and terrified. He catches her and presses her up against the trunk of a great tree. With his hand at her throat he reaches down to the dagger in his sock. They call the dagger a dirk in Scotland, we could include that for the British release. Folk in the US might get confused.

The intertitle declares, 'Stop struggling or you shall feel my blade!' Emily goes limp in his hands and Ben starts to cut away her costume. She is all alone and helpless in the deep forest. There's nobody to step in and help her. Or is there? We discover that all the while the ancient spirits of the trees have been watching, and they step in to protect the innocent girl.

This is where Bert Savage, who plays a tree sprite, reaches down and takes the Laird's dagger just as he has cut away the laces of the girl's bodice and is pulling the fabric apart with his eager, rude fingers. We see barely anything of what's under the bodice, just enough for it to be titillating, but enough for us to understand what's going on. The Laird is a foul rapist and no respecter of beauty or innocence.

By this time the girl has fainted clean away in terror, and she slumps to the ground. Bert stands before her and throws the knife into the bushes. But the Laird still wants his prize and fights back against the protective spirit, pounding at him with his balled fists. The hero staggers back under the onslaught and falls to one knee. The Laird kicks him in the face and he falls backwards. The Laird reaches for the girl once more.

But Bert is the mighty and ancient spirit of an oak. He leaps to his feet and lifts the struggling man away from his victim with a single hand. With a roar of defiance (which of course we can't hear but can plainly see) Bert throws the shrieking Laird out of the forest and clean over the edge of a cliff. The doomed figure vanishes down into the mists to be swallowed by a great waterfall, never to be seen again.

The fourth reel, and the movie, ends with the oak spirit walking back through the trees, with her unconscious body limp in his arms. He reaches the pastures and we watch him approaching her home, an ancient bothy with a peat covered roof. It looks as if it has been there since the beginning of time, hunkered down in the lee of a mountain.

All the while, as he gets closer to the building and further from his forest, his appearance changes, until, by the time he arrives at the stout door of the bothy, he is no longer a tree spirit but a handsome, muscular man wearing a kilt and a simple, collarless cambric shirt.

The girl's father, Ben again but now transformed into a kindly old man thanks to Patch's make-up and costume skills, rushes out. Bert explains about the Laird, his attack on the girl, and tells the father that the nasty man is dead and his daughter has nothing more to fear.

The girl is held safe in Bert's arms, and when she comes round and looks up into his warm, loving eyes she smiles at him. He smiles back. Father smiles at both of them. Everyone embraces. Fade to black, *The End*, and not a dry seat in the house.

That was the script. Maurice's carpenters had their work cut out to provide effects that Art wouldn't have time to do in his studio, including Bert's tree spirit costume – and a realistic flat for the bothy. The inside of the building wasn't shown, so it just needed a convincing front and a working door for the father to dash out from when he sees Bert and his daughter draw near.

Other sections of the movie would be done on location. There were forested areas and hills around Edendale that were perfect for the chase, and back lots where we could shoot the shepherdess with her lambs. The fact that the ground was scorched yellow, sun-baked grass, rather than lush green meadows, wouldn't matter. We shot everything in black and white.

What we didn't have was a waterfall. Art had already told me he could ink the Laird falling to his doom against a real background, but creating a waterfall from scratch, at least a convincing one, would take years instead of months. We needed a waterfall, and I had no time to go find one.

I was chewing my gums and lamenting my lot when Ben leapt to his feet and hurried past me. I knew I'd been boring everyone but I considered that to be something of an extreme reaction. Then he returned with a slender, olive-skinned man in tow. The stranger had a thick cap of tight chestnut curls on his head, and the kind of bashful smile I always warm to straight away. I stood up to be introduced.

Ben nodded at his companion, 'This here's Frenchy Marivaux and he's looking for work. I heard what you said about needing help and he's your man. He cranked the handle for Pathé over in Paris but he didn't like the look of the situation on the Somme. Instead of jumping on a bus for the front he jumped on a boat and came here. Frenchy, meet the Major, your new boss.'

I shook hands with the stranger and looked him over. I couldn't help but notice that his back was slightly twisted, which gave him a barely noticeable hump, and that on his left foot he wore the heavy boot of a man with a club foot.

I smiled, 'Frenchy? That your name?'

He shrugged, 'It's what they call me. My *maman* called me Paul.'

Paul had a pleasant accent, much like some of the folk we'd met in Canada. I continued my interrogation. 'Okay, Paul it is. Pathé have their own cameras, you know your way around an Edison rig?'

He shrugged again and coloured slightly, 'If it uses celluloid film, and has a lens and a crank handle I can make any rig dance.'

Paul had the hungry look of a man who's had to live for too long on the free buffet for the price of a beer. His face was that of a saint, drawn lean to the point of cadaverous, but with huge, liquid chocolate eyes. I could tell he wasn't usually boastful and was finding it difficult. He needed a job more than he needed a bath – and he really needed a bath.

I had to put my mind at rest on one subject, 'What Ben just said, you didn't run away from the fight over there did you? They turned you down.'

I would get used to Paul's shrug after a while. He raised his shoulders and indicated his twisted body – his grimace said everything I expected to hear.

'They only want able-bodied men for the Boche to shoot at. I am as you see, and my lungs are weak. I caught a fever as a child, what you say, tuberculosis? Yes? When I was young. So, the army told me, no! I am not fit enough to breath poison gas. But I can work as hard as any other man, even this great mountain of a man, Ben.'

'Okay, sounds promising. You're on trial starting now. Join us in the commissary for lunch and I'll tell you what I need.'

That little Frenchman's eyes lit up when I mentioned lunch. He was a hungry boy. I told everybody to take five and the troupe ambled out to the chow line. I made a point of letting Paul go first, but he turned to me with frustration in his eyes.

'I've no money for lunch, I'll wait for you back on set, yes?'

'You'll wait back on set *no*! Lunch is free here, one of the perks. Fill your plate and come back for more, there's plenty.'

He did, and it made my heart sing the way he attacked his plate and went back to the serving table twice more. I'd heard tell the French served the best food on the continent, and maybe they do, but nothing tastes better than a free meal does to a broke and starving man.

While he ate, I told Paul what I wanted, and he nodded. With each of his mouthfuls I could feel energy returning to his wasted frame. 'The forest is easy, and there's a waterfall in Eaton Canyon. Not much mist, but we can make that with a wind machine and water vapour. I can do it this afternoon if you like.'

'You know the area well?'

'When your belly is empty and you have no money the only thing you can do is walk and look for food where you can find it. Yes, I know the area very well.'

I had him under contract before he marshalled his little team of special effects people out into the wilderness, and I gave him half his first week in advance. I told him I wanted him back with the camera the next morning, and I wanted to see the footage he produced. If he used a camera as well as he used a fork, we'd struck pure Gallic gold.

[26]

Melia and I had set up home in a ranch-style place perched in the hills, less than a mile from the studio. We had a good view and enough land for me to practice driving my bright red and sporty version of the latest Fiat Tipo Zero without hitting bystanders. I'd invested in the car to celebrate the launch of *Tremendous Tales*.

As I said, back then people would pay good money to watch just about anything, but we gave them something more. A great deal more. We gave them something special. They queued around the block and with my cut of the profits I was earning cash by the bushel.

That was before Washington got greedy for the tax dollar, back when a man with a great idea could earn a good living with his own hands. Later it changed. It became so we worked more for the revenue men than we did for ourselves, but in 1918 we were doing alright.

Paul was as good as his word, and better. He had a way with the camera that matched anything Bisset was doing for the Boss, and Bisset may have been a weasel but he was also one of the best lensmen walking God's earth. Paul was as good if not a regular cut above. But I may have been biased, I preferred my twisted little saint to the Boss's weasel any hour of any day.

Two months later, we were well into the swing of things. The *Undersea Terror* had proved a smash in the US, Canada, Britain, South America... You get the picture.

The war was on and stuck firmly in the Flanders mud, but people still wanted to be entertained. We put some sparkle into their lives and as a result Melia could enjoy ice cream and Champagne for breakfast. They paid for our ranch house and my racy little red Fiat.

In his spare time Horace had been teaching me how to drive without stripping the gears. I wondered aloud if there was anything he didn't know how to do – while practicing my double declutch on the fly the way he'd taught me. He didn't answer straight away and became very thoughtful.

He said, 'Fact is, I envy you. I never learned how to make a lady happy the way you have with Miss Melia. I tell you, that's a man's gift I haven't got. And that little lady would be lost as a kitten in a sack that's been thrown down a well if she had to face the world without you. She depends on you for the sun to rise in the morning and the moon to shine at night. I put my hand on my heart.'

So saying he pressed his hand over his crotch and burst out laughing so loud I nearly lost control of the automobile and put the thing into a long swerving skid. We had been racing at fifty miles an hour and we kicked up a heavy cloud of dust when I hit the brakes. Horace and I coughed as much as we laughed. I reached over to the back seat and fetched up my ideas book.

Horace shook his head in amused exasperation. 'Man! You write *everything* down? Why do you do that, Major? It's not like I'm Shakespeare or Mark Twain and worth quoting. I'm just old Horace who flaps his trap and foolishness slips off his tongue.'

I wrote that down too and he roared like I'd just told the best joke he'd ever heard. I pointed at his groin with my pen.

'Is that really where you keep your heart? Big-hearted man like you?'

Horace chuckled, 'You trying to say something, Major?'

He rolled his eyes suggestively. 'You saying I'm a big-*hearted* man? Thank you kindly, Mr Murdoch, that's right civilised of you. You got a mighty powerful pump of your own trapped behind those ribs – and if you didn't know it already, well, I'm proud to be the man to tell you. God bless you and the horse you rode in on.'

He slapped the dashboard and roared, 'Okay, we done with all this back slapping now? You want to learn how to drive this beast or you just want to wax it come Sunday morning?'

When we finally got back to the house, we found Melia waiting for us in the shade of the covered porch. She was sipping Champagne from a flute and eating strawberries from a wide, Spanish style, Majolica bowl that she liked. As soon as she saw us approaching, she put up her parasol and stepped out into the late afternoon sun.

Thanks to the work she was doing for the Boss, my girl had to stay out of the sun. She couldn't afford any burn marks on her skin. I enjoyed putting perfumed moisturiser on her every night after her bath to keep her smooth as a child, just so I could rub it off again while we spent a pleasant half hour or so getting better acquainted before sleep. We were young, married, and in love.

Melia was feted as one of the most desirable women in the world, but, to me, she was much more. She was everything that made the day worth facing. That seductive character up there on the big screen was a stranger to me. In the flesh she was funny, vulnerable, loving, and, sometimes, as sharp as a viper's tooth.

Her mood could change faster than I could change gear in the Fiat, but I had learned when to leave her alone in her darker moments. Sometimes she would sit with her nose in her book and nothing could disturb her. Other times I would find her weeping silently. It broke my heart to see her face a mask of pain; and her fists gripped so tight her nails left bloody crescents in her palms.

Other times she was so high and gay she reminded me of Ben saying he was so happy he could 'bust clean out of his skin'. She would brighten any room with pure joy. She could be so light she could fly and so dark it would break your heart, but there was no middle ground.

It was as if she had to plumb the most incredible lows in order to reach the heights. I guess there was some kind of balance to it. Sigmund might know, but I didn't have his number to ring him and ask.

Melia stood on the running board of the Fiat to reach Horace's cheek with her lips. Then she ran around the automobile and climbed onto the running board on my side to plant her sweet gift on my mouth. I felt her smile while she kissed me and I grinned back like a goof in love with the best girl in the world.

'You beautiful folk break my heart,' guffawed Horace. 'But the world demands its price. Somewhere in this world are two people miserable as Harlem in mid-winter. They your shadow people, the dark to your light. They go through hell so you can live in heaven. You should find them and shake their hand. Tell them thank you.'

Melia and I gazed at our friend for several seconds. I reached for my ideas book while Melia's pretty face almost crumpled. 'Oh, Horace, do you really think so? Those poor people. We have so much, we're so happy aren't we, Major? Their lives must be awful. Can't we do something for them?'

Horace shook his head, 'It happens and there ain't nothing you can do to change things. That's the natural order. Some live in the sun and others live in the cellar with nothing but rats for company.'

He leaned across me and caught Melia's face between his thumb and forefinger, pushing her full lips out in a delightful open pout. Her eyes flared wide in surprise and she sucked in a sharp breath.

His voice was gentle, 'You must remember the day you was in heaven, sitting there ready and waiting to be born. And God himself leaned forward and took your face just like that. He lifted you into his arms and kissed you. Remember?'

He released her and continued, 'He said, "Make my world a brighter place and you will always be happy. I promise." Then he put you down and you got born – and ever since then you've had those darling dimples. That's where God touched you; and marked you as someone special.'

I said, 'Hey! What about me?'

His grin broadened, 'Man, you got dimples on your ass, I seen 'em. You really think the Lord's gonna kiss you on your little baby fanny? He's God, not your grandmother. No, man, you just a lucky cuss and long may it last. Oh, man! Look, he's writing it down again. He writes everything down – I should get royalties.'

This gave me pause to think. *Why not?* Horace came up with ideas the way water bubbled up from a spring. Why not bring him into the troupe as a writer? *Tremendous Tales* was earning enough to feed another mouth, and Horace would fit right in with the other geniuses and help make me look good. I told him what I was thinking.

He rocked back in his seat as if I'd punched him in the face. His eyes were big as saucers and his mouth opened and closed as if he was tasting his words before they spilled out. For perhaps the first time in his life Horace was rendered speechless and it left him gawping at me like a beached fish.

Melia broke the silence. A serious scowl darkened her brow and her mouth creased in a moody moue.

'Horace is my best friend on set! Why do you want to take *him* away? You've already got Bert and you've got Ben. You've got Frenchy now and you work with Art Cobal every day, and he's a solid gold darling. And you've made Emily so famous, they're comparing her to *me*! And *she* gets to keep her clothes on! Most of the time.'

She made her boiling kettle squeal and bounced on the running board so hard the whole car shuddered. I noticed she was gripping my door so tightly her knuckles were white, as was her jaw. She locked her eyes tight shut and rocked backwards and forwards, making a keening sound through clenched teeth.

Horace regained the power of speech. 'Melia, girl. If you need me, I'll be there. I won't leave you alone I promise. Old Horace is your fire blanket and your safety curtain. He'll look after you, of course he will. I put my hand on my heart, see, I promise. I'll stay with you, promise.'

This time he pressed his palm to where he kept his wallet. Melia stopped rocking and took a deep breath. She sounded like she was breaking back into fresh air from deep underwater and was desperate to fill her starved lungs. She opened her eyes and gazed at Horace as if seeing him for the first time.

'You'd do that?' she asked. 'You'd give up the chance to work with the best production team in the studio just to keep me happy? You'd do that?'

I suddenly had a lapful of lively woman when she climbed over me to throw her arms around Horace's neck. He was as surprised as me and his mouth was still open when she kissed him. Her eyes were closed; but his were boggling and he was looking across at me as if terrified I might think he was trying to steal my lunatic wife from me.

I grabbed her by the waist and lifted her off him, 'That's enough, that'll do. Put the poor man down. He won't be able to sleep tonight as it is. Are you going to calm down? I think he knows you like him. That's it, calm down.'

I stroked her shoulders and she settled more comfortably on my lap, but she never took her eyes from Horace's stunned face. He was a picture sure enough.

Melia sounded dazed, 'You wonderful, kind, thoughtful man. No, Horace, it's no good. I can't let you do that for me. You've got to do it! You've got to join the Major. It's your big chance. I'll never forget this, but you've got to do it, that's settled.'

'So,' she turned to me, 'Major, will you take me to see that disgusting man Jarr? He rang and asked me to go to his house about some changes to my contract or something. Do you mind? Can you take me?'

The sudden change of direction took me by surprise. 'Sorry, honey, no. I'm seeing Paul and Art in an hour to go over the *Babe in the Woods* edit. I was planning to walk into the studio it's such a nice day.'

'Oh, okay. Yeah, fine. So, duty calls as always. I'll call a cab.'

Then Horace chimed in, 'Hey, Major, if I can borrow your car I'll drive Melia to the pottery pot. I know where the man hangs his hat. How's that?'

And I gratefully accepted. I watched them driving away in my Fiat, then set off towards the studio on foot. I didn't know it then but it would prove to be a very long night.

27

Paul had delivered the goods alright. His atmospheric landscapes provided the perfect backgrounds for Art's clever artwork. The result was pure genius. Even the intertitles were less stilted. With someone to carry some of my load I'd been able to concentrate on giving the words more energy. I put plenty of sting into the Laird's threats and whipped some sass into the shepherdess's replies.

Maurice was watching the edit with us. He loved to see his team's work up on the screen and was able to make useful comments about what he described as their 'special mechanical effects'. The tree costume they had designed for Bert was a thing of pure craft, and Paul had filmed it in a way that suggested more than he revealed. It worked beautifully.

When the twenty five minutes of running time was over, Maurice and I burst into spontaneous applause. We had been transported to a place where trees came alive and triumphed over evil. Emily had never looked lovelier; and heroism settled on Bert's broad shoulders like mist on a mountain: but it was the wonderful ingenuity of Art and Paul that made it all possible.

The day of the single-reeler was at an end. Our audience was no longer satisfied with the crude fare we had provided before. Barely a few years earlier, movie-goers had run away trying to escape from the footage of an approaching steam train. By early 1918 that same train was merely one of the elements of a much more complex story.

Our *Tremendous Tales* productions had become a transport of delight, a window onto a more magical world. The only limit to our storytelling was our imagination, and we had our own goldmine filled with fancy.

Other studios were exploring American western history. They invented the myth of tough gunslingers, honest sheriffs and wild Indians on the warpath. War, romance, comedy, drama, every thread in life's rich tapestry was plundered to provide tasty victuals for the movie theatre buffet. Even Melia's sultry offerings had their place.

'If Leonardo da Vinci was alive today this is where he'd be,' said Maurice. 'Don't get me wrong, I like the work Pablo Picasso and Henri Matisse are doing, but it's the movies that make the real fine art for the twentieth century. We got picture houses instead of picture galleries and I'm proud to be involved.'

Art grinned, 'How're you spelling "real" Maurice? That "reel" with two Es? I agree with you if it is. Not everything up there on the silver screen is fine art, my friend. Some of it's a child's scribble done with a big crayon, but the punters still pay to watch it. They pay to watch anything.'

My head was too full of *Babe in the Woods* to comment. We had set a new creative benchmark that we would have to match or exceed from now on. This was our latest masterpiece, fine, but what were we going to do next? Where I used to have thoughts was a whirl of noise. Paul came to the movie's defence.

'What we do is head and shoulders above the usual Nickelodeon fare. Some filmmakers are lazy. They're happy to put anything up there for their audience and most of it will be forgotten the next week. Not this. Not us. We care. We try harder. People will be watching our work in arthouses a hundred years from now. This stuff matters.'

Art stuck out his mitt, for Paul to shake. 'And here I thought it was just me. I thought I was fooling myself into thinking we were doing something special. You really think that, Frenchy? You're not just saying it?'

'I'm saying what became obvious to me the first day I started working with you. You people know what you want and how to do it. You have vision and direction. The Major doesn't need to step on your gas to make things happen. You too, Maurice, your team are craftsmen.'

Maurice shrugged, 'I'm a man of my wood, Paul, man of my wood. You ever seen the work of Grinling Gibbons? If the war ever finishes you should go over to old England and see what a true genius *can* do with wood. Take a look in Hampton Court Palace or St Paul's Cathedral.'

He smiled, 'If I put so much as a half of that man's talent into the things we do I'm happy. It's nice to be appreciated, but it's what you people do with a camera that makes the fat lady sing.'

I couldn't stay quiet any longer, 'Take any single element out of the team and we'd struggle to do what we do. Maurice and his craftsmen, Art and, well, his art, you, Paul, and your camerawork.'

I warmed to my subject, 'And our players, our wonderful players. They get better with every production. Do you see how natural they look up there? Even Ben! Some villains belong in the pantomime for kids to hiss at, but not Ben. "Not too much ham" as the Boss would say, but plenty meaty enough. You really believe Emily has fainted in terror when he grabs her, and when he kicked Bert in the face...'

Cobal butted in, 'Not being funny, Major, but there's an important name you left off your list. Maybe the most important one.'

Maurice and Paul made sounds of agreement. I leaned forward and looked along the trio of grinning faces. Who had I missed? 'Okay,' I said, 'you got me. Who did I leave out?'

Cobal nodded at me, 'Fellah called Lance Murdoch has an important hand in making the magic happen. You don't want to be leaving him out. Even if all he does is sweep up the mess after us clowns have finished, he uses that broom with his very own unique style. I'd raise a glass to the man if somebody pressed a full one into my hand. What do you say?'

The lump in my throat blocked my snappy rejoinder and something burned in my eyes. Maurice was a sensitive man who saw my difficulties. He pushed himself to his feet and thanked the projectionist who was waiting for us to leave so he could go home.

'Come on guys, I need a smoke and a cold one before I head home. You geniuses willing to share a beer and a quiet hour with a carpenter? My treat.'

I nodded, my voice still choked. Paul said, 'Jesus was a carpenter. He preferred wine, so do I.'

Art piped up, 'I thought He was a shepherd.'

Maurice said, 'He was a fisherman, wasn't he?'

I got my voice back, 'He was all that and a king too. Where we going?'

Art led us to a recently Cobal-approved bar called The Sombrero, which was set back from the highway about half a mile from the studio's front gate. Art claimed the place got its name because its first owner, a Mexican, had earned his stake by dancing around his big wheel of a hat for money.

The current owner was a lean type called Jake Olives who had the doleful face of a condemned man – one who had just learned that the kitchens couldn't supply his preferred last meal. He welcomed us, and while we drank he added more colour to the story. His voice was so dry his audience developed a fierce thirst just listening to him, which was a fine talent for a barkeep.

'José was a good dancer, it's true, but his audience mostly paid to watch his guitarist, his wife Rosita. She was a beautiful firebrand of a girl and she played the strings like she was making love to them. She danced and kicked as high as a prancing pony while she played. She wore her skirts high at the front and low at the back, flamenco fashion. José could have kept his hat on his head and fallen asleep in the corner for all the notice the men took of his dancing.'

He took a long pull on the light beer he'd accepted from us with mournful thanks. We quickly realised how much of his character was an act; and happily sat by his bar enjoying the show while eating red hot chilli beef with beans and sipping ice-cold beers. Paul was also on the beer, Jake had advised him that no vineyard ever produced a vintage that went well with a bowl of good chilli beef.

'So,' I asked, 'what happened to José and Rosita after they bought this place? They go bust?'

Jake's face concertinaed like soft folded leather and I realised he was smiling.

'No way. I told you the lady was a firebrand and she danced like a young boy's dream. I know, you ever seen that *Salome* movie with Melia Nord? Rosita was like that. Every man in the room wanted her. Then José found out she was giving private dancing lessons to any man could afford it. Lot of men saved up their dollars to take their half hour lessons with Rosita.'

I felt a sudden chill when Jake connected Melia's name with that of a cheap Mexican prostitute. The spicy beef congealed on my tongue. Art put a calming hand on my arm. Maurice steered the tale away from my wife.

'So, did José divorce her?'

Jake made the concertina face again, 'Nope.' He pointed to a box mounted on the wall behind his bar. 'See that knife in that box? That's the cheap kitchen knife José used. Always kept it sharp as a straight razor. Carved his own steaks. Carved his own wife when she came back from one of her dancing lessons with the man's smell still on her. That little framed photo there, see, that's José swinging in his noose after they dropped the trapdoor under his boots.'

He took a long pull on his drink, 'They say his soul was burning in Hell before his legs stopped jerking at the end of that rope. I guess that was Rosita's last dancing lesson – she taught José the gallows foxtrot. You gentlemen ready for more beer yet?'

My mouth was dry and my head had gone numb. I gazed at the little framed photograph of a man hanged for the murder of his wife. Jake followed my eyes, 'Funny,' he said, 'Most folk look at the knife but you're looking at the man who used it. Now, why is that?'

'Just thinking. Man gets driven to murder his wife – he must have loved her an awful lot. Other men might have thrown her out, but he sliced her like steak you say? How?'

'Cut her from crotch to ribs, slashed upwards. Some of the jury got sick when they heard the coroner's report. Yeah, he opened her up and everything spilled out. There were a few customers out here drinking in this very bar when it happened. They were sitting right where you are now.'

He looked over his shoulder, 'They heard the screams coming from back there and some of them rushed out and found the man holding his wife and crying like a baby. Said she was trying to push everything back into her belly and she died like a butchered hog.'

He looked at them, his eyes bleak as midwinter. 'Some say they can still hear her screaming on quiet nights. I been here over twenty years and I've never heard her. But sometimes I think I can hear him, José, weeping over the body of his murdered wife. I've often wondered what he told his priest in confession that last morning. He never said a word in his own defence. Not one.'

Jake leaned forward conspiratorially, 'Hey, guys you know what he had for his last meal? I'll tell you. Chilli beef with beans. That's right, a man knows he's going to hang and he chooses chilli beef with beans as the last thing he's going to taste on God's earth. And there it is right in front of you, gentlemen. That good bowlful's still made to the exact same recipe they served José. How 'bout that for a recommendation!'

It was a thoughtful quartet that left The Sombrero that evening. The next day was a Sunday so we agreed to meet early on the Monday morning and wished each other goodnight before heading home. I knew one thing – the images Jake had planted in my head would never be filmed by me. I wanted to wash them away with something more wholesome. I set my feet towards the ranch house.

28

I was surprised when I reached the house to find it pitch dark and the curtains still drawn back. The sun had set a couple of hours earlier and Melia was fanatical about switching on the lights. She said she wanted no shadows where a person could hide to spy on her. Then she would draw the curtains tight closed so no chink of light could escape, and no prying eyes could peer in to get a glimpse of our private lives.

The night had become much cooler during my walk home from The Sombrero, but, inside, the house still retained most of the day's heat. I took a shower and tried to wash the story of José and his wife out of my imagination. It was replaced by growing concerns about *my* girl. Where was she?

I had Mason Jarr's phone number in the book so I rang him. I got no answer. Then I tried Horace with the same result. I was beginning to get frantic with worry. I walked out onto the front porch. The night was silent and the house felt lost in its empty acres. Melia had all sorts of plans for those miles of land but nothing would happen until she had some free time to put them into action.

The sky was a featureless black. It was as if God had taken a leaf from Melia's book and drawn his curtains to shield the stars from inquisitive eyes. I was adrift in the darkness. I believed I knew what Jonah must have felt like inside his whale. And that was when a little light came on in my head and a story emerged, its pattern stitched from whole cloth.

Dancing Mexicans, murder, and even my missing wife were pushed into the background while I grabbed my ideas book and a pen and started scribbling. The story flowed out of me as if it had been germinating for months. I chuckled to myself while I was writing. *Thank you, Jonah.*

For once Ben would have to get by without his moustache twirling and pull on a pair of seaman's boots. Bert could be the brave skipper, or a crew member. Emily could play the plucky heroine – but this time without facing a villain. This time she would be swallowed by a whale.

Paul had told me about a month he spent filming in the North Sea where the crew got close enough to the ocean giants for him to capture them throwing themselves into the air like playful dreadnaughts. He shot hours of film, including close-ups of their strangely intelligent eyes and their great tails rising out of the waves and slapping down again.

He had also caught the hunt, which featured men in steam-powered ships firing explosive harpoons to kill the massive beasts and harvest their treasures. Paul told me he had eaten the meat, which he described as very much like bland venison and not at all fishy.

He had also eaten rendered blubber, the whale's fat, which was crispy and served like a fritter. When I asked if he liked it, he shrugged. 'Food is food to a hungry man.'

Pathé had never worked out what to do with the footage so Paul still had hours of film we could salvage for the new project. I jotted the word 'mermaid?' in my book, alongside the line, 'could a person survive inside a whale long enough to be rescued?' And then, 'does it matter? Jonah did, so it must be true.' I lost myself to the joy of invention. Melia, José and Rosita dissolved like phantoms from my mind. I filled pages with notes.

And then I became aware of a strange sound in the silence. It was like a high-pitched insect whine combined with the harsh grinding of metal on metal. *Somewhere,* I thought, *a machine must be in great pain. Where?* I put down my book and pen.

The sound was drawing closer and ever louder. It was a screeching bedlam by the time I saw the headlights and my Fiat came howling out of the night. If the poor creature had been a horse my father would have put a bullet between its eyes. It's screaming sounded terminal.

The car juddered to an agonised halt and the tortured engine received a merciful quietus. It ground down to silence, the only sound that of ticking metal cooling in the evening chill.

Melia climbed out from behind the wheel, 'I don't think your car works very well,' she said. 'It made a horrible noise all the way here, dreadful. You should get it fixed.'

She walked past me into the house and started drawing the curtains while I stretched out a hand towards the bonnet of my beautiful car. It was too hot to touch. I got behind the wheel and tried the starter. It growled painfully into life. I engaged first gear, released the handbrake, and the car rolled forward with an excruciating zinging and popping noise. I got it under the lean-to at the side of the house and left it there. It had suffered enough, I thought. Let it sleep in peace.

I followed Melia into the house. Every curtain had been drawn tight. She wasn't in the lounge. I went wife-hunting. I found her in the kitchen. In the brief time I had spent moving the Fiat she had downed over half a bottle of Merlot. Her amber bottle of tablets was open at her elbow. I said, 'You in pain?'

Her answer was flat, 'Migraine, a stinker. That rotten car of yours didn't help. Noisiest damn car in the state. People kept hooting at me.'

'What happened to Horace? I thought he was driving.'

'Give me a minute, will you? My head's killing me. What do you know about it anyway? You're not a woman. *You* don't get migraines, do you? Aren't you the lucky boy! I might need to lie down. I feel sick.'

'What happened to Horace?'

'Is that all you can think about? Your precious Horace? *What's happened to Horace? What's happened to Horace?*' She said this last in a high-pitched, nasal falsetto.

I poured myself some of the wine and took a sip. If she had to go fetch another bottle and open it, it might at least slow her down a little. Her eyes were already unfocused and her head wobbled as if her neck was too thin to hold its weight.

I persevered. 'Yeah, so, what happened to Horace? And what's happened to you? Tell me and I'll shut up.'

She gazed at me with black, hostile eyes. 'He's been arrested, okay. You happy now? Your precious Horace has been arrested and I had to get myself home. I've got a headache and you're making me feel sick with all your stupid questions about damn *Horace*! He's been arrested, okay? Finish. Now, shut up.'

She lurched to her feet and wove an unsteady path into the wine store cupboard. I heard her uncorking a fresh bottle. She came back to the table and flopped into her chair. Carefully she topped her glass up and put the bottle down beyond my reach. I moved around the table and grabbed it before she could slap my hand away. She screeched, sounding tortured like my poor injured gearbox.

'I need a drink, you bastard! What's it to you? Gimme that bottle, you go get your own!'

I kept my voice low and calm. 'Tell me why they arrested Horace. Tell me that and you can have your bottle back. Why did they arrest him?'

She slammed the table, jolting a little wave of wine over the rim of her glass. It splashed onto the light wooden table top and stained the rich, honey-coloured surface I liked so much. It looked like blood.

She looked at the stain for a moment, then spat her words at me, 'All right! You want to know? Murder! Okay? They got him for murder. You happy now? Gimme that damn bottle – I've told you everything you want to know!'

I handed over the juice and sat back in my seat, pushing until the front legs left the floor. Melia took a great gulp of wine and almost choked on it, swallowing with difficulty. Little slender neck, man-sized drink. I knew the signs. This was going to end in tears.

I growled, 'I'd slow down with that if I was you. You'll be bent over the porcelain and yelling for Howard at that rate. I'm here for you, if you need me, but I'd rather see you stay sensible if you don't mind.'

'Who's Howard? I don't know any Howard.'

I bent sideways in my chair as if vomiting and moaned 'Hoowaaaaaard!' Ending on a retching sound. 'Drunks always call for Howard, him or Raaaaalph! They're twins. You find them lurking at the bottom of the bottle.'

She pulled a bleary-eyed face at me. I said, 'So, Horace. He's a sweet guy. Who did he kill? Did he get in a fight? Were you involved? What happened?'

The wobble to her head was looking critical. I wondered how much she had drunk before coming home. She wasn't much of a driver sober, but drunk? That would explain her trying to melt my gearbox and kick the teeth out of its mouth.

'He shot Mason Jarr. Shot him twice. Bang, bang. People heard the shots and came running. The police arrested him when he tried to drive away. I was in the car. He didn't fight it. He looked at me and told me everything was going to be okay, then they took both of us. They took me in your car and Horace in theirs. They found the gun in the bushes by Jarr's front door. It was horrible.'

'How do you know they found the gun? Horace didn't have any gun. Why would he? What would he want a gun for?'

'The policeman told me while he was questioning me in a room with a metal table and chairs welded to the floor. I tried to ring you. They said I could have one call and I tried to ring you.'

She hiccoughed and her upper lip was beaded with sweat. Her voice became ragged. 'You weren't here. What's the use of you? Never there when I need you. And that creep Jarr. He had his hands all over me. What was I supposed to do? I had to... I, urgh!'

Melia staggered to her feet and ran for the little bathroom off the kitchen lobby, her hands pressed to her mouth. She didn't make it. A spray of almost neat red wine burst around her palms, into her hair, and flowered around her head. I could smell the acrid bite of stomach acid.

I followed her into the bathroom to stop her hair flopping into the toilet bowl. This was the second time since Niagara. I hoped it wasn't about to become a habit. We had been married nearly a year and I didn't want to be the husband of a dipsomaniac. If she carried like that she would soon be sending me off to the temperance hall in town so I could talk about the evils of drink.

To distract myself from the vomiting sounds and the smell I sang quietly, 'One day at a time, sweet Jesus, one day at a time, sweet Lord...' All the while my mind was chewing on the bone Melia had thrown me before running to the can. *That creep Jarr. He had his hands all over me. What was I supposed to do? I had to...'*

I wondered if the booze had unhinged her tongue enough for her to make a plain admission of guilt. What had she had to do? Why was Horace giving her assurances if he was the guilty shooter? Had he been defending her? Or was he covering up for her guilt?

Melia knelt gasping at the toilet bowl, her body empty at last. I looked down at her and wondered, *did I have a killer on my hands?* Had Melia murdered Mason Jarr? And what would I do if she had? She fell limply to one side and murmured gibberish words. Time to clean her up and get her to bed. Murder could wait until morning.

29

'Mr Murdoch, there are over one hundred thousand people in this city and fewer than two hundred police officers. You do the math. We're heavily outnumbered, and we're expected to guard against racketeering, German fifth columnists, communists, and citizens smoking in a public place in front of children.

'When fate hands me a corpse with two fresh bullet holes in his body, a killer at the scene of the crime, and the murder weapon, I don't go looking for more suspects. I put the man in a cell to cool his heels, wait for the coroner's report, and get on with my day.'

Captain Marshall Henderson was one of those slow talking men who sounded as if they'd reached the end of their tether several years ago and finally stopped tugging on it. I had learned a lot from him since a constable steered me into his office and presented me with a cup of a liquid he described as 'joe'. The brew's only saving graces were that it was wet and warm.

Fifteen per cent of Henderson's effective force had been conscripted into the armed forces and he didn't have enough feet on the ground to deal with the steady increase in traffic violations, let alone the vice that plagued his city. Prostitution, drugs and gambling vied for his attention – alongside the war between management and organised labour.

Horace Goodman and the late Mason Jarr had arrived as a gift with a big red bow tied around them. Henderson wasn't worried about motive or where the killer had got his gun. He didn't care that the victim had been found on his back with his arms crossed on his chest, nor that his blood was sprayed across a large sofa against a far wall while the body was over by the fireplace.

Captain Henderson was too exhausted to care.

Earlier that morning I had walked into the studios with Melia, who had recovered from her debauchery the night before. She was flighty as a goose and acting as if the previous day's events hadn't happened. When I asked her how she felt she had offered me a dreamy smile and kissed me thoroughly on the mouth. I could still taste a hint of sour wine on her lips.

I delivered her across to studio one and told the Boss about Jarr's murder. I did it where no-one could overhear. I also told him that Horace had been held as the prime suspect for the killing. I omitted any mention of Melia's drunken semi-confession.

'This is ridiculous,' snarled the Boss. 'That fool Jarr deserved everything he got... it was coming to him. He was sitting at tables with people you and I wouldn't share a room with, let alone break bread. I'm talking dangerous people who wouldn't think twice about murder. No way Horace was involved. What was the poor man doing there anyway?'

I explained about Melia's call from Jarr, 'I think it was just a ploy to get her alone,' I said. 'I need to talk to Horace and find out what he has to say about it.' I explained how Melia had wrecked my automobile in her mad dash home the previous evening and asked if the studio had one I could borrow for a few days.

'Horace's jalopy is still out in the studio parking lot,' he said, 'I saw it when I came in this morning. If you borrow that I'm sure he won't mind. Sounds like he's not going to need it for a few days. Say, have the cops spoken to Jarr's butler yet? He ought to have an idea about all this if anyone does.'

The butler was a guy called Shaw. He was a Southerner and looked powerful. Boss said he was more like a great ape in a white butler suit. He told me, 'If anyone looks like a hoodlum, it's Shaw, I think he was probably employed as a bodyguard rather than to pass the drinks around at a cocktail party. They should speak with him, the cops.'

Before leaving for 2015 East First Street and the Boyle Heights Police Station, which was where Melia told me Horace was being held, I spent an hour with my troupe in studio two. We talked about whales. Paul tried to douse the whole story by telling me that anyone swallowed by a whale – a sperm whale for example – would drown or get dissolved by its strong stomach acids.

He shrugged, 'Maybe Jonah was a saint and he had divine help, I don't know about that. But Emily wouldn't last five minutes, don't do it to her, Major.'

I wouldn't be downhearted, 'We're doing it. She can have something that stops her getting down the creature's throat, you geniuses think about it. We need a doo-hickey that chokes the whale so it has to keep its head above water. That way Emily can breathe. We're not going to be stopped by common sense, are we, guys?'

I handed my ideas book to Art and left everyone to it. When I next saw them the story would be twice as long and would have become as elaborate as anything Mr Lewis Carroll had ever imagined Alice finding down any rabbit hole.

Henderson coughed to get my attention and I brought my wandering mind back to Boyle Heights. I wriggled trying to get comfortable in my straight-backed wooden chair, planted directly before the big police captain's desk. My people were always full of ideas. Captain Marshall Henderson, however, was coming up empty.

After giving me the facts as he saw them he allowed me a few minutes to fire my questions, then shook his head. 'Mr Murdoch, you see any children in this office?' I told him no and was tempted to add one of Paul's shrugs. They could be mighty contagious. Henderson sighed, opened a drawer in his desk and pulled out a large, overflowing ashtray in the shape of a ship's wheel.

He then opened a grey steel box and offered me a cigarette, which he lit before flaming his own. I recognised the Camel brand.

He took a deep lungful, sighed with pleasure, and intoned. 'We're not breaking any city laws so long as we're not undermining the healthy lungs of a minor with "nicotinoids and filthy tars", whatever they are. I hear say more American doctors smoke Camel than any other brand. Just means doctors are as stupid as me. So, speaking as one smoking man to another, tell me everything you know about this butler fellah,' he looked down at his doodle pad, 'Shaw.'

I told him what I knew which wasn't much. Then I asked what Horace was saying. He looked at me through the haze of fragrant smoke. 'I'll let you go ask him yourself. I want you to see how we don't treat suspects like criminals until we find them guilty. Mr Goodman is here as our guest, he's an amenable man. He just don't have the key to the door. Not yet.'

Without leaving his seat he reached up and fetched a cardboard file from on top of a cabinet behind him. He opened it and examined what he found there. He took a deep breath and offered me another smoke which I accepted. There had to be about a hundred nails in that box, he could afford to be generous. We were both blinking and squinting at each other in the pungent haze.

Henderson stood and opened a window, then came back to the table. The fog began to clear. 'I enjoy a smoke but I don't plan to go blind for it. Let's see, now, what does it say here?'

He mumbled while he read, then said, 'Your friend Goodman says he never went into the house. He says he was waiting outside in the automobile until your wife came out with the victim, Mr Mason Jarr, who had his hand at her elbow. Goodman says your wife was agitated and peeled Jarr's hand off her arm like it was poisonous.'

He looked at me with raised eyes, 'What kind of crazy people named Jarr call their boy child Mason? *Mason Jarr*? He must've gone through hell at school.' He shook his head, 'This guy was a victim way before he got shot.'

'He was a filthy creep. Maybe he had a tough start, but I'm told he mixed with the worst kinds of gangster. People you would want to avoid.'

'Noted, and thanks for that. Afraid I don't get to avoid them, much.' He looked down at the folder, 'Anyhow, Goodman says he started the automobile, a red Fiat, and was pulling away when he heard two gunshots from the property. He stopped the vehicle, climbed out, and approached the door, despite Mrs Murdoch's "vehement" protests.'

He paused and smiled, 'My officer had to ask him to spell "vehement". It's not a word we hear at Boyle Heights too often. Anyhow, he claims that as he approached, he saw a hand drop something from the window by the entrance doorway. That's where we found a Colt Woodsman .22 rimfire. That's a nice little pistol, an expensive piece of ordnance for a man to throw away. It had been fired twice.'

I heard a sharp double rap on the door behind me, I turned to see a uniformed officer's head poke through and nod at Henderson before retreating back out into the corridor. Henderson stood up and extinguished his smoke.

'If you're ready, Mr Murdoch, your friend Mr Goodman is ready to see you. Follow me and I'll take you to him.'

The corridors were painted in a depressing two-tone – smoke-stained cream and sage green – with a scuffed wooden dado rail separating the two. Chunks of plaster had been hacked out of the paint, some of it a while back. The damage to the architecture spoke to me of sudden explosions of violence. Perhaps not all the guests had been as 'amenable' as Horace.

Henderson watched me while I gazed at the walls, he followed my eyeline and grimaced ruefully. 'You a thinking man, Mr Murdoch?'

'While we're smoking partners, please, call me Lance. And yes, I guess so.'

'That's right neighbourly of you, Lance. Please, call me Captain Henderson. We can think about first name terms when we know what we're doing with your friend. I see you're looking at the walls.' I waited for more, he continued after a brief pause, 'That's why we cuff people with their hands behind their backs these days.'

144

He brought his wrists together in front of him, 'Shackled like this a desperado starts thinking the cuffs make a handy weapon and lashes out. Knocks lumps out of the walls and any convenient police constables. Took a while to learn the lesson, but it's one worth remembering.'

We paused outside a reinforced steel door with shallow dents in the panelling. Henderson tapped on it.

'This is where we have a quiet and friendly head to head with our suspects. If he has confederates, we talk to them elsewhere. We try to make them think that their buddies have admitted to everything and we just need to clear up a few details. It's an art that would suit a thinking man.'

He made to open the door, then faltered. He turned to me. 'You're a movie man, aren't you?'

'I cannot deny it. Guilty as charged.'

'Yeah, you might need a lawyer,' he grinned showing a heavy smoker's teeth and tired eyes that lacked sparkle. 'Can you explain something to me?'

'I'll do my damnedest. What can I tell you, officer?'

He leaned against the door. 'The police have a thankless job. There's not enough of us and there's too many people who think their life would be improved with easy money, cheap women, and too much booze. They like to run around with the wrong kind of crowd and get in trouble. We have to deal with all that to protect the innocent. You hear what I'm saying?'

I nodded, 'I can see it's a tough way to make a buck.'

'Yeah, it is. So why is it movie people like you make us look like idiots? We try to keep the peace and people laugh at us in the movie houses. Why is that? Can you tell me?'

'In my defence, your honour, *I* never have. But I know what you mean. I guess it's because you're authority figures. You can arrest people and lock them up. Maybe they're scared of you because of that. Some folk like to laugh at people they're scared of.'

Henderson looked at his boots and nodded, 'Yeah, like I say, you're a thinking man.' He opened the door and said, 'Mr Goodman, you got a visitor.' Then he ushered me inside.

[30]

It felt too much like a film set to take the scene that greeted my eyes seriously. Horace sat at the far end of a table topped with hammered metal. The table was about six feet square. An armed and uniformed officer sat behind him in the corner. He cradled a rifle across his knees. His peaked cap was pulled down so far his eyes were in shadow. His grimly downturned mouth looked as if he'd never learned to smile.

The room smelled stale and felt claustrophobic. There were no windows and just a single electric light up on the ceiling. It was in a steel cage, I guess to stop it escaping. The light cast a checkerboard grid around the room and across Horace's bowed head. I had only ever seen Horace as an upbeat man who could laugh at anything. The figure sitting at that table looked beaten down by despair.

He raised his head and squinted at me as if unsure what he was seeing. The hint of a smile creased his lips but never reached his eyes. He lifted his hands towards me and I saw his wrists were chained to the table.

'Sorry, Major,' he said. 'But just now I cain't be standing up to greet you as a gentleman should. I am in a somewhat restricted condition. Something of a quandary, as you can see.'

Henderson had entered behind me and shut the door. I turned to him, 'Captain, can I talk to my friend alone? I'll be fine.'

He pursed his lips and shook his head, 'Lance, did we strip search you before allowing you in here?'

'Strip search? I don't...'

'I'm saying did someone ask you to remove your clothes and search them, and you, for weapons? We call it a strip search.'

'No, but I'm not the one...'

'Of course not; but Mr Goodman here is helping us with a murder enquiry, and a good friend might think about bringing him a little present. You see the "quandary",' he paused and nodded at Horace, 'you see the "quandary" that puts me in? Best if I stay.'

He moved to a chair in the corner opposite the armed guard and sat down. I felt caught between two powerful jaws about to snap shut and shuddered involuntarily. I grabbed the chair facing Horace and tried to pull it away from the table. It didn't move.

'They weld them to the floor.' My friend shrugged. Paul had infected the whole studio with his Gallic tic. 'I suppose if you cain't lift them from the floor you cain't use them as a weapon. Mind you, after a night in one of the beds here, this chair feels mighty comfortable.'

'How they treating you?'

'No better than they treat white folk, but no worse neither. There's a guy here that killed his wife while they were on honeymoon. He was drunk and got mean. He's crying and howling all the time, wants to know where she is. Makes it tough to settle. The other tenants are sweet enough when they're sleeping. How's Melia?'

'She wrecked my car while driving home. She shouldn't have been allowed behind the wheel. I don't know how she got it started.'

'Stripped the gears?'

'Like they were being searched before visiting time.'

He chuckled, a familiar sound in an alien place. 'Sorry about that. At least she wasn't invited to sample the local bed and board. Good job I like salt pork and beans for breakfast and supper.' He glanced at Henderson, then the eyeless guard. 'Yeah, I've eaten worse in my time. I'm sure some guests think the food here is the best they've tasted. The price is right, anyhow.'

Behind me Henderson grunted, he said, 'Mr Goodman, I have some good news for you. Salt pork is on the menu again for lunch. Glad it suits your refined palate. We hate our guests to leave a poor report in the visitor book.'

I tried to turn to face him but the chair wouldn't move, 'Captain, you ever seen a movie called Pudd'n Head Wilson? It's based on a book by Mark Twain.'

'I enjoyed the book. I don't think the movie did it justice. Like I said you're a thinking man. You're talking about fingerprint evidence?'

'You got the murder weapon. Might help.'

'I already thought of that. I've called a guy to come down from Oakland, one of the International Association for Criminal Identification people. Fingerprint expert. He'll be here tomorrow morning. Mr Goodman will be able to enjoy our cuisine just a little while longer.' He gazed at Horace, 'Mr Goodman, did you touch the gun at any time?'

Horace shook his head, 'I never touched a gun in my life, and I never hurt a man I ever met. I don't know what a fingerprint is, but if it gets me out of here, I'll buy me a bushel of the things and hand them out to the officers here.' He turned to the eyeless guard, 'You can have two.'

I was wrong, the man could smile after all. The old Horace had climbed back into his skin and started taking command of the situation with his very particular brand of humour. Even Henderson chuckled.

I explained, 'Horace, look at the tips of your fingers.' He did. 'See those ridges there? Those are your fingerprints. Nobody else has fingerprints like them, fact. Scientists proved it. If you touched the gun and they find your fingerprints on it you'll be guilty. If they don't, you'll go free. When you walk out of here, I know a great place for chilli beef and beans, I'll take you there to celebrate.'

He groaned, 'You know any place don't do beans? I'd be mighty grateful. Fresh fried fish or chicken with a mess of greens sounds like heaven just about now. And good white bread for mopping up those sweet juices. Is that too much to ask? I think I need to take a break from beans.'

'I hear yah.' I passed a thumb over my shoulder towards Captain Henderson. 'I hope we *can* help the good Captain here catch the man who shot Mason Jarr. I'd like to thank him. I'd happily shake his hand. Jarr was a bastard.' I turned to Henderson. 'He tried to get his hands on Melia yesterday, and got a good slapping for his troubles. She won't put up with that kind of rough behaviour, never has. She acts scarlet but she's a professional actress. It's what she does. In life she's pure cream and a good girl through and through.'

Henderson strode to the table and confronted me. He had his 'thinking man' face on again, and curiosity boiled hot behind his eyes. 'Lance, Mr Murdoch,' he began, which pinned my ears back. *Oh-oh,* I thought. 'Mr Murdoch, where were you at about six thirty yesterday evening? And do you have witnesses who can corroborate your whereabouts.'

Horace coughed, 'I didn't teach the Captain that one. They must learn "corroborate" in the police school. That's a whole four syllables, a greedy word.' He turned to the eyeless guard. 'They teach you to say "corroborate" in guard school?'

The man's mouth twitched. Horace looked askance at Henderson, 'Does it help if I say that *I* know that the Major was nowhere near Jarr's place? I had his automobile, that red Fiat. It would take all day to walk there as a pedestrian.'

Henderson mulled that one, then looked me over, 'Then how did you get here today, Mr Murdoch? You said your car was wrecked by your wife. How did you get here, today?'

I slapped the table and pointed at my friend, 'That's right. Seeing you in this place drove it clean out of my fool head. Horace, I borrowed your jalopy.

You left it parked in the studio lot and Boss saw it this morning when I told him I needed a ride. We thought you wouldn't mind. That okay with you? I'll pay for the gas.'

Horace laughed, a genuine roar that was sweet to hear. 'Hear that fool man? Hear that darling fool of a man? He comes to see me in jail and he wants to know if it's okay to borrow my beat-up old Ford? Captain, sir, you really think a man like that's going to run around punching bullets into a person, no matter *what* he did? You'd need a knot in your thinking the size of your fist to consider such a thing for so much as a New York second. Wouldn't happen!'

Henderson scrubbed at his iron grey hair. 'How long *is* a New York second?'

'It's how long a thirsty man waits at a bar before he starts yelling for the keep.'

'That quick, eh?' He turned to me, 'Still, it'd be nice to know where you were and if anyone can...' he paused, '*verify* your alibi. For the sake of completeness, you understand. After all, you said the victim had – designs – on your wife. That sort of thing can rile a man. It would light my fuse I must say.'

I nodded, 'I understand. I wanted to knock Jarr down a few times, and if he was still standing, I might have laid him out flat this morning for trying to paw Melia in his house last night. But I was with my talent in a bar called The Sombrero, just a few minutes' walk from the studio. That's where they do the chilli beef. I was there from about five to around eight. The owner, guy called Jake, tells a story would turn your hair white.'

Henderson stood straight and squared his shoulders, 'Yeah, I know the place. Little Mexican there cut his wife like a opening a clam. Jake used to be an officer here, he got a good price on that little bar. Should be a regular goldmine now the studio's opened down the road. Movie folk enjoy a drink?'

I grinned, 'A drink, a good meal, and a horror story, what more could we ask? Still, Captain, if it would put your mind to rest, I'd be happy to leave my fingerprints with you. And I'll bet my pension you won't find Horace's neither.'

'Lance, I think you know what I think... But we have a protocol we got to adhere to, and I'd thank Mr Goodman for keeping his opinions about my vocabulary to himself. Your friend will be fingerprinted in the morning. We won't need yours. If we don't find anything to convict him on the murder weapon, should we ring you to collect him? You can take him where they serve fried chicken with greens – or wherever he wants to be.'

'No need to call. Give me a time and I'll be here waiting. Horace is no more a killer than I'm the King of England. I'll be here ready and waiting, and he can drive out of town in his own vehicle. I won't let him wait here one second longer than he has to. That all right with *you*, Captain?'

I agreed to be there at eleven the next morning. Horace found it difficult to shake my hand with his wrists shackled to the table, but he did his level best. I hated leaving him behind in that place. The man brought so much light and laughter to the world it seemed wrong to shut it all away in that lightless box.

After being in that place for just an hour the air outside tasted sweet as a mountain stream. I stood just sucking it in for a long time before climbing into Horace's old Ford. Then I drove back to Century Pictures in Edendale. The day seemed brighter, somehow. I hoped it would last.

31

While I was away the troupe had taken my Jonah idea and expanded on it, as I knew they would. They called me over as soon as they saw me and began excitedly firing scenes at me before I'd even got my jacket off. I quietened them and gave them my news about Horace. When I'd finished, they all sat there looking at their fingertips and compared the lines they found there. Except Art, who told me that he too was a great fan of Mr Mark Twain.

The parts of the new plot I heard got my instant approval. It included everything I wanted and then some. Emily put the back of her hand to her forehead and rolled her eyes in mock despair at the idea of getting wet again. Bert put an understanding hand on her shoulder and kissed her neck. She purred like a cat. Their relationship was fully out in the open now, and they looked very well together.

Fact is, we would spend very little time on or under the water. We had Paul's Pathé footage to add some documentary truth to the action, the rest could be created in the studio with clever sets and lighting, and by Art's skilled brushes.

Paul had put his foot down regarding the impossibility of Emily surviving inside the whale, but his antic imagination and Art's mad ideas had conjured a way around the problem which meant she could still be swallowed by the big fish without being drowned or turned into soup by its stomach acids. It all started with a plank.

Emily, her father, Ben, and her beau, Bert, were out with the whaling fleet. Theirs was a smaller boat but had a rocket propelled harpoon gun in the bow, to fit in with Paul's documentary footage. The guys also had to dress to match the French style in Paul's scenes or it would look disjointed. Emily was in the stern so she could wear whatever we wanted. We dressed her like the men, why not? She still looked good.

The boys harpoon a whale, it's a big one, and the boat gets jerked several feet forward. Bert turns to smile at Emily just in time to see her get flipped overboard. Luckily the boat has been undergoing some much-needed repairs, so he grabs a loose plank off the deck and throws it to her. She swims to it and grabs hold.

This is when one of the whales rises up out of the ocean and swallows Emily whole, including her plank. We show Bert and Ben watching it happen with horror on their faces. Bert wants to jump overboard and rescue her, but

Ben holds him back. A single man would be helpless against the beast. They gaze at the ocean, helpless.

The whale dives down into the deep, shaking its mighty head to loosen the plank caught in its teeth. We see Emily jolted around in its mouth. The whale starts to choke, and like a cat ejecting a fur-ball spits the plank – and Emily – into the sea. Luckily it spits her straight into an underwater cave, complete with air and a pirate's treasure chest. The grinning skeleton of a pirate is still in there.

'Wait,' I said, 'how can we see all this? She's in a cave under the sea. Wouldn't it be too dark?'

Art explained, 'Light coming up from the sea, the cave is lit from underneath. And we think there might be some volcanic action down there for a touch more light. Of course, that means the cave is very hot.' He smiled at Emily.

She rolled her eyes, 'I guess it's a little *too* hot in there for a girl in a big sea coat, trousers, and boots? Would I be right?'

Art nodded, 'Well, yes. You almost pass out from the heat so you strip down to your underthings. You look flushed and beautiful, your eyes wild and your hair artfully tousled. Of course your scanties are soaked too so they cling to you like a second skin. It will be a charged moment, but you'll be backlit, just a silhouette. Our audience will think they see everything but actually they see nothing. A tease, just a little tease.'

Emily turned to me, 'Are we ever going to make a movie where I get to keep my clothes on until the credits roll?'

A surprise voice broke in, 'Darling, you think you've got troubles! You should walk a mile in my shoes, if they'd let me wear any.'

Melia was striding towards us like lightning in a skirt. After the quietness of our intense plot discussion she had arrived in an explosion of furious energy that shattered the mood. I could sense her anger boiling close to the surface, much like Art's volcanic heat in the cave. I got to my feet and met her halfway across the stage.

I took her arm but she flung me off and stood, arms akimbo, glaring at me. I wondered what I'd done to make her so angry but my mind was a blank. She supplied the answer in a bitter hiss.

'They've taken me off the movie.'

'They've what? How?'

'Boss just told me. The papers are full of the Mason Jarr killing and my name's all over the story. He says that some kinds of publicity can be great for box office but murder paints the wrong kind of picture. Best if I take a little break until the situation calms down. Major, will you take me home? I don't want to be here. If they say I'm no good for their lousy little picture they can kiss my sweet ass goodbye.'

'Wait there, have you got all your stuff?'

'Everything I need.'

'Okay, I'll be right back.'

I hustled over to the troupe and told them the news. Emily, ever the sweetheart, leapt to her feet and hurried to Melia's side, her arms open for a sisterly hug.

Melia stepped back. 'Don't you come near me with your precious sympathy. If I can't spend it or drink it, I don't need it, thanks. Get back to your chums and your silly little striptease. I hope they get their kicks out of it. Typical men!'

I told the guys sorry, said the story sounded great, gave the shattered Emily a hug in passing, and pushed Melia the heck out of there before she could wreak any more of her particular brand of havoc on my innocent gang of geniuses. It was obvious why she was angry, but it was best she should bottle it up until we were alone.

'I see you had to give your sweet little Emily a squeeze on the way out. I bet she likes that, especially in front of me.'

'Don't talk crazy. Anyway, she's with Bert.'

'Bert! Bert the moustache twirler? Now who's talking crazy?'

'He's our leading man. We found a good-looking guy under all that hair. We've got Ben Usher for moustache duty if we need him, but we don't do that so much these days. We've moved on. We're doing okay with the new stuff.'

'Oh? And I suppose the Boss is stuck in a rut getting me peeled like a banana every time they crank the handle?'

'That isn't what I said...'

'My ass has made this studio millions!'

'Well, for now you can give it a rest. Take a break. Catch up with the real world for a while and smell the coffee.'

Melia stopped and glared at me. She was only a little lady but she could pack an awful lot of fury into her neat little frame. You know how they say some women are beautiful when they're angry? Well – between you and me – my wife looked like a spoiled brat who would benefit from a firm dusting where she sits. Spoilt and spiteful. She took a breath but I butted in before she could get too much momentum going.

'By the way, I saw Horace today. There's a chance he'll be loose tomorrow morning. They got some guy coming down from Oakland to look at the evidence. He's a fingerprint expert. If Horace's fingerprints aren't on the gun, he's free and clear. I'm going to bring him home. Isn't that fantastic?'

'What're you talking about? What kind of evidence? Finger *what*?'

'Fingerprints, look I'll show you.' We were outside by then in the California sunshine and heading towards the main gate. I took Melia's hand and showed her the swirling patterns on her fingertips.

'Fingerprints, see? Everybody's got them and they're always unique. No two sets of fingerprints are the same, not even with identical twins. They can take Horace's prints and if they don't match the ones on the gun, he's free to go. It's pretty new but the science is well proven.'

Melia seemed to shrink into herself while she studied her right hand. She looked like she wanted to tear it off and throw it away. She massaged the palm with the thumb of her left hand and sped up, marching past Wallace the gate guard as if he wasn't there.

I returned the friendly tip of his hat. 'Things on her mind,' I said.

He nodded, 'What woman hasn't?'

I lengthened my stride and caught up with my girl. I could see thoughts reeling through her mind like a personal movie show. She wasn't looking at me or the road back to our house, she was literally lost in thought. I was already nursing a sick certainty – that I didn't dare lend a voice – when she spoke.

'Tell me. How do they take a person's *fingerprints* so they can check them against the evidence? Do you need to be there?'

'I'm not sure but I think they press the fingers against an ink pad then press them onto blotting paper to make a print. Something like that. I've never seen it done, but that's how I'd do it.'

'So, you need the person to be there. Fine. Just so I know.'

We continued our fast walk to the ranch house. It was two hours to sundown and the sky was clear, but Melia still went around pulling curtains closed and turning on the lights as if it was pitch dark outside. Whatever she had to say to me must have been said already, because the next thing I knew she had locked herself in the big bathroom and I heard water running.

I went and got changed in the bedroom. Despite the early hour I'd had a long day, and I had the feeling it was about to get longer. I thought I might as well be wearing fresh duds when the firebrand reappeared. It was too late for lunch and too early for dinner so I took a cold one out of the chill box and went to sit on the porch. I was thinking Horace would probably welcome a beer about then.

Melia's voice sounded creamy and relaxed from the doorway. She was wearing slippers and a light robe. Her damp hair was pinned up in a tousled mess that looked wonderful. Thankfully the spoilt brat had melted away in the bathwater. The beautiful woman had stayed behind. She reached out and took my beer, then took a long swallow. She handed it back.

'You say I should relax and take a break?' she asked. 'The way I want to relax we best not do out here in the open.' She opened her robe, 'Do I need to draw you a map?'

She stepped backwards into the house. I followed her. My heart knew she was guilty but my body didn't care. Not yet.

32

I awoke the next morning to that warm sensation you get after an intense and exhausting night followed by a long, refreshing, and dreamless sleep. I discovered that I was alone in the rumpled bed and the house was silent. Apart from me it was empty. It wasn't the first time and it didn't worry me.

I'd grown used to Melia's eccentric comings and goings, and I had too many ideas flitting around in my head to spend precious minutes fretting about her whereabouts. She'd come home when she was hungry, and I'd welcome her with open arms, as always.

My priorities that morning were whales and Horace – in that order – but first, coffee, a bath and a shave. I could breakfast with the guys in the commissary while they outlined the rest of their lunatic plot. I whistled happily while hot water soothed my body and enhanced my already buoyant mood.

Melia had been impressed by the his 'n hers wardrobes at the Clifton and had insisted we had them in the ranch house, which suited me. She had so many outfits, I swear she could never wear them all, and back in New York she had taken up most of the wardrobe space, both in her loft and my apartment.

I like room in my wardrobe so my threads don't get creased in the crush. A man's suits need to breathe to be happy. Melia's packed rainbow rails of happy apparel looked like one of those French landscapes from the last century; lots of colour but little substance.

Things were crammed in there like cattle in a cart. Her invasion of my space was inevitable so I enjoyed what I had while I still had it. It was only a matter of time before Melia moved in on my territory.

An hour later I strolled onto the Century lot with a dance to my step. Don Sherwood met me in the prop-filled space between the studios, and he whistled like a siren.

'Woohooooo, I see a happy, red-blooded fellow. Nice to see someone's getting some at this time of great hardship for the American male!'

'Hey, Don. You heard Melia's been dropped by casting until this Jarr business gets settled?'

'The rest will do the poor lamb a world of good. She works that little caboose of hers far too hard. In fact I'm surprised to see *you*! I thought you might enjoy a little "we two lovebirds roosting in the nest" time together.'

'We will, but first I've got rub the magic lamp and thrash this latest script with my genii and then I'm down to rescue Horace from the LA constabulary. Truth to tell, by now he probably needs the rest more than me, and who knows what a steady diet of pork and beans has done to the poor man's constitution!'

Don took on a tragic pose, 'That poor, poor man.' He held the pose for a moment, then he relaxed, 'But, take my advice, Lance darling, *pork and beans*! Once you have Horace in the car, keep those windows open. I know whereof I speak. Please accept a word from the wise.' He tapped his nose.

I was done with the studio in plenty of time for the drive to Boyle Heights and my promised appointment with Horace. I parked on East First Street and checked my watch: it was a quarter after ten. Early.

Reluctant to spend a minute longer than I had to in the police station I fetched myself some coffee and scrambled eggs at a diner on the corner of the street. I sat at a bar in the window and read the newspaper. It was full of war news. They said the dough boys were shaking up the Boche but there was still no sign of an end to the conflict.

The eggs were good, I wondered if our boys 'over there' were eating as well. I got a refill for my coffee and drank it slowly before I paid and tipped the pretty Italian girl behind the stick.

'You over to the cop station?' she asked.

'Yeah. You get a lot of trade from there?'

'We do okay. You been looking at the place every five minutes. They finger you for something? You got to present to the desk sergeant? Shame, a nice-looking guy like you. What did you do?'

'Not me, no. A good friend of mine. I'm here to take him home. New evidence means they'll have to let him go, and I'm going to spring him the minute they sign the releases. Get him out into the fresh air, you know.'

She smiled at me, 'Yeah? Well, if he likes good coffee bring him here first. The coffee's on the house, anything else he can fork out for. Okay?'

'That's real kind of you. I'll tell him, thanks.'

On the way in I'd read the sign at the bottom right hand side of the big window. 'No Dogs, no Irish, no Negros, no Jews, no Mexicans, and no panhandlers (no offense)' I had nearly walked straight past the place to somewhere a little more liberal, but it smelled good and I didn't want to go too far for a joe. I'd swallowed my pride and stepped inside.

I accepted her smile, looked around at the all-white, dog-free room, then stepped out into the untainted air. I felt guilty for giving such people my cash, but she had been pretty in a slightly overly sensuous way, and I'd smiled back. I set my chin towards Boyle Heights and crossed the street. A dog scampered past me the other way and disappeared up the alley beside the diner. *You'll get no joy there, buddy* I thought.

Twenty minutes later Captain Henderson fetched me from the bench the desk sergeant had pointed me to, after giving me a suspicious once-over. I was tempted to tell him that at least *I* was welcome at the diner over the road, and if the broad Blarney in his accent was anything to go by, *he'd* be given the bum's rush. And so would his dog. If he had one.

Henderson explained that Horace had a tented arch where the killer had an ulnar loop, which meant nothing to me except he was free to go as soon as he had been processed. His fingerprints, however, would remain on file in Oakland. They were building what they called a 'database'.

'Tell me,' Henderson asked, 'has your wife got big hands and man-sized fingers?' He held his paws up, 'Like these?'

'No, not at all,' I answered with a grin. 'You met her. She comes in the little miss petite size, you know? Prettiest little hands and slender little fingers. So, nope.'

'Okay, it's purely a formality, but could she come in for printing? If she could come in today that would be great, the Oakland guy's down here for the day. He's clearing up a backlog of cases for us: or trying to.'

'I can't make any promises. I don't know where Melia is just now. She's her own boss, you see, and she's on holiday. I'll ask her when she comes back, if that's all right with you?'

'What? Your wife just takes off when the fancy takes her? I don't know if I could live with that? My wife stays home with the kids, and she's always there when I get in. She's her own boss too, but at least I always know where she is. How can you allow that? Your wife wears the pants in your house?' He shook his head, 'Sorry, that's none of my business. Forget I said that, sorry.'

'No, it's okay. Melia's always had an independent streak. I knew who I was marrying when we walked down the aisle. We lived in separate houses for a while back there, and she still needs her own space. It's just the way she is. She always comes home, and I know she's not out wildcatting. Sounds nuts, but she's a good girl, and I trust her.'

I don't know why I was justifying our relationship to this bull cop, but it seemed important that he understood. I guess I liked the big lug. He had played square with Horace and that was aces with me.

He shrugged, 'They say we all make our own beds before we lie in them. I wish you well of it, Lance. You movie people, you write your own rules, while we ordinary folk live ordinary lives. I guess it's like, if you had to eat rib roast every day you'd get bored with it and look for something else, some novelty. Don't get me wrong I love rib roast, but I love meatloaf in gravy – and pork and beans too.

'Between you and me, sometimes I'll dream of different women. Sometimes I'll see a girl and wish I was young again, you know? But that's just fancy, it's like trying to catch every bubble in a glass of beer in the hope that one day you'll swallow enough you'll be able to fly. Can't happen, best go get yourself a kite.'

He paused, 'Your Melia, I think she's one of those dream women, yeah? Woman like that, there comes a time you want to wake up. But she's your headache, not mine. There's only the one girl I'll ever go home to, and that's the good Mrs Henderson.'

I was wrong-footed by Henderson's insight and went for humour in response, 'I bet Horace would swap your mess of pork and beans for meatloaf and gravy just now.'

He chuckled, 'You sang the entire mass right there. But then, we never planned this establishment as the hostelry of choice; and the pen is worse, I can tell you.'

'Pen? Mightier than the sword? I don't follow.'

'Pen! Penitentiary, like San Quentin?' I shrugged, and he gaped at me, 'What kinda ivory tower do you live in? And how high is it? Guys sent down to the Big Q write to us with fond memories of their stay with the gentle bulls of LA. Ah, good, here's Mr Goodman. Are you ready to fledge, Mr Goodman?'

Horace grinned, tiredly. I could see the effort it took for him to be cordial, 'Push me off *this* branch and I'll fly,' he said. 'Even if I fall like a stone and it punches me six feet into the ground, I'll take the risk. Am I done now?'

Henderson held out an arm, 'Please, Mr Goodman, allow me to escort you.'

With a genuine laugh Horace linked arms, 'By the way, Captain, thanks for the books. I left them on the bunk in the cell. Without them I'd have caught cabin fever in that little twelve by ten. Enough of this, kick me blinking into the light like a newborn, I'm ready to stretch my wings.'

'Around here we call it "stir crazy". You did all right in there, Mr Goodman. My officers said they've never met a bird so polite.'

We reached the outer door and the top of the steps leading to the sidewalk. Horace literally blinked, 'Man alive,' he breathed, 'I forgot how beautiful this world is. Will you look at this place.'

Henderson took a deep breath himself, like a diver up for air and about to return to the depths, 'I envy you, Horace. You'll remember this morning with a smile for the rest of your life. Maybe we should offer a few nights in the can for folk who've lost touch with the good things in life. But,' he warned, 'you want to keep that warm feeling? Then stay out of Minelli's Café over there on the corner. Now, good luck, and scram, both of you.'

I swear that man wanted to escape with us. He almost buckled under the weight of that building when he walked back inside. Horace watched him go, then shook himself and squinted up at the sky.

'Major, if you're of a mind to take me away from here, I've sure got an inclination to be elsewhere. Which way to the jalopy?'

'Do you want to drive?'

'Not yet; I've too much to ponder, too much to see. Take me home, please, Lance, take me home. And I'll drink deep from the cup of freedom all the way there. No rush, so, why not go the scenic route?'

'What's the scenic route?'

His chuckle bubbled up, 'I say we get lost, and then we drive around until we're found once more. Sound like a plan?'

'Sounds like a great plan, let's go.' But all the while I was thinking of Henderson's words, *Melia, I think she's one of those dream women, yeah? Woman like that, comes a time you want to wake up. But she's your headache, not mine.*

33

Horace cried off on my offer of fried chicken and greens in a diner. Instead we found a big general store in a small town and we had the clerk fill brown bags with plenty of fixings. The whole time we were in there the fat boy at the counter only addressed me. It was as if my friend was an invisible shadow at my side. Horace let me do all the talking.

I realised Minelli wasn't the only man with jaundiced eyes in the Golden State – and it left a bitter taste. In New York a man might be judged by the cut of his suit, but never by the colour of his skin.

As we walked back to the jalopy a stick-thin, leathery old fool in an ancient three-piece suit – and a wide-brimmed, straw hat – hawked noisily and spat on the boardwalk. He muttered, plenty loud enough to hear, 'They selling *niggers* in Porky's store now? Got to get me one of those!'

I turned and glared at him. I opened my mouth to respond but Horace stopped me, 'Lance, you can't change centuries of wrong by shouting at an ancient bucket of bile like him. Forget him. Let's get me home where I can take a bath and scrub that prison cell stink off my skin. The black will still be there, but the dirt'll be gone. I can live with one but I'd rather do without the other. Grandpa don't matter. Come on.'

We climbed into the car. The comedian shouted after us, 'Best thing, you take your tame darkie back to the plantation. Make him work 'til he bleeds. They lazy as sin but sure look prettier with blood on their hands.' He laughed at his own humour until he began wheezing with the effort. Then he started a harsh, wet, tubercular coughing fit that doubled him up.

Horace urged, 'Hit the gas, let's get out of here! I mean it.'

We were several hundred yards away and still accelerating when Horace told me the old bastard had collapsed in the middle of the road. As long as he had been watching, nobody had come to the ancient bucket's aid.

I said, 'Shouldn't we go back and help him?'

Horace shook his head, 'Best just drive, get us out of here. Think about it, a black man standing over a collapsed white man in this burg had better make his will, and so should his friends. They'll fetch the rope to us before they think to call the sheriff.'

He turned to face the road ahead a bitter expression on his face. 'That nasty old man made his bed, and now he got to lie in it. I'll swallow my guilt like a Christian and call on the Lord to give him peace, but I'd rather not do it while swinging from the branch of a tree. For the love of all that's holy, drive!'

Horace was the gentlest, and kindest, man I ever knew. But that day we left a guy dying in the street rather than face the risk of the noose from his neighbours. I heard those words ringing in my head like a warning, first from Henderson and now Horace; you make your bed and then you lie in it. Is that what killed Mason Jarr? He made his bed and someone made sure he died in it?

We were out of town and moving at a healthy lick but I had no idea where we were headed. There were precious few road signs, and the few we did see only advertised the farmsteads we were passing. Horace asked me the time and then checked out the shadows.

He started to point me in what he assured me was the right direction. 'We need to be heading northeast from Ku Klux Klansville. Keep going thataway and I promise you we'll be home before sunset. I'm enjoying the company but I think I've had enough sightseeing for one day. I dearly want to see my hearth and my bath before another snake comes out of the sagebrush and tries to bite us.'

'If oranges could speak, we could ask the locals.'

'They sure like oranges hereabouts, don't they? Personally I'd rather see the noble grape. It's been too long a dry spell since I had a civilised drink.'

As if in answer to his prayer we rounded a bend through a small forested area and found ourselves on a road following a valley floor that threaded its way through steep hills covered in vines.

'My God,' sighed Horace, 'a man could suffer from the Sahara Desert of all thirsts and never drink his way through all this. We must have died and gone to heaven. Where are we, anyway?'

'We're still in Los Angeles, I think. What does that sign say?'

'Wine Street! Well, I'll be damned.'

We broke through another tree line and entered a more mundane agricultural region with green leafy plantings. Off to our left I noticed a distant pall of grey, staining the blue sky. I wondered aloud what it was.

Horace squinted at it. 'Building work. See that? The municipality is growing fast enough to kick up the dust. One day soon, Los Angeles is going to eat itself alive. Enjoy the view while we have it, Lance. Here come the roots of a brand-new city. Next year this will all be streets and building works. These hills will be swallowed whole by fresh new walls.'

'Yeah? So, where will we go for a view?'

'Who knows. Alaska?'

We drove in sober silence for long minutes, but it was difficult to remain downhearted with the mild afternoon enlivened by fresh breezes. The grasses here were greener than around the ranch house, and sometimes we drove through shallow streams of running water that kicked up diamonds of silver spray. We had the world to ourselves for long empty miles.

'I woke up this morning in a prison cell.' Horace drank in the countryside with liquid eyes that darted around while he tried to see everything at once. He said again, 'I woke up this morning in a prison cell; and I was going crazy.'

He looked down at his hands which were twisting and knotting together as if he was trying to mash the memory into ball small enough to swallow. Then he flipped them in the air in surrender.

'That cell was everything I hate about the world. I never want to go back there. You find yourself trapped with nothing but the inside of your head for company because there's nothing to see but the bars. And there's nothing to hear but a drunk two cells down who kept calling me nigger and asking me what I was looking at? "Hey, nigger," he shouted, "you looking at me?" Why would I want to?'

He took a deep, shuddering breath, 'You got me out of that nightmare. When you came to me yesterday, I was in a bad place. I hated my life. In the studio I'm a respected person, but in there I was just another black man behind bars. Henderson did what he could, but you came like an angel of grace and gave me hope. What I mean is, thank you, I owe you more than I can say.'

At first, I felt humbled by the man's honesty. If our roles had been reversed, could I have opened my heart to him in the same way? I doubted it. Then the devil sat on my left shoulder and whispered, *if he owes you so much why won't he tell you what happened when Jarr was killed? Go on, ask him.* I fought it with all my strength but the question burned too hot in my mind, I had to know.

'So, okay, please tell me, what really happened back at Jarr's place? You said Melia came out with Jarr, they spoke together, then she got in the car. He went back inside his house and you started the engine, ready to drive away. Jarr was alive at that point.

'But you say that's when you heard two shots. You got out of the car and saw someone drop the gun out of the window. Discretion being the better part of valour, you got back in the car, hit the gas, and tried to get out of there same as we did back in Klansville just now. But the neighbours had heard the shots and came out of their houses and the cops turned up to stop you. Is that true? Is that the whole story?'

'Henderson buys it, why can't you?'

'Look, it's murder! And none of it makes sense. Jarr was found on his back laid out for a burial, two bullets in him and his hands crossed over his chest. I never shot anyone but I say there's no way he fell down so neat like that. And where he was laid out – it wasn't even where he was shot. His blood was the other side of the room. There's something wrong about all this. Help me out here.'

He sat back in his seat and closed his eyes. I apologised, 'Sorry, you're tired. You've had a rough few days. What was I thinking? I'm sorry. Look, you catch up on your sleep. I think I know where we are now so you just rest your eyes and I'll take you home.'

He didn't move and he didn't open his eyes but he turned to face me. 'I'm thinking, Lance. I'm thinking you're better not knowing anything about that day. I'm thinking you're a good friend, so why should I make your life miserable? I'm thinking that if the situation was reversed and it was me asking you about all this, you'd say nothing to protect your friend. And, you know what? I'm thinking you'd be right.'

'Horace, I know she did it. You can't hide it from me. I know!'

'How? I don't! I can't be so sure and I was *there*. Even with a stack of *Bibles* in front of me I couldn't swear to it. Don't bury that sweet lady without proof. Don't they say a person's innocent until proven guilty?'

'Man, listen to me! She's run away, she's gone.'

'She what?'

'Last night I told her, I told her you were going to be released and why. I told her about fingerprints and how they can be used as evidence to prove guilt and innocence. I told her you were sure to be proved innocent and that a specialist could identify the real killer. Last night we went to bed together...'

I paused, and for the first time I realised that my subtle wife might have deliberately – and pleasurably – exhausted me into a deep sleep so she could escape without rousing me the next morning. I kept that part to myself.

I continued, 'This morning I woke up and she was gone. There was no note, no nothing. Henderson said he wanted her in for printing, just a formality – but she's gone. What does that tell you? Melia's like an April shower, you never know which way she's going to blow nor how hard, but everything tells me she's running scared. Come on, Horace, spill it. What happened that day?'

He opened his eyes and looked at me. He was a young man in his early thirties, hardly older than me, but the light in those eyes was old and tired and his mouth was turned down in a crease of pain. He looked like he had drunk acid. I pulled over into a clearing by the side of the road and cut the engine. The silence was shocking after the constant blare of the motor and the rumble of tires on the road. Horace sat up.

'All right,' he said. 'You got to know? Then I guess I got to tell you.'

34

Horace's house was a half-hour walk from the ranch house. I needed all that time to get my ducks in a row. I had dropped him off and helped him carry his groceries into his kitchen, then took a glass of good Merlot with him to celebrate his release. The house was neat, clean, and filled with books. He wore it like a second skin. It suited him.

I thanked him for the loan of his car and refused to use it to drive home. I told him it was a luxury I wouldn't need if I didn't have him to chauffeur around. We shook hands, then he leaned forward and kissed me on the cheek. It was a light touch, barely a brushing of his lips against my skin.

'Things will be fine,' he said, his voice quiet in my ear, 'You'll see. Things will be just dandy. God looks after good folk and you and Melia are good folk. He'll make a special dispensation just for us, he's got to. We earned it. Jarr made his bed...'

'Yeah, you said. And the bastard had to go die in it with two bullet holes in his chest. Okay, enough, go have your bath, I'll let you know if I hear anything from Melia. Wash that prison stink off you and get civilised. Enjoy a good meal, drink good wine, read a good book. Put some good things between you and the last few days. I'm going home to do the same. See you at the studio tomorrow? You and I need to talk.'

He saw me to his gate and we shook hands again, then he watched and waved until I was a good few hundred yards down the road and he was lost in the gathering twilight. Los Angles had barely encroached on that part of the world by then. I walked alone down a dark and empty road with flat darkness either side of me and a scattering of stars above me.

Physically I felt small, but my mind was filled with a murmurous horde of thoughts and images that scratched at my nerve endings with razor-like claws. I thought of Horace in his civilised house, his wonderful mind filled with light; and then I thought of the blind fools who couldn't see beyond the colour of his skin and treated him like dirt.

He and I were too old for the draft into the army – we were both over thirty one, but he told me that members of his family had already volunteered and gone overseas. However, he had heard of a cousin down south who had filled in his registration card and torn a piece off the corner, so his selection committee would know he was black. That way, he was told, the army would fast track his application.

Postal workers deliberately lost the man's card and he was arrested as a draft dodger. It was only because he gained the sympathetic ear of a police officer like Henderson, and the testimony of a white neighbour who had seen him hand the card in at the post office, that the poor devil didn't go to prison. Proof that more people like Porky, Minelli, and the Ancient Bucket were trying to put their fellow men down. Why?

But all the time I knew I was trying to think about anything else rather than let the facts about Melia and Mason Jarr stew in my mind. I had told Horace I knew she was guilty, but what he told me about that day proved it to me without a doubt. Horace had lied on oath. He had perjured himself in the eyes of the law, and he had done it for Melia. If discovered he would go to prison – and that would kill him.

In my imagination I watched what happened that day through Horace's eyes. The sky was a little cloudy but Melia had insisted they rode with the Fiat's top folded down so she could feel the wind in her hair. He drove her up the road to Jarr's house and she asked him to wait, promising not to be more than an hour.

The door was opened by a man Horace didn't recognise, a big man with shoulders that filled the doorway. He was dressed all in white except for his black formal tail coat. It must have been tailored to fit, said Horace – they wouldn't do that size off the peg. It still looked tasteless. The man beckoned Melia in, then stood for a few seconds looking down at Horace and the car.

'I thought he was going to come down and ask me what I wanted. He had that suspicious look in his eyes. He sure wasn't thinking about fetching me a coffee, I was certain about that. He looked more like he was wondering whether to use something on me, like a lead weighted sap, a cudgel or a steel bar. He wouldn't use anything subtle. I smiled and waved, just trying to be friendly, you know? He shut the door.'

Jarr lived in an upmarket crescent of freshly-minted classic housing. Greek pillars and pediments at the doors, Georgian styling at the windows, cut stone finials to finish flaring gables and mansard tiled roofs. Horace described it with a sour face, saying it was, 'as if an architect had eaten a dish containing every style of building he liked, then vomited that mess onto the foundations.'

He continued, 'I was becoming the star of the show for Jarr's neighbours. So many curtains twitched it was as if the buildings in that crescent had developed nervous tics. I started winking back. They didn't like the idea of a black man sitting in their street, even if he was in a nice red car with matching maroon upholstery.

167

'I think somebody must have rung the law about then, because there's no way the cops could have arrived when they did after the shooting. No way there was enough time between the sound of the shots and the police wagon turning up. We're talking minutes, less. No way there was enough time. I lay good money those neighbours reported a suspicious character, no doubt in a stolen car.'

He swallowed, hard, 'I should be grateful. No doubt if I'd been sitting in Klansville I'd have been fitted with a hemp necktie and left swinging from the nearest hanging tree with the cops none the wiser. I guess Jarr's neighbours wouldn't dirty their hands with a rope. Probably wouldn't know where the help kept them, anyhow.'

He rubbed his hand at his throat, 'Can you even imagine what that feels like? To hang? I can. That and burning must be the worst way. I'd rather drown or freeze to death. Or go like Jarr. Bang, bang, finish, that's all she wrote.'

Bang, pause, bang. Horace heard the shots and just afterwards Melia came out the front door and ran down to the car. She bundled into the passenger seat and shouted 'Drive, get away, oh, get away!' Horace turned the engine over and he must have panicked it because it didn't catch first time, or second, or third.

He was on the point of giving up on the automatic starter and climbing out to crank the starting handle under the Fiat's radiator grill when he gave the ignition one more twist and the automobile roared into life. He had released the brake and engaged the gears when he saw a hand come out and drop something from the little window to the right of Jarr's front door. He couldn't be sure what it was at the time, but that was where the cops found the pistol.

Melia was in a strange state. She kept looking back at Jarr's house and shuddering as if she was seeing something loathsome, all the while repeating, 'Come on, come on, come on,' but it was already too late. Horace hurled the Fiat around the crescent just as the paddy wagon slewed across the street and blocked their path. Officers spilled out and surrounded them.

Melia made a grab at the steering wheel as if trying to wrench the automobile in a different direction, but Horace killed the engine and climbed out of the driving seat. And that was when everything started to happen in slow motion. He was an innocent man trying to deal with an hysterical woman. Surely the police could be reasoned with? They'd soon be on their way once more.

Then a clutch of neighbours hustled up and started bleating about gunshots. They cried murder and pointed at Horace, who had never moved

168

from the car. He had been seated in plain sight the whole time, but he must be guilty of something. He was a black man. Who else was there?

Horace told me he was already cuffed and sat next to a burly cop in the paddy wagon when the first brace of officers approached Jarr's open front door. They knocked and entered.

Horace couldn't see Melia, but he could hear her berating everyone around her. He clearly heard the words, 'Don't you know who I am?' One of the cops answered. Horace didn't hear what the guy said but he heard the laughter afterwards. He also heard Melia's screech of fury which was cut short when a man barked at her to 'Shut up, please, ma'am!'

One of the cops ran from Jarr's house and sprinted to his fellows. He said something and they all looked across to where Horace was sitting. Two of them climbed into the wagon with Horace and his guard and the vehicle pulled away from the crescent. They ignored Horace's questions until eventually he fell silent.

He looked through the rear window and saw the Fiat following them. Melia was still in the passenger seat, looking like a frightened child beside a thug of a man in a blue uniform. He would later recognise him as the eyeless guard with a rifle in the interview room. He felt sick and frightened.

He wondered what the cops had found in Jarr's house; but was afraid he already knew. He also wondered what had happened to the big butler in white wearing a black tail coat. There had been two shots – were there two victims? He looked back at the tiny woman in the red car following them. With a sick certainty, he believed he knew what must have happened.

But wait; if the butler guy was dead, who dropped something out the window? If he had been shot and survived, why would he do that? In fact why do that at all? Something there didn't add up. He tried to tell the cops around him what he was thinking but they ignored him.

One of the men at the front of the wagon barked at him to keep quiet but the burly man at his side grunted, 'Let him have his say, after us the next person he talks to is Henderson, then the judge. Let's see what he has to tell us. Go ahead, mister, what's on your mind?'

Horace started to tell them about the butler back at Jarr's house, and that he had seen something falling or being dropped out of the window. Before he'd finished, the brute by his side balled his fist and slammed it into Horace's belly. It knocked the wind out of him and he almost threw up.

'Sorry,' growled the brute. 'Was you saying something? I think I missed it. Would you care to repeat it for my buddies and me?' Then he punched him again, harder this time. Horace got the message. For the remainder of the trip to Boyle Heights he rode in silence.

The rest I knew. The horror of everything that had happened buzzed around in my head while I walked the miles from Horace's house to mine. Melia had been released and an innocent man had been thrust into a cell for two nights. But now I knew he wasn't innocent. He had perjured himself to protect that crazy little woman I loved. And if Melia was guilty so was Horace. He was an accessory to murder – and now, so was I.

[35]

Melia wasn't home when I got there, but then I hadn't expected her to be. Nor was there anything from her in the mailbox, just a few messages from the studio including one addressed to her. I checked her wardrobes to see if anything was missing. I was greeted by a dense wall of colourful frocks and dainties, drawers of scanties, and banks of shoes.

She could have taken enough clothes to last a month without denting her stash of fashionable couture. She liked clothes – a lot. It was one of her favourite subjects, along with psychiatry.

The place was too empty without her. I kept hearing the echo of my own footsteps ringing off the walls and looked around, expecting to find her standing behind me. I chose to get a drink and a hot meal at The Sombrero. Maybe I could fill the vacant space in my life with food and alcohol. I locked up the dark house and headed out under that big sky once more.

Jake welcomed me by name, poured me a beer, and pointed to a corner from which I could hear peals of bright laughter.

'Your friends are over there,' he told me, 'and tonight's specials are chilli beef, brisket with gravy, southern fried chicken, and pork and beans. They all come with the fixings. You want some?' I thanked him and said yes to the chicken. I couldn't possibly say yes to pork and beans out of respect for Horace.

The place was busier than the last time I'd been there so I got close to the table before I recognised the troupe. There were a few bottles in front of them. They had obviously been celebrating something. I wondered if I was in the right frame of mind to join them. I was afraid I might cast a pall over the proceedings and I almost turned away, but Art saw me and leapt to his feet.

'You got the message! Great! Isn't it marvellous news?'

I remembered the notes from the studio. They were still sitting unopened on the telephone table by my front door. Ben hustled me a chair from somewhere and I joined them. I told them I'd come straight from Horace's place so I hadn't seen any messages. They insisted I tell them about him before sharing their news, then we all toasted his release.

It was a few minutes before I finally learned that *Babe in the Woods* had been put forward by the studio for the 1918 Studio Excellence Awards. They expected us to stand a chance in three categories; best short comedy drama, best art direction, and best technical engineering effects. Yes, fact is my kids were telling me we had brought home the bacon in big fat slices. Beer was no good for celebrating this news, I ordered Champagne.

Art told me, 'They want us to work on full-length features from now on. Bigger budgets, bigger casts, whatever we want. By the way, Boss told me they've found something odd about Jarr's accounts. The studio brought some boffo accountant down from New York to look at the paperwork and see where we are financially. Said the poor man ended up buried in a mess of skeletons when they started falling out of Jarr's closets. He thinks the studio might owe us more money. How about that?'

'Yeah, how about that!' I said. 'Have we heard any more about his killer?'

Ben leaned forward, 'I got a friend down at the *Herald*. Sweet newshound called Pep Durfee. Honest guy for a journo. He covers the LA crime scene and dearly loves blood and thunder. Pep tells me the cops are already looking for a guy they like for Jarr's death. Guy called Arlo Shaw.'

He grinned, 'And there's more, more about Jarr. They've been trying to write up a biography about Jarr for an in-depth piece, but the story don't pan out. They track him back as far as New York in 1911, but then the trail vanishes. Turns out Mason Jarr is a mystery man without a past!'

I stared at him, 'Hold that phone right there. Shaw? I've heard of him. He was Jarr's butler. Built like a redwood with shoulders out to here. Horace saw him and told the police. They'll want his fingerprints I bet.'

Ben shook his head, 'Nah. If he's the guy who handled the gun the cops already got his prints on file up in Oakland. His physical description matches to a tee. Up there he's listed as one, Wheeler Oakie. Seems our suspect runs a regular list of shady aliases.

'He's already a wanted man; he beat a rival near to death in a bare-knuckle ring and crippled another man for life over a card game. God knows what else. Jarr must have spat in his soup or something to earn his slugs in the belly.'

I said, 'Sounds like Shaw's a cannon with a real short fuse.'

Ben agreed, 'A bomb waiting to go off. Could have happened at any time. Jarr's clock was ticking the minute he employed the guy.'

Emily said, 'But, yeah, so, why would he?'

Ben shrugged, 'Why would he what?'

'Why would Jarr employ this Wheeler guy? Don't you get butlers from an agency or something?'

Bert and I agreed. I said, 'Maybe there's more to all this than we know. Say, why don't we let the cops work it out? It's what they get paid for after all. We get paid for making movies – and now we've got ninety minutes to fill instead of twenty five. Do we expand the whale story or start something new? What do you say?'

I ate chicken when it arrived and we all drank too much wine, and we bounced ideas around like a ball on a ping-pong table. By the time I headed for home we had so much material we could have made a movie five hours long – and I also had the germ of an idea planted in my brain.

I was sure about Jarr's butler. I was sure that he didn't do it, but I was also sure that if he was hanged for it he deserved it. My heart was easy about that. The man deserved his noose. Would it matter so much which crime he finally swung for?

I slept soundly, as if my crazy world still made sense. I dreamed about Melia being swallowed by a whale. She escaped by shooting it and climbing out through the bullet holes. Even in my dream I heard the Boss telling me, 'Corporal, improbable is fine but try to avoid the impossible. People won't swallow impossible. Keep it real.' In my dreams I would always be the Corporal.

After breakfast the next morning I was joined by Walt Benson from Benson and Drake auto repairs. He was the 'miracle mechanical marvel' who was going to repair the hurt Melia had done to my Fiat. Maurice had heard good things about him. He was told that if he could cure what ailed the Fiat he would become the go-to guy for the whole studio, including our stunt cars. He had a strong incentive to be my car doctor.

He gave the car a long look-see, then strode to my side looking mortified. 'Mr Murdoch, what in the Sam Hill did you do to that poor vehicle? Some of that gear box is *melted*! Why didn't you just take a shotgun to its workings and put it out of its misery?'

'Wasn't me, Walt. A tiny spit of a girl did all that in a single evening. I heard her screaming all the way from LA.'

'The girl was screaming?'

'No, the automobile. She's an innocent poor creature who needs a lot of care, can you heal her?'

'I don't know much about women, Mr Murdoch, but they shouldn't be allowed to drive cars. I've only been married twenty three years but I'd never let Mrs Benson loose on anything more complicated than a bicycle, and nothing more technical than a washing tub. What your girl did to that car was close to attempted murder. I can take her away and fix her, but don't let the lady loose on that gear box ever again. Promise?'

'I won't, Walt, that's a promise.'

I offered him a cigarette and we smoked while a few of his boys loaded the wounded Fiat onto the flat bed of a truck. He winced at the squeal from the car while it was winched into place.

'I swear they suffer like we do. Hurt like that would break a man, break him like a twig. She'll be with me a week, Mr Murdoch, and thanks for the smoke. If there's a problem, I'll give you a call. Please tell Maurice I'm on it. See you in a week's time. By then she'll be good as new, better.'

The truck clattered off towards town and I put my best foot forward and headed towards the studio. I had felt a twinge in my gut when Walt accused Melia of attempted murder. I thought of all the things we say to each other in all innocence, not knowing how it might hurt. I tried to let my mind rest and concentrate on my job – telling 'improbable' stories and entertaining my audience.

The Boss was holding court with the troupe when I strode onto the set. They looked none the worse for wear after our celebration the night before, which was a relief. Boss let anyone do whatever they wanted with their free time so long as they turned up for work on the hour and remembered their marks.

Bert and Emily were sitting close together. They had a dazed, happy look about them that made me think they'd carried on celebrating together after leaving The Sombrero. I silently wished them joy of each other and hoped their path together wouldn't throw up too many tangles to trip them up. I envied them their simple lives.

Boss rushed at me, took my right hand in both of his and pumped it hard. He pulled the extreme sourpuss face that told me I was about to hear some extremely good news, then he offered me a cigar and waited patiently while I got it lit. It was a sweet smoke, I could taste whisky in the tobacco. Expensive.

He was repeating a litany of words, most of which were 'You guys, you wonderful guys, you guys...' I was glad I wasn't being singled out for praise. There was nothing I'd done that hadn't depended on the whole troupe to make it work. I was pleased to see Maurice had been included, then worried that with all the talent in one place nothing else was happening. No filming meant we were losing money.

Boss said, 'You've got a lot to do so I won't take up too much of your valuable time. You guys have got to pay for these cigars I keep giving away. Tobacco doesn't grow on trees you know...' He paused and pointed at Paul, 'You say anything, Frenchy, and I'll feed you to the whale myself. I know tobacco grows on bushes, okay? I don't need to be told by an émigré from Pathé.'

The troupe laughed dutifully. When the old man was in this good a mood it was best to go along with his terrible sense of humour. Even I attempted a smile, which earned me a punch on the shoulder.

He continued, 'So, we're okay for *Tremendous Tales* to go full scale?' He listened to everyone's enthusiastic agreement. 'Great, then we need to speed up Art's side of the process.'

Surprised I looked at Art. He grinned then raised his thumb at me. The Boss saw the gesture, and I got another punch on the shoulder. 'Major, I'm surprised! You think I'd talk about this without talking to the talent first? Artie agrees. It takes too long to paint straight onto the film all the time. So, he's just been promoted – from now on you're head of film production and Artie's head of animation.'

He scowled, 'Make it worthwhile, you deadbeats!' Then he shook everyone's hand except Emily's, who had earned a cigar-flavoured buss on the cheek. He took my arm. 'Major,' he snarled, 'lend me your ears, I'd like a quiet word.'

He led me off set into the prop room and leaned towards me, 'Okay, Lance,' he said, quietly, 'what's with this note I got from Melia? What does she mean, she's "taking a rest"? We got a movie to finish!'

At first the Boss didn't believe me when I told him I had no idea where Melia had got to. He prodded a hard finger into my chest and told me he wanted her back on set, and used words like, 'now', 'pronto' and 'yesterday'. It took me a while to convince him I was telling the truth.

'The police are after her too, Boss. They want to fingerprint her. Anyhow, what's the rush? She told me you rested her. She said you told her that murder was the wrong kind of notoriety, and that the movie was on hold until the Jarr thing was resolved. Was that a lie?'

He regarded me with hooded eyes, then he smiled with a flash of teeth. I began to feel nervous. He looked like the shark about to bite and I was the only meat in the water.

'She told you that? Yeah, that's true. That's what the money men said. It's what they told me to say to her, so I did. But that was before the movie houses started hollering for more and more Melia Nord movies. They can't get enough of the scarlet woman. They love her now. She has history *and* a touch of mystery, all wrapped up in that neat little package of hers.

'People are queuing around the block to watch her entire back catalogue. We're going to have to come up with a new description for something this popular. We must get her back. You hear from her, you tell her that. You got any way to get in touch, you call her in. You hear me? That a promise, Major?'

I nodded and he stormed away still muttering to himself. Once he was gone I flopped down on a crate and fought to control my pounding heart. I took deep, slow breaths, hearing the rhythm of my pulse in each exhalation. When I was ready, I walked on unsteady feet back to my team. I had to pull myself together – we had a movie to make.

We had yards of good footage in the can by the time I dragged my weary ass back to the ranch house. Emily had told me that the studio girl's bush telegraph was whispering that Bisset had started secretly screen-testing girls – naked girls wearing long black wigs – so they could finish *Jezebel* if Melia remained AWOL.

'You can bet that footage will become prime exhibits in his personal collection,' she sighed. 'Thank God I'm with the troupe or he'd insist I take the test. I'm not even the same shape as Melia, it would be pointless. If he approaches you about it slap him down for me, promise? Please?'

Everyone wanted me to make promises that day, but even with my mind humming like a telegraph wire we still managed to shoot great footage. We had a script almost locked down into six, fifteen-minute chapters but the troupe were coming up with new ideas by the hour.

We would still use Paul's archive footage, and Art was going to be using new and faster techniques that he said he had been experimenting with for the past few years. When we finished on set he introduced me to his team of 'animators'.

They were all pretty, young and female, and they had all met Art on the model circuit. They saw him as a friendly route out of the posing spotlight, and if they were talented enough he was pleased to help. He tried to explain how the technique he called 'cels over painting' worked, but I told him I was a simple fool who had only recently worked out which way to point the funny box with an eye in the front.

'It's up to you and your beautiful witches to make your magic come to life,' I told him, 'I don't want to know. I don't need to know. To me it's a secret art, Art, and I do my level best to match it in the studio. They tell me we're good at this stuff, let's not prove them wrong too quickly.'

I bailed on another evening in The Sombrero. I needed to get home and see if there were any messages from my errant lady. I also wanted a bath, and I needed a change of clothing.

I didn't know what I'd find in the cool box but my needs were simple. I would happily eat pork and beans if there was nothing else. Most of all I felt ready to face my empty house. But when I got there I found it wasn't empty. It was filled with nearly seven feet of ex-butler.

Maybe his name was Arlo Shaw and maybe it was Wheeler Oakie – hell, it could have been Tom Sawyer for all I cared. But that evening he was sitting in my lounge drinking one of my beers, and he was pointing a gun straight at me. He was every bit as big as Horace had said he was, his shoulders spread wider than the back of my armchair. His neck was as thick as my waist.

He had smiled at the expression on my face when I'd turned the lights on and saw him for the first time. I didn't know how to react, and at first I took a deep breath to yell at him and ask him what the hell he was doing in my house. Then I saw the gun gripped in his big paw and I let the air out slowly. The gun looked small; but a cannon would have looked small in that massive fist.

I looked back towards the door thinking of making my escape, and in a surprisingly light voice he said, 'You can try, but you'll have three bullets in you before you go a single step. If you don't believe me I'll put one in your leg right now as a little taster. I promise I'll try not to hit anything vital. At least, I'll do my best.'

I've seen marble sculptures with more warmth in their eyes than his. My mouth was dry and my voice caught in my throat. I croaked, 'Can I grab a beer, I'm parched.'

He replied, 'When we've completed our conversation I will leave. Then you can have your beer.' He raised his bottle, 'Pabst, you have taste.' He took a long swallow and sighed, 'Ahhh, that's good.' He raised the gun, then belched slightly. 'Excuse me. Now, Mr Murdoch, where is she?

'Where's who?'

He clicked back the hammer of his revolver, it looked small but deadly in his big fist. 'We both know who. Where's the bitch who shot my brother? Where's your wife, Melia Nord?'

With absolute certainty I knew I was going to die, right there in my own lounge. I would never see how Art's new technique would work, nor discover how Maurice's guys would put together a convincing whale's head capable of swallowing Emily and her plank. That seemed a shame.

All the strength drained from my legs and they turned to rubber. I staggered and sat down on my floor. I was ice cold and sweating. My stomach churned and I had to fight hard to stop my bowels from emptying.

The human redwood leaned forward – he somehow managed it without creaking. I was astonished to see a touch of real concern on his face. He examined me silently, weighing me up. Then he closed the hammer of his pistol and stuffed it into one of his jacket pockets. He stood up.

'Mr Murdoch, you need to know something. You need to know I'm no hoodlum. I came here looking for your wife because she killed my brother. You weren't involved, neither was her driver, that black friend of yours. I seen you together. You're nice people. Look, I just want your wife to admit what she did.'

He pressed his hands together as if in prayer. 'The cops like me for it and if they collar me I'll swing for sure, is that fair? Her? It was self-defence, she'll walk for sure. I saw it, I'm a witness. Trust me, she'll walk.'

I blurted, 'Your fingerprints are all over the gun. You're already on file in Oakland under the name Wheeler Oakie. You got history. You put one man in hospital over a card game and nearly killed another guy bare-knuckle fighting. You want me to think they've painted you blacker than you really are? You're a wanted man. If you appeared as a witness they'd arrest you before you said a single word. Ain't that the truth?'

178

He sat back in his chair and shook his head. 'That guy at the card game had a knife and didn't like that I caught him cheating and called him on it. The bare-knuckle fight should have been called off but the referee let it go on. Mo was a good friend but he never learned when to lie down. He was a big man. I had to stop him or he would have put me in traction.

'I did my time in the big house. You had to earn respect there or they take advantage. Milk-fed calf like you, they'd be picking bits of you out of their teeth the first day, unless someone took a liking to you and took you under his wing. They like tender boys in the house. They didn't mess with me. So, what I'm saying is, your information's wrong, Mr Murdoch. I'm not a wanted man.'

I made myself more comfortable on the floor. The way Oakie was talking I was beginning to think I might survive and I didn't want to suffer from sore ankles.

'Yeah? I've got news for you mister. Captain Henderson has you on his list of wanted men. He wants to know why your fingerprints are on that gun. You're top of his list.'

'That's why I need your wife to come clean. They can't hang me for being stupid, and that's all it was. Look, why don't you get off the floor and grab a chair? I told you, I'm no hoodlum. Sit down. No, go get that beer first, and I'll tell you what happened. I'm innocent as you are, I swear that's a fact.'

I went to the cool box in the kitchen, opened two bottles of beer and handed one to him when I returned to the lounge. I sat to one side of him and took a pull on my drink. He thanked me and did the same, raising the bottle to me in salute. We drank in silence for a while. There was nothing companionable about it – the atmosphere was electric with tension. But I wanted to hear what he had to say.

He started by telling me about his brother, Harlow Oakie aka Mason Jarr. The giant's name wasn't Wheeler, it was Chester, after his maternal grandfather. He told me he had grown up big and gentle. He got the name Wheeler when he single-handedly lifted a cart's axle so his Pa could change a broken wheel.

Like a lot of naturally powerful men he had tried not to hurt his playmates at school and treated everyone with reserve. Harlow, however, was wiry and mean. He would goad other children until they attacked him and Chester would have to come to his defence.

'It was the way we grew up. Other kids tried to tell me Harlow was spiteful but I couldn't see it. I thought they were just being nasty. Blood is blood, Mr Murdoch. You got any brothers?'

179

'No, I'm an only child.'

'I envy you. Me and Harlow, there was just the two of us. And two was plenty. Harlow ran around sticking pins in the world and I had to deal with the problems he caused. Thing is, I was good at it. It was him got me into the bare-knuckle game. It didn't hurt *him* at all and we made money.

'Of course it all went wrong. I made my mistakes and did my time and came out looking for something legit, but brother Harlow was always there pulling me down. Then he started running with a filthy gang of crooks, a real bad posse of pureblood scum. They used to meet in the back of a place called The Angel Tavern. I tell you, any angels made it there had fallen a long way from grace, a long, long way.'

[37]

Chester was earning my sympathy. And I wished I had my ideas book handy so I could make notes. Even so, I was very aware that he'd broken into my house. I couldn't forget the loaded pistol in his jacket pocket, and that a few minutes earlier he'd threatened to shoot me with it. I decided it was safer to hold my tongue and listen while he unburdened his strange life into my ears. The tale of the gentle giant and his twisted brother, the crook.

My mind was gathered up by the story he told me in his soft, light voice. While he spoke I could almost see the back room of the Angel Tavern, a bar in the darkest part of New York's East Village. A room tarred yellow by years of tobacco smoke. And the jaundiced faces of the men gathered there, sallow and smeared with open greed.

The way Chester told it these men were wealthy from crime but were gut sick that they couldn't openly spend their ill-gotten gains without attracting the attention of the authorities.

He explained, 'A man can ride a mile on a cop's back if the bribe's big enough, but the money's only truly safe if it looks legit. That's where Harlow came in. He spotted a new investment with a guaranteed return and he'd found his way in through the front door.'

The movies. The goose that lay solid gold eggs. Harlow Oakie had re-invented himself as Mason Jarr, because, as he told his mobster friends, 'I will keep your produce fresh. The revenue won't get a sniff if the money don't spoil in the barrel.'

Chester had changed his surname to Shaw because his brother promised he had reached his 'safe haven' at last. But he chose Arlo as a given name to remind his brother where they came from. It was close enough to Harlow to ring bells.

We, 'The Talent' had thought the move from New York to California was all about finding better light, bigger locations, and cheaper rents, and that had genuinely been a part of it. But, it turns out, Jarr's 'bankers' had headed out west to get out from under the revenue men's spotlight and we had meekly followed. Sheep led by wolves.

But we were making good money, the studio was making millions, and the bankers could openly drive around in big cars and live in mansions. Everyone was happy. Even Arlo Shaw had settled comfortably into his role as butler

181

and bodyguard. Life was easy and his bank account looked as healthy as a grass-fed spring lamb.

'But Harlow got an itch in his breeches that just wouldn't settle,' Chester continued. 'He was coming home from the film set every day and talking about the things Miss Nord was doing. She got deep under his skin, real deep. He had his little movie screening room at the back of the house and he would take the latest processed footage in there with a bottle of something and then he would lock the door. She was burning him up. I'm sorry, Mr Murdoch, but Harlow was bit bad by your lady wife. He got himself infected.'

It was only a matter of time before the sad sack would try his hand at a little seduction. Chester told me, 'He had two baths that day but the sweat was still rolling off him like water through a broken dam. Then Miss Nord was at the door. Every nerve in my body twanged like a cheap piano when I opened the door and saw just how little and sweet she looked. She looks taller on the screen, but in life she's just a bitty little thing. Sorry, I know she's your wife, but I ask you, how could anyone want to hurt anyone so tiny, so exquisite?'

He was on his third beer and I had sunk a good portion of my second. He asked, 'Did you know she had a gun?' I was afraid to speak in case I interrupted his train of thought, I just shook my head. 'Harlow sure didn't. He took her into his office, got me to pour them both a drink, thanked me and told me I should leave. I was being the butler so I did as he bade me, but I left his door open.'

Chester stared at his bottle, 'You might not believe me, but I thought that if I saw Harlow try anything I would step in and stop him. I'd never seen him like that before. He was lit up. You know how pigs don't sweat much? That's why they cover themselves in wet mud if the sun shines too hard. If a pig sweated and wore a suit it would have been the spit of Harlow that day. The honest spit.

'He shut the door, and he grinned at me when he did it. It was a secretive grin, like he had the cream and he wanted it all to himself. I didn't like that look, not at all. Well, I don't know for sure what happened next but I can take a guess at it. I'm sure Miss Nord was defending her virtue from a man trying to take advantage.'

He took a deep breath, 'She didn't scream or shout none, if she had I swear I would have come running, but after a few minutes of silence there came those two shots, bang, bang, one after the other. I froze at the sound and she lit out of that room like a hare with its tail on fire, lickety-split. I ran in and saw Harlow lying over by the big sofa. He was bleeding bad. I grabbed him and pulled him out of that blood, he didn't like blood much, not even on a steak, you know?'

He raised his eyes to mine, 'He sighed so sad, just once, and he was gone. My brother was mean but he was still my brother. There was nothing else I could do so I made him look respectable. Then I went after Miss Nord. I wanted to tell her everything would be okay, you know? That was when I saw the gun and at the same time I heard a car firing up outside. I wasn't thinking, I just picked up that gun and I ran to the window by the outer door.'

Chester acted pointing a gun using the fingers of his right hand. 'I wasn't going to shoot anyone. I thought that if I shot at the car it would scare them enough to hold them and I could talk to them. But when I reached the window and poked the gun out I saw the cop wagon coming into the crescent. I tried to snatch that gun back but I caught my hand on the window's catch and I dropped it.'

He lifted those big hands into the air, 'The cops were all over Miss Nord's car like a rash and they were talking to the neighbours. They headed for the house. Smart money would have said, Chester, you stay where you are and you tell them what happened. But I didn't. Like a fool I hightailed it out the back across the yard and over the fence down to the river. That's it, Mr Murdoch, that's everything. Is it right I should swing for what happened that day? Is that fair? Anyhow, thank you for listening. I appreciate you giving me the time.'

And then he was gone. For a big man he moved fast and very quietly. It took me a few seconds to realise he had walked out and I was alone in the house once more.

I followed him to the door and looked out after him but he had faded into the night. His words echoed around in my skull like caged rats. *Is that fair?* No, Chester, it isn't. Could I do anything to help him? Like what? Must I surrender my crazy wife to the police because a self-confessed gentle giant had put himself in the firing line without thinking? Could I? And what about Horace? He was just trying to protect Melia from herself. How would all this affect him?

The whole thing was a mess. The confusing enormity of it all gave me a headache. What should I do? What *could* I do? I got myself another beer and looked for something to eat. I was hungry and the pangs in my belly took a firm grip on my attention. I couldn't think on an empty stomach. I wasn't really hungry but I would *make* myself eat. And then I paused.

Chester had been calmly sitting in my lounge when I turned on the lights. If he could just walk in then so could anyone. He wasn't a mouse to crawl in through any hole, he was massive! In a quiet panic I scuttled through the house, tightly closing windows, drawing curtains, and firmly locking and bolting outer doors. Even then I still didn't feel secure.

I realised I had become lax and complacent living in my remote home. I would never have behaved like that in New York. It pays to be cautious and have strong, effective locks in the big city. But here Chester had been able to walk straight in and wait for me with a gun. That must never happen again. I was quivering like a harp string by the time I returned to my kitchen.

I couldn't stop my hands shaking and I almost spilled the glass of red wine when I was pouring it out, which would have added to Melia's stain from the other evening, ruining that fine table. I put the bottle down and sat with my head in my hands. I thought back to that day when Horace had been sitting with me while I roared around my grounds and practiced my double declutch in the Fiat. So much had changed since then.

With a gasp of surprise I realised I was weeping. Fat tears fell onto the tabletop where they left perfectly round dark shapes on the honey-coloured wood. I watched in fascination until my sight blurred. My headache grew worse. And then I remembered Melia's amber bottle of painkillers. It couldn't hurt to take two. They might even help calm the pounding of my wretched heart.

I found them in the cabinet in the big bathroom off the master bedroom. Out of habit Melia had tucked them at the back of the middle shelf behind my shaving tackle. The bottle was three-quarters empty. I supposed she had taken a good supply with her. She wouldn't have gone far without her 'medication'.

My head was pounding, I took them down to the kitchen and sat looking at the label. Compressed tablets/No. 726/ASPIRIN/PHENACETIN/AND CODEINE by Parke, Davis and Co. Ltd. England. I took two and washed them down with some wine. There was a faint aftertaste but nothing too bad.

I thought about Melia sitting at the same table doing the same thing and I wondered how many of the little pills she had swallowed since the day of the sandbag. How often had she refilled the amber bottle? After a few minutes a heavy lassitude fell over me and my thoughts softened and flowed without direction. It was as if they were circling me, swimming through warm water. I began to chuckle, but I didn't know why.

Hey, I thought, *I must really be tired. It's all the strain of the last few days. I need to go to bed. If I'm this tired I need to go to bed and sleep.* There came a muffled yet shrill sound from the lounge. It was the telephone, but I was too tired to care. I lifted one leaden foot in front of the other and half walked, half pushed myself to the stairs.

I staggered up to the bedroom and began to undress, pulling my pants down as far as my ankles, then gazed down at my shoes. The tied laces presented themselves with a baffling complexity that was way too much for my fuddled senses to deal with just then. The shoes could wait, bed could not.

I tried to take the few steps towards my bed, which billowed its open arms at me in welcome. My pants tangled around my ankles, I stumbled and fell headlong. I fell so slowly and hit so hard it seemed unfair, the wind was knocked out of me in a whistling groan. I felt no pain. Life was too complicated to make sense of it. I succumbed to unconsciousness, floating down into the depths of a bottomless dark pit, and I forgot everything until the morning.

[38]

Floating down into that dark, soft pit had been effortless. Dragging myself back up into the light the next morning was like pulling my body out from a tarpit of screaming agony. My head hurt. My face must have struck the bed's wooden base as I flopped to the floor, bruising my cheek and mashing my lip against my teeth. I had bitten my tongue and my face was glued to the rug by blood.

My right side was stiff after my night stretched out on the bedroom's hard hessian matting and every movement provoked new discomfort. I'd fallen off horses and caused less damage; hell; I'd crashed cars and come out better. I tried to stand up and fell to my knees once more, my feet still caught up in my clothing. I'd had better mornings.

I was glad I was alone. It would have been embarrassing to do all that in front of a witness. I was a pitiful mess. I ran myself a hot tub and soaked away some of the pain, then I gingerly shaved and brushed my teeth.

Luckily, as far as I could tell, I hadn't cracked or broken anything; but the face in the mirror was already purpling from cheek to lip. I was just beginning to feel some semblance of normalcy when I finally descended to the kitchen and saw the barely touched, open bottle of wine next to the amber bottle of tablets.

Two bottles of light beer, part of one glass of wine, and two little pills. The alcohol wouldn't have been enough to put my maiden aunt Tilly into such a drunken stupor, and she was an active supporter of the temperance league. Those little pills had hit me like a roundhouse to the jaw and I'd gone down for the count. Melia had been eating them like candy, she must wander about in a constant daze.

I winced my way through breakfast and sipped at coffee that burned my injured tongue. My head still pounded but I decided it was safer to see the quack at the studio than risk another brace of Melia's dynamite caps. Trying those once had been a good plenty. I wrote down everything on the label so I could ask the doc if my reaction had been normal; and I also wanted to get some quiet advice about the damn things. What were they?

I would have flushed the poisonous contents of that bottle down the toilet, but what had the local fish population ever done to me? I put it back behind my shaving gear, contents complete bar the two I'd taken the night before and another two I wrapped in the paper on which I'd noted their prescription.

I wanted to find out what was really in them, because I doubted it had much to do with Messrs Parke, Davis and Co. Ltd of old England. While I walked to the studio, after carefully locking the house behind me, I tried to do some comparative anatomical mathematics in my aching head.

How many times could my half-pint-sized wife fit into my quart-sized body? How *could* she take those things without getting put down for the count? And how many was she taking? Too many questions – what I needed was answers.

Wallace peered at me when I reached the gate, 'Morning, Mr Murdoch,' he said, 'I sure hope the other fellah looks worse than you. You okay?'

I grinned and winced a wink at him, 'Here's a tip, Wallace, make sure you take your pants all the way off before climbing into bed. Saves a great deal of confusion during the night and reduces the number of questions you have to answer the next morning.'

'Okay, Mr Murdoch, if you say so. But what I say, I say you take my advice. You see that guy coming again you walk the other way, that's all I'm saying. You're good people and you don't need that kind of hurt. I can put you in touch with people if you need them, you hear what I'm saying?'

'You're good people too, Wallace, and thanks.'

I found Doc in the commissary performing an autopsy on some sausage links and fried eggs. When he caught sight of me his jaw swung open so I could see that hadn't yet finished chewing his last mouthful. He prodded a yolk smeared knife blade at me.

'You going in front of the camera today? If you are it's not me you want, it's make-up. Give them a few hours they could make you look at least halfway human again. Take me days, at least. What did you do, kick a gorilla out of bed again?'

He was referring to the time I had woken an actor who had fallen into a deep and bad-tempered sleep due to the stifling heat in his gorilla suit. He was required to perform a tug-of-war against a black bear – using Melia as the rope. The gorilla took issue when I kicked the soles of his feet after shouting got me nowhere; and he had chased me around studio one screaming abuse. In Spanish.

The bear and Melia watched everything from on set. Unlike the gorilla the bear was real. Melia was sitting on its lap with its paws around her waist while she fed it pieces of honeycomb. That was back when life made more sense.

I told Doc what had happened to me the night before and he examined my note and the two white tablets it contained. 'I know the product,' he mused, 'it might make you a little sleepy but nothing more. Sounds like these put you on your ass. You sure it wasn't a gorilla? Or did you meet any other large, man-like creatures?'

I was tempted to tell him about Chester, but I figured with the pills in his hand he had enough to deal with. When he finished eating I followed him to the dispensary where he fetched out a small, square, brown bottle containing round pills. He told me to take two when I needed them, beginning straight away, but no more than two every few hours.

'You might start seeing crazy animals and people acting like lunatics, but don't worry. That just means you're awake and working in an insane asylum. If you have any other side effects come and see me. You want an eyepatch for that shiner? An eyepatch is a very romantic look around here.'

I held up the bottle. I had become wary around tablets. 'So, Doc, tell me, what are these?'

He raised his eyes to the heavens, 'What? Are you studying for a medical degree now? Look, do I ask you what you do with the funny wooden box on legs? No. So don't ask me about medicine. They're special magic pills make nasty pain go bye-bye, that's all you need to know from me. You want to know more ask that cute wife of yours. She already knows too much in my opinion. Oh, and tell her I want to see her. Soon. Capisce? Soon.'

I got more sympathy from the troupe, at least they looked worried. And I was pleased to see Horace sitting in with the discussion group. When I walked in, he was laughing and animated, and he had that look that fit right in with the movie asylum I was trying to create for precious intelligences just like his.

The crazy gang accepted my story that I had been practicing a stunt that went wrong and taken a tip head first into my furniture. Only Horace flicked me a sideways look that was weighted with doubt. However, with the big whale project to plan out and get underway, the state of my sorry puss got pushed back into the shadows. As did my absent wife, Chester, and the murderous events at Mason Jarr's house.

We had our title, *Jonah's Gold*, and since I'd last seen them the troupe had come up with enough business to put ninety minutes of action up on the silver screen. As the leader of the troupe I thought I'd have to knock some raw ideas into shape. Not so. What they laid out before me unfolded to disclose a fully realised gem of a plot.

It would change some during the shooting – fresh ideas always floated up to the surface while we filmed – but I liked the story, and, crucially, not a yard of the footage we'd shot so far would be wasted.

We now started our tale in a fisherman's cottage where we meet Captain Ishmael and his beautiful daughter. They're happy together and make a great team on his boat. She's a lark and a free spirit, while he's a tough old bird but also an indulgent father who dotes on his flesh and blood.

However, daughter's in love with the handsome young guy who works on her father's boat. They wish to marry, but the captain won't allow it until the young man can support his daughter in a fitting manner, which is unlikely any time soon because Pa pays the wages and money is tight.

We move out to sea and for a while the story follows my original idea, right up to the point where the whale spits Emily – who, of course, plays the daughter – and her plank, into an underwater cave. The girl clings to her plank, and, unconscious, floats upwards into a bubble of air. She rises into a pool by a little beach. The waves gently nudge her onto a narrow band of white sand.

We take a close look at her lovely face, then pan back until we see a skeletal hand apparently caressing her hair. We hold there and the screen goes dark. We're back on the boat, and we see the two men frantically searching the waves looking for Emily. They almost come to blows, blaming each other for the accident.

Boyfriend (Bert), pushes the captain away, kicks off his boots, throws off his sea jacket and dives into the water. We see him looking around frantically, bubbles exploding from his mouth. Vaguely below him he sees a mighty whale bucking and pushing against a crop of stone on the seabed, all supplied, of course, by Art and his clever witches.

Bert darts back to the surface, fills his lungs with air, then dives down to discover what the whale's up to. It's his only hope of finding Emily. The whale has disappeared. Desperate for air he finds the entrance to the cave, but it's no good, he's drowning and must return to the surface. That's when the whale attacks from behind and thrusts him into the mouth of the cave in a helpless confusion of arms and legs.

The sheer force of the whale's attack blasts him to the surface of the pool like a cork and he shoots up to crack his head against the rocky roof of the cave. He's knocked out and would have drowned but Emily saves him and drags him to the beach. Bert's scalp is bleeding into the water and the scent of his blood enrages the whale which starts trying to rip the cave apart...

I read through the rest of that magnificent outline with my heart in my mouth. The bony hand belonged to a skeleton stretched over an ancient treasure chest filled with gold and jewels, the answer to their prayers. If they could get just a portion of it to the surface they could get married. But there's a problem. Gold is heavy. Extremely heavy.

The couple couldn't swim to the surface with their treasure, and anyway, the whale's going mad, battering at the entrance to their cave. The roof is beginning to collapse and rocks are pounding into the water. What to do?

In desperation Emily fills the deep pockets of her sea jacket with gold and jewels, as much as she can carry (In this version she remains fully clothed). Bert takes off his shirt and creates a makeshift sack so he can carry more treasure. He also finds a rusted sword and vows to die trying to kill the great beast if that means Emily can escape.

That's when a huge effort by the whale brings down some of the wall at the end of the little beach and they see stairs cut from the natural rock that had, until then, been hidden by a centuries old rock fall. They run for the stairs, just as the whale smashes into the little cave in a flood of seawater.

The skeleton and treasure chest are washed away, never to be seen again, and the whale roars and twists like a frustrated demon, enraged by the smell of blood. Bert and Emily have made their escape and they're safe – for now. And that's where the draft ended.

'So, what happens next?' I wailed, 'We got at least another half hour of movie time to fill, we can't stop there.'

Paul grinned at Art and they both grinned at me. Art said, 'We'll tell you that over a beer and a plate of special at The Sombrero this evening, our treat. We have an idea for a grand finale will turn your hair white. Can you wait?'

'Have I got a choice?'

They chuckled, 'Nope,' they said in unison. 'No choice at all.'

[39]

An abandoned husband shouldn't feel so happy. It was over two months later and there was still no sign of Melia. I was worried – of course I was – and I missed her with a bone-deep ache, but I was too occupied to fret. The troupe were rising to our new challenge like champions, and anyhow, I believed Melia would come home when she was good and ready. She could look after herself, she had told me so. Often. And loudly.

Fact is, we moviemakers were needed more than ever. The war over in Europe was stuck deep in the mire, and we had begun hearing rumours of some kind of coughing sickness or pneumonia sweeping across the nation. Word had it that some folk had caught it bad. I heard some were dying. Whole towns were suffering.

But there was nothing about it in the newspapers. Funny that, maybe newsmen preferred to avoid people in their sick beds – or maybe they were all too busy trying to catch pictures of famous movie stars dancing in their birthday suits?

Those were real sorry times and people wanted and needed to be entertained. They needed the release from reality that the big silver screen up there in the darkness provided. We traded in dreams, and my gang were amongst the best dream spinners in the business. I was happy and proud as a new father to be part of the work; every day was an adventure. Every day we reached new heights.

But we were outgrowing Edendale. Don't get me wrong, it was a great place. The big lake nearby could stand in for the sea when we needed a watery location, and the surrounding hills and woodland could stand in for almost anyplace on Earth. You'd think we would be satisfied with our lot, but we were already thinking of moving again. Smart money (the all-seeing Maurice) was talking about us going to some place called Hollywood.

The length of Allesandro Street between Berkeley Avenue and Duane Street, where the studio was located, had become the site of a lot of busy construction work. If sound arrived, as had been promised, we'd be shouting to be heard above the clatter of saws and the pounding of riveting hammers, pile drivers and heavy trucks. We needed peace and that industrious dale could no longer claim to be Eden.

But *Jonah's Gold* was coming together beautifully, even if it was getting birthed into one of the noisiest maternity wards under God's sky. And that last half hour of magic was going to have the audience jumping out of their seats. My troupe started early and stayed late. Art's witches had to be physically turned out of their studio or they would have worked through the night. The team from *Tremendous Tales* was an inspiration before a single movie frame was processed. I was afire with it.

The Fiat was back on the road and better than ever, but I needed the quiet thinking time I enjoyed during my walk from the ranch house to the studio and back. I got a clearer look at the work when I was away from the creative whirl and electric atmosphere of the set.

The gang had even tracked me down to my hideaway inside the giant whale's head built by Maurice's award-winning mechanical effects team. For me there was no longer any escape on the Century stage.

Any witness to my solitary stroll home would have thought they were watching a demented man. I talked to myself, performed little dance steps, and sometimes stopped to make notes in my latest ideas book. That particular evening I had stayed for a beer at The Sombrero, which now sported a printed sign on its door stating, 'All welcome, but sorry, no work clothes or boots'.

One late afternoon an influx of sweaty construction workers had driven away Jake's regulars – we studio folk – and he had the sign made the next day. When I pointed out that I worked in the duds I was wearing, as did the troupe, he told me that every sign was open to interpretation by the proprietor.

'The day you guys come in here trailing building dirt and brick dust I'll rethink that sign's wording, okay? I run a clean house and I had to pay Monica extra to sweep up after those builder guys. And that smell of sweat! Urgh. So, until then you're welcome in your work duds, and the specials tonight are chilli beef, catfish, and pork chops so big and fresh you can still hear the squeal if you squeeze them hard enough!'

Jonah's Gold would be ready for the busy Thanksgiving weekend, which timed its release date perfectly for the Studio Excellence Awards season early next year. I was excited by the crazy masterpiece we were crafting; but I was already thinking about the next movie script.

I had an idea for a drama about two brothers growing up together; one a scheming weasel the other a gentle giant. The weasel is always getting the giant in trouble, but the real problem arises when a beautiful girl comes between them, and the giant has to choose between blood and his true love.

We could take everyday folk down into the seedy backstreets of criminal life, show them how a good woman can reach into the hardiest, broken soul and find love there.

I even knew the final scene, it was perfect. The giant is saved and walks away from his pleading brother into the arms of his girl. Perhaps it was because I was thinking about such things I wasn't surprised to see a massive shape detach itself from the shadows of my porch as I drew nearer to my house.

I had expected to see Chester. I thought he'd come to see if I'd heard anything from Melia, and I nearly called out a hello, but I was soon disabused. It was Captain Henderson from Boyle Heights who stepped out into the waning light. His face looked drawn and his powerful shoulders drooped as if weighed down by his long coat.

'Can I talk to you, please, Mr Murdoch?' I told him sure and invited him inside. I asked him if he preferred coffee or beer while he hung up his hat and coat. He thanked me for a beer and asked if he could use my restroom, observing that I obviously worked a really long day. He had been waiting, he said, several hours.

I pointed out the small bathroom in the lobby off the kitchen and fetched our beers. He joined me at the wooden table and settled into one of my kitchen chairs with a sigh of gratitude. He chugged the neck of his Pabst then sat squeezing the bottle in his big paws. He looked lost in thought. I was reminded of Chester Oakie talking about his brother and wondered what revelation I was about to hear next.

He coughed and chewed at his words as if they were too hard to say without a little softening, then without raising his eyes to mine he said, 'We found Mrs Murdoch. The Ramsey County police of Minnesota found Mrs Murdoch. I'm sorry Mr Murdoch, there's no easy way to say this...'

'Where is she?'

He looked at me. 'You really didn't know? She's been gone months and you just carried on working. I thought you must know. Any man would go crazy if his wife just upped and left him. You didn't; I thought you had to know.'

I felt cheap, sitting there and drinking my beer in front of his big, square, honest cop's face. He was trying to work out what kind of man he was looking at, the kind of man who let his wife go missing and just got on with his day like nothing had happened.

He shook his head and breathed hard, 'Damn, I was sure you knew. She was in St. Paul, Ramsey County. She was staying at the big hotel there, the St. Paul. I thought you knew.'

'Sorry, I've been waiting to hear. She does odd things sometimes. Melia, she's her own worst enemy. Thinks she can look after herself. She always has, since she was a girl. Always swept her own path. I suppose she needs me to go get her?'

I fetched us both another beer, but I wanted something stronger. All this talk about Melia was spoiling the mood.

Henderson's eyes were bleak. 'No, she doesn't. She's here in LA. She's with the county coroner. I'm sorry, Mr Murdoch, but she's dead. She was murdered.'

I couldn't swallow the beer in my mouth, it caught in my throat. The cold froth felt too stupidly frivolous on my tongue. I didn't feel real. Like a hollow man I stood up and walked to the kitchen sink and spat the liquid out. I turned on the faucet and watched it drain away. Henderson watched me, silent. I didn't know if the feeling of bitter reproach was coming from him or me.

I fetched two glasses and a full bottle of good Scotch malt. I poured each of us a healthy belt. It warmed me but did nothing to add substance to the empty sensation creeping up from my feet to my head. Perhaps it was the jolt of hard alcohol that caused tears to spring into my eyes.

Henderson held his glass without drinking. I could tell he was waiting for me to ask my next question. He wanted to know what I knew. I pulled my thoughts into order and fired the first thing in the queue.

'Was it Arlo Shaw? Did he do it? Did he kill her?'

He leaned forward, 'What do you know about Arlo Shaw? Why do you ask?'

'Arlo Shaw, Wheeler Oakie, Chester, whatever name he's using now. He was Mason Jarr's little brother. Jarr's real name is Harlow Oakie; and if a skunk ever needed shooting it was him. Chester was okay. *I* thought he was okay. Was it him?'

I took some more whisky. I was still hollow inside but at least my head was on straight once more. There was a long distance between where I sat with Henderson in my kitchen and Melia somewhere in the county coroner's office. I wondered if she was feeling cold.

Henderson took a sip from his glass then examined the bottle. 'Smooth,' he said. Then, 'No, it wasn't Oakie. Boys from the Heights tracked him down to a rooming house off Central Avenue. He resisted arrest. That man's built like a big mule but he's fast. He injured two of my men before pulling a gun. They had no choice but to bring him down. So no, it wasn't him killed Mrs Murdoch.'

He took a sip, 'Funny thing. That was the last thing he said, he said, "It wasn't me, this is stupid". But no, it wasn't him.'

I was sad about Chester. I think he knew what was going to happen. I guess that's why he came to see me. Melia was his last hope. I wondered what kind of cannon they had used to 'bring him down'.

I drank a little more whisky then found my glass was empty once more. I refreshed it with a steady hand. I was surprised how calm I felt. How very calm.

'Curiosity killed the cat,' I said, 'but I got to know, and I'm all out of guesses. If not Chester, then who? Who killed her?'

Henderson reached over and took my glass. 'This would be better heard with a level head, Lance. It's hard enough to tell, but I think it's going to be real hard for you to hear. You ready?' I nodded.

He took a breath, 'Your wife's body was found in the Chinese quarter of St. Paul, down by the river. She had spent the evening at an establishment called The River Queen. Let's be polite and say that place is the lowest kind of dive frequented by river rats and boatmen.'

'Why was she there?'

'Best guess? Drugs. She was a guest at the St. Paul hotel which had a perfectly good bar, but we think Mrs Murdoch was looking for something a little more potent than a glass of wine.'

I took a deep breath, 'A mixture of heroin and cocaine would be my guess. Potent enough to kick a horse's ass. Tablet form, I'd say. They find them?'

Henderson shook his head, 'Whatever she got was probably stolen along with her clothes after she'd been attacked, raped, and strangled. They think there were at least four of them. Barkeep at the River Queen said a small gang of river rats left directly after Mrs Murdoch. He said he didn't know them and couldn't be sure he'd recognise them again. Guess it's safer for him that way.'

I wasn't sure how I got there. There was a blank moment and then I came round to find myself vomiting in the small bathroom. I think I brought up my soul and found my heart once more. It was broken. I thought of my funny little girl when I first met her. I saw her dancing as a showgirl for a roomful of men dressed like cowboys. What a terrible way to extinguish such a bright light.

Henderson spent the next hour with me. I couldn't stop shaking and he stayed to make sure I was okay. I took two important things from our conversation during that hour. Melia's body had been fingerprinted in St. Paul in an attempt to discover who she was.

The prints were distributed and ended up at Oakland, where they were matched to the second set found on the Mason Jarr murder weapon – alongside and under those of Chester Oakie. That's why Henderson had become involved. He was the officer in charge of the case. He said he would also need to talk to Horace to verify a few things and would be in touch.

The second thing was from the coroner's report. He had found bruising to the victim's brain that had nothing to do with the attack. The coroner was of the opinion that such bruising might cause mood swings and abnormal behaviour; which might be why the victim had gone to such a 'low dive'. I thought of that damned sandbag slamming her into that solid door.

Even after Henderson finally left I could think of nothing but the way that sweet little girl had been destroyed by a dumb prank. I decided to get Bisset on his own the next day. Before going to bed I rang Horace and warned him the police would want to talk to him soon and why. I wished him goodnight.

I got fired. I was given until we had completed *Jonah's Gold* to find something else to do for a living; and warned that I would never work in movies again. But by God and all his little angels it was worth it. I'd better explain.

I'd had a rough night. The thought of everything that had happened to Melia churned in my mind like sand and gravel in a cement mixer. Okay, true, she had become a helpless drug addict and she had also become a murderer in self-defence, but when she stood in front of a camera the world was a brighter, better place.

When that sandbag swung down towards us and I stepped out of its way it smashed Melia from the doorway of studio one like a hit to the centre bleachers. It was a home run and threw her straight out of her beautiful, funny life until she landed, a long agonising time later, in some filthy backstreet down by the Mississippi river in St. Paul.

Beaten, raped, murdered. It pounded like a drum in my head. Beaten, raped, murdered. And her poor beautiful body left naked and discarded like garbage in a filthy alleyway. She didn't deserve that. Her life had been torn away by a bunch of men who followed her from some sleazy bar where she would never have been if she hadn't been buying the drugs she needed to feed her habit.

I hoped she was stoned when it happened, maybe that way she wouldn't suffer. Maybe she didn't know what was happening? That was best. Cold comfort.

I felt guilty, because she'd had to run away and I didn't know why. Was it to escape the law? To escape me? To escape our lives together? Had she had enough of the movie star life? Or was she acting out some crazy scene that only made sense to that bruise on her brain? Everything bad that had happened to Melia led back to that stupid stunt with the sandbag.

Every time I dozed off I saw that bag swinging towards us. I saw it smash her against the door. I heard that solid crack of her head and I imagined her brain jolted around inside her skull. Henderson hadn't given me too many details about her murder, but I imagined that too. I have a strong imagination.

Shame I don't have a strong stomach. I had taken a pail into the bedroom and placed it by the bed. I filled it that night, retching my agony into a bucket. I still slept on the left side of the bed – that was my side. I had the whole bed to sprawl around in but I curled up on the left. I was waiting to feel Melia's soft warmth on my back, to hear her voice softly whisper, 'Are you asleep?' But, I knew I'd never hear it again.

I fought against self-pity. I'd lost one of the most wonderful women who had ever lived – and her life had been stolen from her in a terrible, unimaginable way. Except I *could* imagine it. The four of them taking turns, each one rutting like a filthy animal while the others held her down. They took everything she owned; her body, her money, her clothes, and her life.

In my mind's eye the attack happened in a dark place. Maybe they beat her unconscious so she wouldn't scream before they did what they did; but in those few frantic seconds she would know what was going to happen. She would know.

The last moments she experienced in her life were spent in violence, pain, and terror. Someone would pay for that. Someone would pay. And I thought I knew who it was going to be.

When I reached the studio the next day and Wallace wished me good morning I just raised my hand in silent greeting. My head was grinding too loud for me to hear anything. I walked fast into the studio buildings, blind and deaf to everything but where I needed to be and the man I wanted to find. I walked straight into somebody and knocked them sideways into a packing crate. I don't know who it was. I muttered something, an apology of sorts, but didn't slow down.

Studio one was almost empty. There were a few men and some women, but none were the man I wanted. I checked the commissary, but he wasn't there. Even so I could smell him. I was like a hound on the scent. Then I went into the editing suite. He shouted at me to 'Shut the door you moron!' I shut the door. There was just us in there. Hal Bisset and me.

He turned back to whatever he was doing as if I wasn't there, but I wasn't in the mood to wait until he was finished. With my left hand I took him by the shoulder and spun him around to face me. With my right fist I struck down into his astonished face. The blow jarred me to my elbow, one of my knuckles cracked. He shrieked and dropped to the floor.

My fist hurt in a good way, exquisite agony. I used it like a club to pound him while he wriggled and snivelled on the floor. In the blue light of the room I saw black blood on his lips and teeth. He was panting in terror but I bet he didn't feel a tenth of the terror Melia must have felt in her last moments. Beaten, raped, murdered. It pounded through me while I pounded him.

I took his neck in my hand and I squeezed. 'She's dead, you bastard. Are you happy now? She's dead, and it's all because of that stupid stunt of yours with that sandbag. You bruised her brain and she's dead.'

I slammed his head against the floor and spat my words at him. 'You weren't fit to walk in her shadow, but you killed her. You killed her sure as if you shot her in the head. Now I'm going to break you into pieces.' I was sobbing with uncontrolled fury and ready to smash Bisset like a bug.

I was slammed to one side away from my prey and I reacted like a wildcat ready to take on the world. Nobody would save Bisset's sorry carcass. I roared and turned on my attacker. I would swat them away, then break Bisset's back. My life was very simple at that moment, concentrated into my need to perform my simple act of revenge.

The Boss stood before me holding a chair, poking the legs at me as if I was a wild animal. I could smell the iron tang of Bisset's blood and I wanted more. I was filled with too much bile to stop. The air rasped into my lungs and I crouched ready to leap. Nothing would stop me.

'Lance, *what*? Have you gone mad? Calm down, man! What are you doing? What do you think you're doing?'

That familiar face, that voice. I had listened to it bellow through a megaphone at me; and heard it in quiet moments of shared confidence. I knew he would understand. I pointed down to the weeping ruin at my feet.

'Melia's dead. They found a bruise on her brain that would have affected everything she did. A bruise on her brain that changed her. And you know where that bruise came from? It happened when this bastard slapped her with that stupid sandbag. It happened when she cracked her head against the door.'

I kicked Bisset, hard. 'The doc said she had concussion and he gave her tablets. They were too strong and she got addicted. Now the coroner says the bruise on her brain would have changed the way she acted. She became crazy. She shot Mason Jarr, by the way. I think he tried to rape her so she shot him. Everything that happened started when this, this, *asshole* here rigged that sandbag. She's dead because of him. She's dead.'

I kicked Bisset again. He started wailing and making bubbling noises. I didn't know it, but I'd broken his jaw and cracked his cheekbone. Now I'd stopped hitting him I could feel my right hand grinding and swelling. Before long I'd be suffering from the damage I'd done to my knuckles. I wouldn't be making any notes in my ideas book for a while.

The Boss put the chair down and sat on it. He looked me square in the eye and crossed his legs, then he folded his arms and scowled at me. It was such a familiar set of gestures that I almost laughed. The Boss taking control of the situation the way he always did. For him, a disagreement was an opportunity to find a better way to do something. He always told us, 'Don't fight each other, fight the enemy. We work together and we win.'

His voice was calm, 'It wasn't Hal, Lance, he didn't do it. He was upset as you when it happened. Poor man, he loved Melia as much as you do, perhaps more. But she always loved you. Other men flirted with her but we all knew, for her there was only ever you. When she found you she stopped looking and she gave you everything she had. So, anyway, no. Hal didn't do it.'

'So, who did? Do you know?'

He looked down at his hands. 'Yes, I do. It was a stupid prank gone wrong; and I've regretted it ever since. I don't know what I was thinking, and I've tried to make things up to both of you in any way I could. I'm sorry, Lance. It shouldn't have been Melia, she shouldn't even have been there. I asked for you and she tagged along and she caught the packet. It was an accident. It was meant for you. It was stupid of me, I'm sorry.'

I felt stunned. 'You did it?' He nodded without looking up. 'You did it?' I felt physically sick. His shoulders drooped. All his authority oozed out of him. He deflated in front of me. His head was too heavy for his body and he sagged down into his chair. I walked to his side, fury boiling in my veins. I raised my aching hand and he flinched, cringing away from me.

'You're not worth it,' I sighed. I looked down. 'Hal, stay there. I'm going for the Doc. I'm really sorry, pal. I thought... Sorry, man, I'll make it up to you.'

Bisset had pushed himself into a seated position. His face crumpled, but his eyes were hard as iron and they were set straight at Carl Lemmon. I couldn't think of that miserable creature as the 'Boss' anymore. He was nothing.

I had nearly reached the door when I heard a terrifying shriek from behind me followed by a meaty sound like a butcher's cleaver slamming into a thick haunch of meat. I turned and froze at the scene before me. Bisset was swaying drunkenly on his feet and he was arcing some kind of weapon over his head. He was screeching like a demented demon but his bubbling, blood-choked words made no sense.

He swung his weapon down like an axe and struck Lemmon a full blow across his back. The impact jolted Lemmon's senseless body out of the chair. Bisset brought his weapon up again and that's when I came to life.

Without thinking I ran forward and thrust out my arms to shield Lemmon's body. I screamed in agony when the pole in Bisset's grasp struck my hands, but I grabbed it and clung on. It was one of those hard, wooden poles with a metal hook on the end that we used to open shutters and windows. There was at least one in every room. It made a very effective club.

Bisset glared at me then spat blood at Lemmon. He was still trying to pull the pole from my hands to continue his attack when the door of the processing room flew open and a posse of people thundered in looking to rescue whoever was screaming loudest.

Lemmon was saying nothing. Bisset's first strike had caught him behind the ear and knocked him out cold. I remember wondering if Bisset had bruised the bastard's brain. Anyhow, as I said, I got fired.

[41]

It was Thursday the twenty-eighth of November in the year 1918. Thanksgiving. The war in Europe had ended at last. The dreadful butcher's bill for that conflict would finally number over a quarter of a million Americans, but for now people were celebrating. They might have had German blood, Italian, Dutch, African, French or English blood, but during that celebration we were all one nation, all Americans.

There were still no official reports about the terrible lung congestion disease that was creeping across the states and leaving too many mourning families in its wake. We had all heard about people who had been affected, but we didn't know the numbers nor how long it would last. Not then.

Lemmon recovered from Bisset's attack. He retained his senior director's position at Century Edendale and found himself another cameraman. He tried to steal Paul Marivaux from *Tremendous Tales* but discovered that Paul, as with all of my troupe, was hired on a movie by movie basis. Paul had no contract Lemmon could negotiate or steal away from us. And he wanted to stay with the team.

None of the troupe had contracts with Century Edendale except me. Art Cobal and his witches were working under his own studio brand *A Brush With Fate*. Bert, Emily and Ben had also set up their own actors' company, *The Artists' Folio*. Bert and Emily had set a date in the new year to become Mr and Mrs Savage. I was to be their best man.

I had already booked them into the Plaza for their first night as man and wife, after promising Monsieur Lavell that there would be no funny business – and that Bert's feet would be correctly attired at all times. Lavell was sorry to hear about Melia and told me so. He and 'Amilton, would raise a glass to her memory at the end of their shift.

'She was enchanting,' he told me. 'She had that rare quality, elfin and beautiful. I wanted to smile just looking at her.'

I agreed, and it hurt. I wondered when the pain of her loss might subside. When would I be able to accept that her brightness had been dimmed forever? I still looked for her to be with me when I awoke alone in the night. I listened for the soft question, 'Are you awake?' In my dreams I heard her. And I answered, 'For you, always.'

Maurice had never been offered a contract by Century, not even after he and his team had won their Studio Excellence Award for Mechanical Effects.

They were considered as piece-workers; artisans rather than artists. When I told him I'd heard about a new studio that was going to open in Gower Street near Sunset Boulevard, and that they would be looking for mechanical craftsmen, he told me to keep him informed.

Hal Bisset could have pressed charges against me, but once he could talk again he told me that he couldn't blame me for what I'd done. 'She was the most wonderful girl I'd ever seen,' he said. 'She was Jake. The real whistle. A peach. When that sandbag hit her I wanted to kill whoever did it. I'm glad for what I did to Lemmon. It was a righteous act.

'You know they won't let me anywhere near the studios now, and none of the other production companies will talk to me. I've got savings that will tide me over, and it was worth it to beat the shakes out of that Goop. I'll manage.'

I told him what I'd told Maurice, 'Don't worry. You're in for sure, I'll have a word with the top man there. You'll be working with friends. You keep your head above water until the new year and life will be duck soup once more.'

Hal was a 'cat' who was 'hep' to the modern lingo, I struggled to keep up. Nothing dates faster than yesterday's slang. No matter, I was contracted to finish *Jonah's Gold* and the lawyers had set down the terms – including my share of the profits. The troupe and I would be riding the gravy boat when our masterpiece hit the screens – and there wasn't thing one the studio could do about it.

I never found out why Lemmon set the sandbag stunt in first place, it made no sense, but Bert had his own theory. 'He's a vain man. Anyone dresses like that and sports that dopey pencil line moustache has to be vain. And you were doing too well as assistant director. People were talking about you. He wanted to bring you down. He wouldn't lower himself to a custard pie in the puss or a water balloon, so he went for a sandbag. Tried to catch you out. And it backfired on him like an old Ford.'

Bert sighed, 'Well, bah hoo, bully for him. He got caught in his own fool trap and slapped his starring lady in the head instead. He'll be picking up the pieces of that stupid mess for the rest of his life. Maybe it'll finally give him a chance to take a good look at himself and learn a few things his Mom and Pa forgot to teach him, like the value of friends and practicing a little humility. Me, I doubt he'll bother. Too busy keeping that dumb moustache of his straight.'

Jonah's Gold premiered on Thanksgiving day at Sid Grauman's Million Dollar Theatre on Broadway, and we were all there. I'd invited Bisset and Captain Henderson to join us for Champagne and platters of expensive bites in savoury pastry. We had ourselves food, drink, a box with a good view of the screen and we were away from the common crowd. Roll the camera.

I'd booked our place in the name of Gower Street Productions, even paid for it from our brand-new official bank account. Art, Paul and I had walked through our studio buildings the day before and seen how well things were shaping up. I had my ideas book with me and shared my thoughts about our first movie – The Brothers; the crooked weasel and the gentle giant. They loved it and had their own ideas, of course. But first we had a premier to attend.

Century had promised to stay away from the troupe and not tie us up in any long-winded legal wrangles, but only so long as they could take my name off the credits. It was still a *Tremendous Tales* production and everyone else got a fair mention, but I had to be off the roll. I agreed, but only on the proviso that I was allowed to include a dedication at the end. We shook on it.

I looked around my gang with real pride. They had none of the usual movie mannerisms, none of the flamboyant peacock gorgeousness and primping that was part of the package with far too many of the 'brightest stars in the movie firmament'. We were professionals. Working folk who made great cinema. And everything about to happen when the houselights went down had been dedicated to our loved ones who couldn't be there on that special day.

The theatre grew dark and the stalls became silent. I could feel the thrill of anticipation electrify the air. I saw Emily clutch Bert's arm with excitement. Art and his witches sat together, still and watchful.

Henderson looked across at me and mouthed, 'Good luck'. I mouthed back, 'Thanks'. The credits rolled without my name but everyone else was there. I sighed with pleasure and settled down to watch. I always loved a good movie.

The first hour howled past at a fierce lick. We heard gasps and sighs, and, even in the semi-darkness, I observed that odd wavelike motion in the crowd that meant people were leaning forward in fascination or bouncing back in shock. There came a few shrieks of horror when the whale ruptured the cave and Emily and Bert barely escaped the flood of seawater before they made it to the stairs.

They climbed those stairs; Bert with his make-shift shirt sack and Emily with her pockets full of treasure. The sea was rising fast behind them, they had to hurry or drown. Then, just as it looked as if they were home clear, they reached the next rockfall and their escape route was blocked. They had no way forward and behind them only icy cold death in the rising sea.

Up on the screen Emily took Bert in her arms and kissed him passionately. The intertitle flashed up, 'At least, if we must die, we shall die together.' They turned to see the black waters steadily mounting the steps. They pressed back against the rock wall barring their path to freedom and happiness. The audience leaned forward in their seats like a rolling wave.

The camera switched to the furious whale gyrating like a mad thing in the sea. We see one of its tiny eyes rolling in its huge head. Back on the stairs Emily screams at the icy touch of the inky waters. We return to the whale, its eye swivels forward and focuses. It heard her. It rears back and rushes furiously at the rock face. It smashes hard into the fractured stone and splits it open.

Emily and Bert are struggling in the rising flood when the whale's great mouth bursts through the wall in a mighty gush of seawater. Emily is thrown up onto the rocks and Bert defends her with the only weapon he has. He strikes at the whale with his sack of gold.

The huge mouth hinges open and the sack disappears into its maw. The whale thinks he's caught one of them and pulls away. Back in the turmoil of the tunnel Emily reaches out her hand to Bert and brushes against something. It's her plank of wood rising on the flood. She and Bert thrust it through the gap made by the whale and launch themselves out into the open sea.

Buoyed by the plank they rise to the surface. They see sunlight dappling the waves overhead. But below them the savage whale has seen them. It flicks its mighty tail and chases after them, its jaws agape. Just as Bert and Emily break the surface the great maw opens around them and they are swallowed. This time there can be no escape.

Once again the plank bridges firm across the whale's mouth and they cling to it, looking tiny in its huge maw. On the fishing boat Emily's father, Captain Ishmael, is leaning against the rocket-propelled harpoon gun and gazing sadly at the cruel ocean, the cold waves that have taken his daughter and the only man he ever respected.

The whale hits the surface, Ishmael sees what is happening and without hesitation swings the harpoon gun around to face the whale, which is rising up out of the sea under the impetus of its charge to the surface. The whale launches itself into the air. It is a truly magnificent sight. Ishmael aims and fires and his powerful dart catches the great whale, piercing its mighty heart.

The whale falls back into the sea, dead, and Emily and Bert are thrown clear. Ishmael rescues them and they celebrate as they tow their catch back to the slipway by the cottage. It is a great whale and will pay for the young people's wedding, promises the captain.

At that moment Emily starts laughing, and she pulls handfuls of gold and jewels from her jacket pockets. Ishmael stares dumbfounded at the treasure, and the three dance a jig on the foredeck. Emily leans forward and kisses the harpoon gun.

The audience is already cheering all around us but the movie is not yet over. When Ishmael and Bert are back on the slipway flensing the whale's huge carcass, Bert finds his shirt lodged in the beast's throat. The pirate gold is still wrapped in the makeshift sack. They're rich beyond their wildest dreams.

The camera pans in to capture Bert and Emily's kiss of pure happiness. Then, when it tracks back, we see they are standing in front of the altar and the parson declares them 'husband and wife'. Confetti falls around them and the scene fades to black.

Our audience explodes. *Jonah's Gold* receives a standing ovation. The troupe slap each other on the back, laughing and cheering with the crowd. Then they see the tears in my eyes. Out of respect they settle back into their seats and read the final printed words with me.

This moving picture is humbly dedicated to the memory of Melia Nord and Horace Goodman. Those stars that shine too briefly shine the brightest of all.

The evening of the next day after I had warned Horace that the police wanted to talk to him about the shooting, Henderson had visited me again. He told me that when he and his officers called at Horace's house they had found the man swinging from a noose tied to his bannisters. He was cold. He must have been there since the previous night.

The thought of going back to that police station had been more than Horace could bear. Despite his fear of the rope he had chosen the noose rather than face the chance of imprisonment. Marshall Henderson stayed with me for a long hour while I wept like a child trying to wash the guilt from my soul. I shed so many tears, but I had lost too much too quickly. Henderson understood. After that we became friends, and I was one of the few men invited to call him by his given name.

The lights came up. I blew my nose, got to my feet and joined the troupe. We linked arms and walked out towards our new future together. Melia and Horace would have enjoyed our little gang. I wished they could have joined us. I guess, in a way, they had.

-End-

Author's note

The early years of the movie era were much as I describe them here. My characters are fictional, as is the plot, but the antics they get up to could have been plucked from the pages of cinema history.

The move from New York to California happened for a number of reasons. I left out the primary one which was to get away from the 'Edison Men' who hounded the fledgling studios for money in exchange for using the patented Edison movie cameras. That would have been too diverting and I wanted to concentrate on Melia and her Major.

Why California? The light was better, rents were low and the landscape lent itself as the perfect backdrop for the creation of the wild west movie mythology; but escaping those Edison Men was a great reason to hitch the wagons and head southwest towards Edendale.

That's right, Edendale. Hollywood the way we understand it didn't exist back then. It wasn't even an address until the studios created it; at first it was just a post box placed for the benefit of fans who came to worship the screen gods and goddesses.

The wealth created by the movie studios was similar to that engendered more recently by dot.com companies. Millions of nickels soon mounted up and fans were devoted to their screen darlings. But there was more to cinema than beautiful faces, custard pies, and crashing cars.

The Great War remains fresh in our minds today because it was caught on film. We see the horror of the trenches and those young men marching to battle. No-one thought to film the effects of the devastating influenza epidemic that would eventually claim more lives than the First and Second World Wars combined. And the press didn't report it for fear of causing a panic.

The early years of the twentieth century were full of events that *were* recorded by movie cameras, but more than anything else it saw cinema mature from a sideshow novelty to the principal entertainment of its age.

During *The Celluloid Peach* I talk about Studio Excellence Awards. These are fictional and must not be confused with Oscars which didn't happen until the late 1920s.

Like *The Celluloid Peach* the idea of the Studio Excellence Awards celebrates a time of explosive creativity and technical achievement in the silent cinema. I like to think my characters and movie scripts reflect just a fraction of the frothing reality of the time, they should have been award winners.

We watch the early triple reelers now in respectful silence and marvel at the athleticism of the actors and comedians. The comedy and acting style is dated, but a hint of the magic remains. We understand event cinema today: *Star Wars, Jurassic Park, Avatar, Avengers Infinity War* – all these instil a similar sense of wonder to that which must have filled the old Nickelodeons when Charlie Chaplin played to packed houses.

Melia Nord never existed; but in her lives the spirit of her time.

Lightning Source UK Ltd.
Milton Keynes UK
UKHW010604240419
341520UK00001B/79/P

9 781912 576845